Classic

CHRISTMAS STORIES

Classic
CHRISTMAS STORIES

Sixteen Timeless Yuletide Tales

EDITED *by*
JULIA LIVSHIN

THE LYONS PRESS
GUILFORD, CONNECTICUT
AN IMPRINT OF THE GLOBE PEQUOT PRESS

The Lyons Press is an imprint of
The Globe Pequot Press

10 9 8 7 6 5 4 3 2 1

Printed in the United States of America

Designed by Claire Zoghb

ISBN 1-59228-055-2

Library of Congress Cataloging-in-Publication data
is available on file.

For my mother and my father
and for Ethan

Acknowledgments

Thanks to Laura Strom, my editor at Globe Pequot, for her guidance and good advice, and to Linda Lowenthal and Jon Zobenica, *Atlantic* colleagues who kindly shared their time and expertise. For his encouragement and generosity, and for all his help with this book, I am especially grateful to C. Michael Curtis.

Contents

Introduction   XI

The Gift of the Magi
by O. Henry   1

Christmas Jenny
by Mary Wilkins Freeman   11

Christmas Every Day
by William Dean Howells   35

From the Garden of a Friend
by Mary Agnes Tincker   49

The Christmas Club
by Edward Eggleston   71

Vanka
by Anton Chekhov   107
(translated by Constance Garnett)

CONTENTS

Reginald's Christmas Revel
by Saki (H. H. Munro)   115

Mrs. Podgers' Teapot
by Louisa May Alcott   121

*The Story of the Goblins
Who Stole a Sexton*
by Charles Dickens   153

The Christmas Shadrach
by Frank R. Stockton   173

Dancing Dan's Christmas
by Damon Runyon   207

*Christmas Storms and
Sunshine*
by Elizabeth Gaskell   223

The Blue Carbuncle
by Arthur Conan Doyle   243

The Bachelor's Christmas
by Robert Grant   279

CONTENTS

*How Santa Claus Came to
Simpson's Bar*
by Bret Harte   321

*The Man Who Was Like
Shakspeare*
by William Black   347

Introduction

Three years ago, you may have noticed, Christmas made it into the news. Not the usual bit in the business section about consumer spending during the holidays, but a real headline-grabbing story. *The New York Times* reported that Don Foster, an English professor at Vassar College, had written a book disputing the authorship of one of the pillars of Christmas literature, "The Night Before Christmas," a poem commonly attributed to Clement Clarke Moore. Something of a literary Sherlock Holmes, Foster marshaled textual and biographical evidence to build a pretty convincing case that the true author of the poem, originally published anonymously in a New York newspaper, was an unknown gentleman poet named Henry Livingston, Jr. The matter has yet to be settled conclusively, but, as far as I know, no one seems to have proven Foster wrong. A real-life Christmas mystery.

What's jarring about this story is the notion that anything having to do with Christmas could be subjected to this spoilsport sort of historical verification. In most people's minds, Christmas and its attendant rituals are timeless and, therefore, essentially without origin. The reminder that our modern conception of Santa Claus—as a jolly old elf who slides down the chimney on Christmas Eve and slips presents into children's stockings—can be traced to a whimsical poem published in 1823 is a little startling. But the fact is that Christmas as we observe it today is a relatively recent tradition, dating not from the dawn of Christianity but from the early nineteenth century. Even such basic customs as decorating the Christmas tree and exchanging gifts became established practices only as recently as the 1820s and 1830s. In earlier times the celebration of Christmas was primarily a pagan affair, tied to the winter solstice and the agricultural cycle, and was characterized by Mardi Gras–like behavior. As it happens, the popularization of the wholesome, family-oriented holiday we know today can largely be credited to the influence of two other literary works: Washington Irving's *Old Christmas*, first published in 1819, and Charles Dickens's *A Christmas Carol,* which appeared in 1843. Which brings us to the stories in this volume.

Practically all of the stories here are products of the second half of the nineteenth century and the early decades of the twentieth, when the Christmas story was a thriving literary genre and people looked forward to the holiday editions of popular magazines like *Collier's* and *The Saturday Evening Post.* One of the pleasures of this project was thumbing through those old issues, with their crumbly pages and handsome illustrations, in search of worthy candidates for this book.

Along with "The Gift of the Magi" and "How Santa Claus Came to Simpson's Bar," which are staples of Christmas anthologies, I have included some lesser-known works by literature's heavyweights—Dickens, Chekhov, Arthur Conan Doyle, Louisa May Alcott—as well as pieces by less familiar writers. Neither *Old Christmas* nor *A Christmas Carol* made it in—primarily because of space constraints. *Old Christmas* is actually divided into several sketches, but while the whole is richly descriptive and brimming with Christmas ambience, no individual sketch, I thought, had a strong enough plot to work on its own. And *A Christmas Carol*, in addition to being too long for this collection, is already widely available. In its place, I have chosen to include another Dickens tale, "The

Story of the Goblins Who Stole a Sexton," which appeared as part of *The Pickwick Papers* and, as you'll see, is something of a precursor to *A Christmas Carol.*

I hope you'll find that all of the selections in this book are good stories in their own right and would make for rewarding reading even beyond the Christmas season. In making my choices, I passed over stories that simply dispensed morality lessons or relied on stock Christmas characters and situations to do the job of storytelling for them. The only other consideration for the collection as a whole was variety—in physical setting, plot, social milieu, narrative voice. The coming pages will take you from a speakeasy on West Forty-seventh Street to a Russian village, from a gentlemen's club to a Good Samaritan's hut.

The magazine holiday issue may be a vanishing breed but over the last fifty years Christmas has continued to exert its extraordinary appeal through television, movies, and music. Until 1997 Bing Crosby's "White Christmas" was the biggest-selling single of all time (it has since dropped to second), and our enthusiasm for such perennial favorites as *It's a Wonderful Life* and *A Charlie Brown Christmas*, the latter of which has aired on television every year since its debut in 1965, seems inexhaustible. Some have even made Christmas a part of daily life—most notably in the town of Christmas, Michigan, where roadside Santas and streets with names like Jingle Bell Lane keep the spirit of the season always in the air. What would the little girl in the story "Christmas Every Day" say to that?

Julia Livshin
September 2003

The Gift of the Magi

O. HENRY

One dollar and eighty-seven cents. That was all. And sixty cents of it was in pennies. Pennies saved one and two at a time by bulldozing the grocer and the vegetable man and the butcher until one's cheeks burned with the silent imputation of parsimony that such close dealing implied. Three times Della counted it. One dollar and eighty-seven cents. And the next day would be Christmas.

There was clearly nothing to do but flop down on the shabby little couch and howl. So Della did it. Which instigates the moral reflection that life is made up of sobs, sniffles, and smiles, with sniffles predominating.

While the mistress of the home is gradually subsiding from the first stage to the second, take a look at the home. A furnished flat at $8 per week. It did not exactly beggar description, but it certainly had that word on the lookout for the mendicancy squad.

In the vestibule below was a letter-box into which no letter would go, and an electric button from which no mortal finger could coax a ring. Also appertaining thereunto was a card bearing the name, "Mr. James Dillingham Young."

The "Dillingham" had been flung to the breeze during a former period of prosperity when its possessor was being paid $30 per week. Now, when the income was shrunk to $20, the letters of "Dillingham" looked blurred, as though they were thinking seriously of contracting to a modest and unassuming D. But whenever Mr. James Dillingham Young came home and reached his flat above he was called "Jim" and greatly hugged by Mrs. James Dillingham Young, already introduced to you as Della. Which is all very good.

Della finished her cry and attended to her cheeks with the powder rag. She stood by the window and looked out dully at a gray cat walking a gray fence in a gray backyard. Tomorrow would be Christmas Day, and she had only $1.87 with which to buy Jim a present. She had been saving every penny she could for months, with this result. Twenty dollars a week doesn't go far. Expenses had been greater than she had calculated. They always are. Only $1.87 to buy a present for Jim. Her Jim. Many a happy hour she had spent planning for something nice for him. Something fine and rare and sterling—something just a little bit near to being worthy of the honor of being owned by Jim.

There was a pier-glass between the windows of the room. Perhaps you have seen a pier-glass in an $8 flat. A very thin and very agile person may, by observing his reflection in a rapid sequence of longi-tudinal strips, obtain a fairly accurate conception of his looks. Della, being slender, had mastered the art.

Suddenly she whirled from the window and stood before the glass. Her eyes were shining brilliantly, but her face had lost its color within twenty seconds. Rapidly she pulled down her hair and let it fall to its full length.

Now, there were two possessions of the James Dillingham Youngs in which they both took a mighty pride. One was Jim's gold watch that had been his father's and his grandfather's. The other was Della's hair. Had the Queen of Sheba lived in the flat across the airshaft, Della would have let her hair hang out the window some day to dry just to depre-ciate Her Majesty's jewels and gifts. Had King Solomon been the janitor, with all his treasures piled up in the basement, Jim would have pulled out his watch every time he passed, just to see him pluck at his beard from envy.

So now Della's beautiful hair fell about her rippling and shining like a cascade of brown waters. It reached below her knee and made itself almost a garment for her. And then she did it up again nervously and quickly. Once she faltered for a minute and stood still while a tear or two splashed on the worn red carpet.

On went her old brown jacket; on went her old brown hat. With a whirl of skirts and with the brilliant sparkle still in her eyes, she fluttered out the door and down the stairs to the street.

Where she stopped the sign read: "Mme. Sofronie. Hair Goods of All Kinds." One flight up Della ran, and collected herself, panting. Madame, large, too white, chilly, hardly looked the "Sofronie."

"Will you buy my hair?" asked Della.

"I buy hair," said Madame. "Take yer hat off and let's have a sight at the looks of it."

Down rippled the brown cascade.

"Twenty dollars," said Madame, lifting the mass with a practiced hand.

"Give it to me quick," said Della.

Oh, and the next two hours tripped by on rosy wings. Forget the hashed metaphor. She was ransacking the stores for Jim's present.

She found it at last. It surely had been made for Jim and no one else. There was no other like it in any of the stores, and she had turned all of them inside out. It was a platinum fob chain simple and chaste in design, properly proclaiming its value by substance alone and not by meretricious ornamentation—as all good things should do. It was even worthy of The Watch. As soon as she saw it she knew that it must be Jim's. It was like him. Quietness and value—the description applied to both. Twenty-one dollars they took from her for it, and she hurried home with the 87 cents. With that chain on his watch Jim might be properly anxious about the time in any company. Grand as the watch was, he sometimes looked at it on the sly on account of the old leather strap that he used in place of a chain.

When Della reached home her intoxication gave way a little to prudence and reason. She got out her curling irons and lighted the gas and went to work repairing the ravages made by generosity added to love. Which is always a tremendous task, dear friends—a mammoth task.

Within forty minutes her head was covered with tiny, close-lying curls that made her look wonderfully like a truant schoolboy. She looked at her reflection in the mirror long, carefully, and critically.

"If Jim doesn't kill me," she said to herself, "before he takes a second look at me, he'll say I look like a Coney Island chorus girl. But what could I do—oh! What could I do with a dollar and eighty-seven cents?"

At 7 o'clock the coffee was made and frying-pan was on the back of the stove hot and ready to cook the chops.

Jim was never late. Della doubled the fob chain in her hand and sat on the corner of the table near the door that he always entered. Then she heard his step on the stair away down on the first flight, and she turned white for just a moment. She had a habit of saying little silent prayers about the simplest every-day things, and now she whispered: "Please God, make him think I am still pretty."

The door opened and Jim stepped in and closed it. He looked thin and very serious. Poor fellow, he was only twenty-two—and to be burdened with a family! He needed a new overcoat and he was without gloves.

Jim stopped inside the door, as immovable as a setter at the scent of quail. His eyes were fixed upon Della, and there was an expression in them that she could not read, and it terrified her. It was not anger, nor surprise, nor disapproval, nor horror, nor any of the sentiments that she had been prepared for. He simply stared at her fixedly with that peculiar expression on his face.

Della wriggled off the table and went for him.

"Jim, darling," she cried, "don't look at me that way. I had my hair cut off and sold it because I

couldn't have lived through Christmas without giving you a present. It'll grow out again—you won't
mind, will you? I just had to do it. My hair grows
awfully fast. 'Merry Christmas!' Jim, and let's be
happy. You don't know what a nice—what a beautiful, nice gift I've got for you."

"You've cut off your hair?" asked Jim, laboriously,
as if he had not arrived at that patent fact yet even
after the hardest mental labor.

"Cut it off and sold it," said Della. "Don't you like
me just as well, anyhow? I'm me without my hair,
ain't I?"

Jim looked about the room curiously.

"You say your hair is gone?" he said, with an air
almost of idiocy.

"You needn't look for it," said Della. "It's sold, I
tell you—sold and gone, too. It's Christmas Eve,
boy. Be good to me, for it went for you. Maybe the
hairs on my head were numbered," she went on
with a sudden serious sweetness, "but nobody could
ever count my love for you. Shall I put the chops
on, Jim?"

Out of his trance Jim seemed quickly to wake. He
enfolded his Della. For ten seconds let us regard with
discreet scrutiny some inconsequential object in the
other direction. Eight dollars a week or a million a
year—what is the difference? A mathematician or a

wit would give you the wrong answer. The magi brought valuable gifts, but that was not among them. This dark assertion will be illuminated later on.

Jim drew a package from his overcoat pocket and threw it upon the table.

"Don't make any mistake, Dell," he said, "about me. I don't think there's anything in the way of a haircut or a shave or a shampoo that could make me like my girl any less. But if you'll unwrap that package you may see why you had me going a while at first."

White fingers and nimble tore at the string and paper. And then an ecstatic scream of joy; and then, alas! a quick feminine change to hysterical tears and wails, necessitating the immediate employment of all the comforting powers of the lord of the flat.

For there lay The Combs—the set of combs, side and back, that Della had worshipped for long in a Broadway window. Beautiful combs, pure tortoise shell, with jeweled rims—just the shade to wear in the beautiful vanished hair. They were expensive combs, she knew, and her heart had simply craved and yearned over them without the least hope of possession. And now they were hers, but the tresses that should have adorned the coveted adornments were gone.

But she hugged them to her bosom, and at length

she was able to look up with dim eyes and a smile and say: "My hair grows so fast, Jim!"

And then Della leaped up like a little singed cat and cried, "Oh, oh!"

Jim had not yet seen his beautiful present. She held it out to him eagerly upon her open palm. The dull precious metal seemed to flash with a reflection of her bright and ardent spirit.

"Isn't it a dandy, Jim? I hunted all over town to find it. You'll have to look at the time a hundred times a day now. Give me your watch. I want to see how it looks on it."

Instead of obeying, Jim tumbled down on the couch and put his hands under the back of his head and smiled.

"Dell," said he, "let's put our Christmas presents away and keep 'em a while. They're too nice to use just at present. I sold the watch to get the money to buy your combs. And now suppose you put the chops on."

The magi, as you know, were wise men—wonderfully wise men—who brought gifts to the Babe in the manger. They invented the art of giving Christmas presents. Being wise, their gifts were no doubt wise ones, possibly bearing the privilege of exchange in case of duplication. And here I have lamely related to you the uneventful chronicle of two foolish children in a flat who most unwisely sacrificed for each other the greatest treasures of their house. But in a last word to the wise of these days let it be said that of all who give gifts these two were the wisest. Of all who give and receive gifts, such as they are wisest. Everywhere they are wisest. They are the magi.

Christmas Jenny

MARY WILKINS FREEMAN

The day before there had been a rain and a thaw, then in the night the wind had suddenly blown from the north, and it had grown cold. In the morning it was very clear and cold, and there was the hard glitter of ice over everything. The snow-crust had a thin coat of ice, and all the open fields shone and flashed. The tree boughs and trunks, and all the little twigs, were enamelled with ice. The roads were glare and slippery with it, and so were the door-yards. In old Jonas Carey's yard the path that sloped from the door to the well was like a frozen brook.

Quite early in the morning old Jonas Carey came out with a pail, and went down the path to the well. He went slowly and laboriously, shuffling his feet, so he should not fall. He was tall and gaunt, and one side of his body seemed to slant towards the other, he settled so much more heavily upon one foot. He was somewhat stiff and lame from rheumatism.

He reached the well in safety, hung the pail, and began pumping. He pumped with extreme slowness and steadiness; a certain expression of stolid solemnity, which his face wore, never changed.

When he had filled his pail he took it carefully from the pump spout, and started back to the house, shuffling as before. He was two thirds of the way to the door, when he came to an extremely slippery place. Just there some roots from a little cherry-tree crossed the path, and the ice made a dangerous little pitch over them.

Old Jonas lost his footing, and sat down suddenly; the water was all spilled. The house door flew open, and an old woman appeared.

"Oh, Jonas, air you hurt?" she cried, blinking wildly and terrifiedly in the brilliant light.

The old man never said a word. He sat still and looked straight before him, solemnly.

"Oh, Jonas, you ain't broke any bones, hev you?" The old woman gathered up her skirts and began to edge off the door-step, with trembling knees.

Then the old man raised his voice. "Stay where you be," he said, imperatively. "Go back into the house!"

He began to raise himself, one joint at a time, and

the old woman went back into the house, and looked out of the window at him.

When old Jonas finally stood upon his feet it seemed as if he had actually constructed himself, so piecemeal his rising had been. He went back to the pump, hung the pail under the spout, and filled it. Then he started on the return with more caution than before. When he reached the dangerous place his feet flew up again, he sat down, and the water was spilled.

The old woman appeared in the door; her dim blue eyes were quite round, her delicate chin was dropped. "Oh, Jonas!"

"Go back!" cried the old man, with an imperative jerk of his head towards her, and she retreated. This time he arose more quickly, and made quite a lively shuffle back to the pump.

But when his pail was filled and he again started on the return, his caution was redoubled. He seemed to scarcely move at all. When he approached the dangerous spot his progress was hardly more perceptible than a scaly leaf-slug's. Repose almost lapped over motion. The old woman in the window watched breathlessly.

The slippery place was almost passed, the shuffle quickened a little—the old man sat down again, and the tin pail struck the ice with a clatter.

The old woman appeared. "Oh, Jonas!"

Jonas did not look at her; he sat perfectly motion-less.

"Jonas, air you hurt? Do speak to me for massy sake!" Jonas did not stir.

Then the old woman let herself carefully off the step. She squatted down upon the icy path, and hitched along to Jonas. She caught hold of his arm—"Jonas, you don't feel as if any of your bones were broke, do you?" Her voice was almost sobbing, her small frame was all of a tremble.

"Go back!" said Jonas. That was all he would say. The old woman's tearful entreaties did not move him in the least. Finally she hitched herself back to the house, and took up her station in the window. Once in a while she rapped on the pane, and beckoned piteously.

But old Jonas Carey sat still. His solemn face was inscrutable. Over his head stretched the icy cherry-branches, full of the flicker and dazzle of diamonds. A woodpecker flew into the tree and began tapping at the trunk, but the ice-enamel was so hard that he could not get any food. Old Jonas sat so still that he did not mind him. A jay flew on the fence within a few feet of him; a sparrow pecked at some weeds piercing the snow-crust beside the door. Over in the east arose the mountain, covered with frosty foliage full of silver and blue and diamond lights. The air was stinging. Old Jonas paid no attention to anything. He sat there.

The old woman ran to the door again. "Oh, Jonas, you'll freeze, settin' there!" she pleaded. "Can't you git up? Your bones ain't broke air they?" Jonas was silent.

"Oh, Jonas, there's Christmas Jenny comin' down the road—what do you s'pose she'll think?"

Old Jonas Carey was unmoved, but his old wife eagerly watched the woman coming down the road. The woman looked oddly at a distance: like a broad green moving bush; she was dragging something green after her, too. When she came nearer one could see that she was laden with evergreen wreaths—her arms were strung with them; long sprays of ground-pine were wound around her shoulders, she carried a basket trailing with them and holding also many little bouquets of bright-colored everlasting flowers. She dragged a sled, with a small hemlock-tree bound upon it. She came along sturdily over the slippery road. When she reached the Carey gate she stopped and looked over at Jonas. "Is he hurt?" she sang out to the old woman.

"I dunno—he's fell down three times."

Jenny came through the gate, and proceeded straight to Jonas. She left her sled in the road. She stooped, brought her basket on a level with Jonas's head, and gave him a little push with it. "What's the matter with ye?" Jonas did not wink. "Your bones ain't broke, are they?"

Jenny stood looking at him for a moment. She wore a black hood, her large face was weather-beaten, deeply tanned, and reddened. Her features were strong, but heavily cut. She made one think of those sylvan faces with features composed of bark-wrinkles and knot-holes, that one can fancy looking out of the trunks of trees. She was not an aged woman, but her hair was iron-gray, and crinkled as closely as gray moss.

Finally she turned towards the house. "I'm comin' in a minute," she said to Jonas's wife, and trod confidently up the icy steps.

"Don't you slip," said the old woman, tremulously.

"I ain't afraid of slippin'." When they were in the house she turned around on Mrs. Carey, "Don't you fuss, he ain't hurt."

"No, I don't s'pose he is. It's jest one of his tantrums. But I dunno what I am goin' to do. Oh, dear me suz, I dunno what I am goin' to do with him sometimes!"

"Leave him alone—let him set there."

"Oh, he's tipped all that water over, an' I'm afeard he'll—freeze down. Oh, dear!"

"Let him freeze! Don't you fuss, Betsey."

"I was jest goin' to git breakfast. Mis' Gill she sent

us in two sassage-cakes. I was goin' to fry 'em, an' I jest asked him to go out an' draw a pail of water, so's to fill up the tea-kittle. Oh, dear!"

Jenny sat her basket in a chair, strode peremptorily out of the house, picked up the tin pail which lay on its side near Jonas, filled it at the well, and returned. She wholly ignored the old man. When she entered the door his eyes realaxed their solemn stare at vacancy, and darted a swift glance after her.

"Now fill up the kittle, an' fry the sassages," she said to Mrs. Carey.

"Oh, I'm afeard he won't git up, an' they'll be cold! Sometimes his tantrums last a consider'ble while. You see he sot down three times, an' he's awful mad."

"I don't see who he thinks he's spitin'."

"I dunno, 'less it's Providence."

"I reckon Providence don't care much where he sets."

"Oh, Jenny, I'm dreadful afeard he'll freeze down."

"No, he won't. Put on the sassages."

Jonas's wife went about getting out the frying-pan, crooning over her complaint all the time. "He's dreadful fond of sassages," she said, when the odor of the frying sausages became apparent in the room.

"He'll smell 'em an' come in," remarked Jenny, dryly. "He knows there ain't but two cakes, an' he'll be afeard you'll give me one of 'em."

She was right. Before long the two women, taking sly peeps from the window, saw old Jonas lumberingly getting up. "Don't say nothin' to him about it when he comes in," whispered Jenny.

When the old man clumped into the kitchen, neither of the women paid any attention to him. His wife turned the sausages, and Jenny was gathering up her wreaths. Jonas let himself down into a chair, and looked at them uneasily. Jenny laid down her wreaths. "Goin' to stay to breakfast?" said the old man.

"Well, I dunno," replied Jenny. "Them sassages do smell temptin'."

All Jonas's solemnity had vanished, he looked foolish and distressed.

"Do take off your hood, Jenny," urged Betsey. "I ain't very fond of sassages myself, an' I'd jest as liv's you'd have my cake as not."

Jenny laughed broadly and good-naturedly, and began gathering up her wreaths again. "Lor', I don't want your sassage-cake," said she. "I've had my breakfast. I'm goin' down to the village to sell my wreaths."

Jonas's face lit up. "Pleasant day, ain't it?" he remarked, affably.

Jenny grew sober. "I don't think it's a very pleasant day; guess you wouldn't if you was a woodpecker or a blue-jay," she replied.

Jonas looked at her with stupid inquiry.

"They can't git no breakfast," said Jenny. "They can't git through the ice on the trees. They'll starve if there ain't a thaw pretty soon. I've got to buy 'em somethin' down to the store. I'm goin' to feed a few of 'em. I ain't goin' to see 'em dyin' in my door-yard if I can help it. I've given 'em all I could spare from my own birds this mornin'."

"It's too bad, ain't it?"

"I think it's too bad. I was goin' to buy me a new caliker dress if this freeze hadn't come, but I can't now. What it would cost will save a good many lives. Well, I've got to hurry along if I'm goin' to git back to-day."

Jenny, surrounded with her trailing masses of green, had to edge herself through the narrow door-way. She went straight to the village and peddled her wares from house to house. She had her regular customers. Every year, the week before Christmas, she came down from the mountain with her evergreens. She was popularly supposed to earn quite a sum of money in that way. In the summer she sold vegetables, but the green Christmas traffic was regarded as her legitimate business—it had given her her name among the villagers. However, the fantastic name may have arisen from the popular conception of Jenny's character. She also was considered somewhat fantastic, although there was no doubt of her sanity.

In her early youth she had had an unfortunate love affair, that was supposed to have tinctured her whole life with an alien element. "Love-cracked," people called her.

"Christmas Jenny's kind of love-cracked," they said. She was Christmas Jenny in midsummer, when she came down the mountain laden with green peas and string-beans and summer squashes.

She owned a little house and a few acres of cleared land on the mountain, and in one way or another she picked up a living from it.

It was noon to-day before she had sold all her evergreens and started up the mountain road for home. She had laid in a small stock of provisions, and she carried them in the basket which had held the little bunches of life-everlasting and amaranth flowers and dried grasses.

The road wound along the base of the mountain. She had to follow it about a mile; then she struck into a cart-path which led up to the clearing where her house was.

After she passed Jonas Carey's there were no houses and no people, but she met many living things that she knew. A little field-mouse, scratching warily from cover to cover, lest his enemies should spy him, had appreciative notice from Jenny Wrayne. She turned her head at the call of a jay, and she caught a glimmer of blue through the dazzling white boughs. She saw with sympathetic eyes a woodpecker drumming on the ice-bound trunk of a tree. Now and then she scattered, with regretful sparseness, some seeds and crumbs from her parcels.

At the point where she left the road for the cart-path there was a gap in the woods, and a clear view of the village below. She stopped and looked back at it. It was quite a large village; over it hung a spraying net-work of frosty branches; the smoke arose straight up from the chimneys. Down in the village street a girl and a young man were walking, talking about her, but she did not know that.

The girl was the minister's daughter. She had just become engaged to the young man, and was walking with him in broad daylight with a kind of shame-faced pride. Whenever they met anybody she blushed, and at the same time held up her head proudly, and swung one arm with an airy motion. She chattered glibly and quite loudly, to cover her embarrassment.

"Yes," she said, in a sweet, crisp voice, "Christmas Jenny has just been to the house, and we've bought some wreaths. We're going to hang them in all the front windows. Mother didn't know as we ought to buy them of her, there's so much talk, but I don't believe a word of it, for my part."

"What talk?" asked the young man. He held himself very stiff and straight, and never turned his head when he shot swift, smiling glances at the girl's pink face.

"Why, don't you know? It's town-talk. The say she's got a lot of birds and rabbits and things shut up in cages, and half starves them; and then that little deaf-and-dumb boy, you know—they say she treats him dreadfully. They're going to look into it. Father and Deacon Little are going up there this week."

"Are they?" said the young man. He was listening to the girl's voice with a sort of rapturous attention, but he had little idea as to what she was saying. As they walked, they faced the mountain.

It was only the next day when the minister and Deacon Little made the visit. They started up a flock of sparrows that were feeding by Jenny's door; but the birds did not fly very far—they settled into a tree and watched. Jenny's house was hardly more than a weather-beaten hut, but there was a grape-vine trained over one end, and the front yard was tidy. Just before the house stood a tall pine-tree. At the rear, and on the right, stretched the remains of Jenny's last summer's garden, full of plough-ridges and glistening corn-stubble.

Jenny was not at home. The minister knocked and got no response. Finally he lifted the latch, and the two men walked in. The room seemed gloomy after the brilliant light outside; they could not see anything at first, but they could hear a loud and demonstrative squeaking and chirping and twittering that their entrance appeared to excite.

At length a small pink-and-white face cleared out of the gloom of the chimney-corner. It surveyed the visitors with no fear nor surprise, but seemingly with an innocent amiability.

"That's the little deaf-and-dumb boy," said the minister, in a subdued voice. The minister was an old man, narrow-shouldered, and clad in long-waisted and wrinkly black. Deacon Little reared himself in his sinewy leanness until his head nearly touched the low ceiling. His face was sallow and severely corrugated, but the features were handsome.

Both stood staring remorselessly at the little deaf-and-dumb boy, who looked up in their faces with an expression of delicate wonder and amusement. The little boy was dressed like a girl, in a long blue gingham pinafore. He sat in the midst of a heap of evergreens, which he had been twining into wreaths; his pretty, soft, fair hair was damp, and lay in a very flat and smooth scallop over his full white forehead.

"He looks as if he was well cared for," said Deacon Little. Both men spoke in hushed tones—it was hard for them to realize that the boy could not hear, the more so because every time their lips moved his smile deepened. He was not in the least afraid.

They moved around the room half guiltily, and surveyed everything. It was unlike any apartment that they had ever entered. It had a curious sylvan air; there were heaps of evergreens here and there, and some small green trees leaned in one corner. All around the room—hung on the walls, standing on rude shelves—were little rough cages and hutches, from which the twittering and chirping sounded. They contained forlorn little birds and rabbits and field-mice. The birds had rough feathers and small, dejected heads, one rabbit had an injured leg, one field-mouse seemed nearly dead. The men eyed them sharply. The minister drew a sigh; the deacon's handsome face looked harder. But they did not say what they thought, on account of the little deaf-and-dumb boy, whose pleasant blue eyes never left their faces. When they had made the circuit of the room, and stood again by the fireplace, he suddenly set up a cry. It was wild and inarticulate, still not wholly dissonant, and it seemed to have a meaning of its own. It united with the cries of the little caged wild creatures, and it was all like a soft clamor of eloquent appeal to the two visitors, but they could not understand it.

They stood solemn and perplexed by the fire-place. "Had we better wait till she comes?" asked the minister.

"I don't know," said Deacon Little.

Back of them arose the tall mantel-shelf. On it were a clock and a candle-stick, and regularly laid bunches of brilliant dried flowers, all ready for Jenny to put in her basket and sell.

Suddenly there was a quick scrape on the crusty snow outside, the door flew open, and Jonas Carey's wife came in. She had her shawl over her head, and she was panting for breath.

She stood before the two men, and a sudden crust of shy formality seemed to form over her. "Good-afternoon," she said, in response to their salutations.

She looked at them for a moment, and tightened her shawl-pin; then the restraint left her. "I knowed you was here," she cried, in her weak, vehement voice; "I knowed it. I've heerd the talk. I knowed somebody was goin' to come up here an' spy her out. I was in Mis' Gregg's the other day, an' her husband came home; he'd been down to the store, an' he said they were talkin' 'bout Jenny, an' sayin' she didn't treat Willy and the birds well, an' the town was goin' to look into it. I knowed you was comin' up here when I seed you go by. I told Jonas so. An' I knowed she wa'n't to home, an' there wa'n't nothin' here that could speak, an' I told Jonas I was comin'. I couldn't stan' it nohow. It's dreadful slippery. I had to go on my hands an' knees in some places, an' I've sot down twice, but I don't care. I ain't goin' to have you comin' up here to spy on Jenny, an' nobody home that's got any tongue to speak for her."

Mrs. Carey stood before them like a ruffled and

defiant bird that was frighting herself as well as them with her temerity. She palpitated all over, but there was a fierce look in her dim blue eyes.

The minister began a deprecating murmur, which the deacon drowned. "You can speak for her all you want to, Mrs. Carey," said he. "We ain't got any objections to hearin' it. An' we didn't know but what she was home. Do you know what she does with these birds and things?"

"Does with 'em? Well, I'll tell you what she does with 'em. She picks 'em up in the woods when they're starvin' an' freezin' an' half dead, an' she brings 'em in here, an' takes care of 'em an' feeds 'em till they git well, an' then she lets 'em go again. That's what she does. You see that rabbit there? Well, he's been in a trap. Somebody wanted to kill the poor cretur. You see that robin? Somebody fired a gun at him an' broke his wing.

"That's what she does. I dunno but it mounts to jest about as much as sendin' money to missionaries. I dunno but what bein' a missionary to robins an' starvin' chippies an' little deaf-an'-dumb children is jest as good as some other kinds, an' that's what she is.

"I ain't afeard to speak; I'm going to tell the whole story. I dunno what folks mean by talkin' about her the way they do. There, she took that little dumbie out of the poor-house. Nobody else wanted him.

He don't look as if he was abused very bad, far's I can see. She keeps him jest as nice an' neat as she can, an' he an' the birds has enough to eat, if she don't herself.

"I guess I know 'bout it. Here she is goin' without a new caliker dress, so's to git somethin' for them birds that can't git at the trees, 'cause there's so much ice on 'em.

"You can't tell me nothin'. When Jonas has one of his tantrums she can git him out of it quicker'n anybody I ever see. She ain't goin' to be talked about and spied upon if I can help it. They tell about her bein' love-cracked. H'm. I dunno what they call love-cracked. I know that Anderson fellar went off an' married another girl, when Jenny jest as much expected to have him as could be. He ought to ha' been strung up. But I know one thing—if she did git kind of twisted out of the reg'lar road of lovin', she's in another one, that's full of little dumbies an' starvin' chippies an' lame rabbits, an' she ain't love-cracked no more'n other folks."

Mrs. Carey, carried away by affection and indignation, almost spoke in poetry. Her small face glowed pink, her blue eyes were full of fire, she waved her arms under her shawl. The little meek old woman was a veritable enthusiast.

The two men looked at each other. The deacon's handsome face was as severe and grave as ever, but he waited for the minister to speak. When the minister did speak it was apologetically. He was a gentle old man, and the deacon was his mouthpiece in matters of parish discipline. If he failed him he betrayed how feeble and kindly a pipe was his own. He told Mrs. Carey that he did not doubt everything was as it should be; he apologized for their presence; he praised Christmas Jenny. Then he and the deacon retreated. They were thankful to leave that small, vociferous woman, who seemed to be pulling herself up by her enthusiasm until she reached the air over their heads, and became so abnormal that she was frightful. Indeed, everything out of the broad, common track was a horror to these men and to many of their village fellows. Strange shadows, that their eyes could not pierce, lay upon such, and they were suspicious. The popular sentiment against Jenny Wrayne was originally the outcome of this characteristic, which was a remnant of the old New England witchcraft superstition. More than anything else, Jenny's eccentricity, her possibly uncanny deviation from the ordinary ways of life, had brought this inquiry on her. In actual meaning, although not even in self-acknowledgment, it was a witch-hunt that went up the mountain road that December afternoon.

They hardly spoke on the way. Once the minister turned to the deacon. "I rather think there's no occasion for interference," he said hesitatingly.

"I guess there ain't any need of it," answered the deacon.

The deacon spoke again when they had nearly reached his own house. "I guess I'll send her up a little somethin' Christmas," said he. Deacon Little was a rich man.

"Maybe it would be a good idea," returned the minister. "I'll see what I can do."

Christmas was one week from that day. On Christmas morning old Jonas Carey and his wife, dressed in their best clothes, started up the mountain road to Jenny Wrayne's. Old Jonas wore his great-coat, and had his wife's cashmere scarf wound twice around his neck. Mrs. Carey wore her long shawl and her best bonnet. They walked along quite easily. The ice was all gone now; there had been a light fall of snow the day before, but it was not shoe-deep. The snow was covered with the little tracks of Jenny's friends, the birds and the field-mice and the rabbits, in pretty zigzag lines.

Jonas Carey and his wife walked along comfortably until they reached the cart-path, then the old man's shoestring became loose, and he tripped over it. He stooped and tied it laboriously; then he went on. Pretty soon he stopped again. His wife looked back. "What's the matter?" said she.

"Shoestring untied," replied old Jonas, in a half inarticulate grunt.

"Don't you want me to tie it, Jonas?"

Jonas said nothing more, he tied viciously.

They were in sight of Jenny's house when he stopped again, and sat down on the stone wall beside the path. "Oh, Jonas, what is the matter?"

Jonas made no reply. His wife went up to him and saw that the shoestring was loose again. "Oh, Jonas, do let me tie it; I'd just as soon as not. Sha'n't I, Jonas?"

Jonas sat there in the midst of the snowy blackberry vines, and looked straight ahead with a stony stare.

His wife began to cry. "Oh, Jonas," she pleaded, "don't you have a tantrum to-day. Sha'n't I tie it? I'll tie it real strong. Oh, Jonas!"

The old woman fluttered around the old man in his greatcoat on the wall, like a distressed bird around her mate. Jenny Wrayne opened her door and looked out; then she came down the path. "What's the matter?" she asked.

"Oh, Jenny, I dunno what *to* do. He's got another—tantrum!"

"Has he fell down?"

"No; that ain't it. His shoestring's come untied three times, an' he don't like it, an' he's sot down on the wall. I dunno but he'll set there all day. Oh dear me suz, when we'd got most to your house, an' I was jest thinkin' we'd come 'long real comfort'ble! I want to tie it for him, but he won't let me, an' I don't darse to when he sets there like that. Oh, Jonas, jest let me tie it, won't you? I'll tie it real nice an' strong, so it won't undo again."

Jenny caught hold of her arm. "Come right into the house," said she, in a hearty voice. She quite turned her back upon the figure on the wall.

"Oh, Jenny, I can't go in an' leave him a-settin' there. I shouldn't wonder if he sot there all day. You don't know nothin' about it. Sometimes I have to stan' an' argue with him for hours afore he'll stir."

"Come right in. The turkey's most done, an' we'll set right down as soon as 'tis. It's 'bout the fattest turkey I ever see. I dunno where Deacon Little could ha' got it. The plum-puddin's all done, an' the vegetables is 'most ready to take up. Come right in, an' we'll have dinner in less than half an hour."

After the two women had entered the house the figure on the wall cast an uneasy glance at it without turning his head. He sniffed a little.

It was quite true that he could smell the roasting turkey, and the turnip and onions, out there.

In the house, Mrs. Carey laid aside her bonnet and shawl, and put them on the bed in Jenny's little bed-room. A Christmas present, a new calico dress, which Jenny had received the night before, lay on the bed also. Jenny showed it with pride. "It's that chocolate color I've always liked," said she. "I don't see what put it into their heads."

"It's real handsome," said Mrs. Carey. She had not told Jenny about her visitors; but she was not used to keeping a secret, and her possession of one gave a curious expression to her face. However, Jenny did not notice it. She hurried about preparing dinner. The stove was covered with steaming pots; the turkey in the oven could be heard sizzling. The little deaf-and-dumb boy sat in his chimney-corner, and took long sniffs. He watched Jenny, and regarded the stove in a rapture, or he examined some treasures that he held in his lap. There were picture-books and cards, and boxes of candy, and oranges. He held them all tightly gathered into his pinafore. The little caged wild things twittered sweetly and pecked at their food. Jenny laid the table with the best tablecloth and her mother's flowered china. The mountain farmers, of whom Jenny sprang, had had their little decencies and comforts, and there were china and a linen table-cloth for a Christmas dinner, poor as the house was.

Mrs. Carey kept peering uneasily out of the window at her husband on the stone wall.

"If you want him to come in you'll keep away from the window," said Jenny; and the old woman settled into a chair near the stove.

Very soon the door opened, and Jonas came in. Jenny was bending over the potato kettle, and she did not look around. "You can put his great-coat on the bed, if you've a mind to, Mrs. Carey," said she.

Jonas got out of his coat, and sat down with sober dignity; he had tied his shoestring very neatly and firmly. After a while he looked over at the little deaf-and-dumb boy, who was smiling at him, and he smiled back.

The Careys stayed until evening. Jenny set her candle in the window to light them down the cart-path. Down in the village the minister's daughter and her betrothed were out walking to the church, where there was a Christmas-tree. It was quite dark. She clung closely to his arm, and once in a while her pink cheek brushed his sleeve. The stars were out, many of them, and more were coming. One seemed suddenly to flash out on the dark side of the mountain.

"There's Christmas Jenny's candle," said the girl. And it was Christmas Jenny's candle, but it was also something more. Like all common things, it had, and was, its own poem, and that was—a Christmas star.

Christmas Every Day

WILLIAM DEAN HOWELLS

The little girl came into her papa's study, as she always did Saturday morning before breakfast, and asked for a story. He tried to beg off that morning, for he was very busy, but she would not let him. So he began:

"Well, once there was a little pig—"

She put her hand over his mouth and stopped him at the word. She said she had heard little pig stories till she was perfectly sick of them.

"Well, what kind of story *shall* I tell, then?"

"About Christmas. It's getting to be the season. It's past Thanksgiving already."

"It seems to me," argued her papa, "that I've told as often about Christmas as I have about little pigs."

"No difference! Christmas is more interesting."

"Well!" Her papa roused himself from his writing

by a great effort. "Well, then, I'll tell you about the little girl that wanted it Christmas every day in the year. How would you like that?"

"First-rate!" said the little girl; and she nestled into comfortable shape in his lap, ready for listening.

"Very well, then, this little pig,—Oh, what are you pounding me for?"

"Because you said little pig instead of little girl."

"I should like to know what's the difference between a little pig and a little girl that wanted it Christmas every day!"

"Papa," said the little girl, warningly, "if you don't go on, I'll *give* it to you!" And at this her papa darted off like lightning, and began to tell the story as fast as he could.

Well, once there was a little girl who liked Christmas so much that she wanted it to be Christmas every day in the year; and as soon as Thanksgiving was over she began to send postal cards to the old Christmas Fairy to ask if she mightn't have it. But the old Fairy never answered any of the postals; and, after a while, the little girl found out that the Fairy was pretty particular, and wouldn't notice anything but letters, not even correspondence cards in envelopes; but real letters on sheets of paper, and sealed outside with a monogram,—or your initial, any way. So, then, she began to send her letters; and in about three weeks—or just the day before Christmas, it was—she got a letter from the Fairy, saying she might have it Christmas every day for a year, and then they would see about having it longer.

The little girl was a good deal excited already, preparing for the old-fashioned, once-a-year Christmas that was coming the next day, and perhaps the Fairy's promise didn't make such an impression on her as it would have made at some other time. She just resolved to keep it to herself, and surprise everybody with it as it kept coming true; and then it slipped out of her mind altogether.

She had a splendid Christmas. She went to bed early, so as to let Santa Claus have a chance at the stockings, and in the morning she was up the first of anybody and went and felt them, and found hers all lumpy with packages of candy, and oranges and grapes, and pocket-books and rubber balls and all kinds of small presents, and her big brother's with nothing but the tongs in them, and her young lady sister's with a new silk umbrella, and her papa's and mamma's with potatoes and pieces of coal wrapped up in tissue paper, just as they always had every Christmas. Then she waited around till the rest of the family were up, and she was the first to burst into the library, when the doors were opened, and look at the large presents laid out on the library-table—

books, and portfolios, and boxes of stationery, and breast-pins, and dolls, and little stoves, and dozens of handkerchiefs, and ink-stands, and skates, and snow-shovels, and photograph-frames, and little easels, and boxes of water-colors, and Turkish paste, and nougat, and candied cherries, and dolls' houses, and water-proofs—and the big Christmas-tree, lighted and standing in a waste-basket in the middle.

She had a splendid Christmas all day. She ate so much candy that she did not want any breakfast; and the whole forenoon the presents kept pouring in that the expressman had not had time to deliver the night before; and she went 'round giving the presents she had got for other people, and came home and ate turkey and cranberry for dinner, and plum-pudding and nuts and raisins and oranges and more candy, and then went out and coasted and came in with a stomach-ache, crying; and her papa said he would see if his house was turned into that sort of fool's paradise another year; and they had a light supper, and pretty early everybody went to bed cross.

Here the little girl pounded her papa in the back, again.

"Well, what now? Did I say pigs?"

"You made them *act* like pigs."

"Well, didn't they?"

"No matter; you oughtn't to put it into a story."

"Very well, then, I'll take it all out."

Her father went on:

The little girl slept very heavily, and she slept very late, but she was wakened at last by the other children dancing 'round her bed with their stockings full of presents in their hands.

"What is it?" said the little girl, and she rubbed her eyes and tried to rise up in bed.

"Christmas! Christmas! Christmas!" they all shouted, and waved their stockings.

"Nonsense! It was Christmas yesterday."

Her brothers and sisters just laughed. "We don't know about that. It's Christmas to-day, any way. You come into the library and see."

Then all at once it flashed on the little girl that the Fairy was keeping her promise, and her year of Christmases was beginning. She was dreadfully sleepy, but she sprang up like a lark—a lark that had overeaten itself and gone to bed cross—and darted into the library. There it was again! Books, and portfolios, and boxes of stationery, and breast pins—

"You needn't go over it all, Papa; I guess I can remember just what was there," said the little girl.

———

Well, and there was the Christmas-tree blazing away, and the family picking out their presents, but looking pretty sleepy, and her father perfectly puzzled, and her mother ready to cry. "I'm sure I don't see how I'm to dispose of all these things," said her mother, and her father said it seemed to him they had had something just like it the day before, but he supposed he must have dreamed it. This struck the little girl as the best kind of a joke; and so she ate so much candy she didn't want any breakfast, and went 'round carrying presents, and had turkey and cranberry for dinner, and then went out and coasted, and came in with a—

"Papa!"
"Well, what now?"
"What did you promise, you forgetful thing?"
"Oh! oh, yes!"

Well, the next day, it was just the same thing over again, but everybody getting crosser; and at the end of a week's time so many people had lost their tempers that you could pick up lost tempers anywhere; they perfectly strewed the ground. Even when people tried to recover their tempers they usually got somebody else's, and it made the most dreadful mix.

The little girl began to get frightened, keeping the secret all to herself; she wanted to tell her mother, but she didn't dare to; and she was ashamed to ask the Fairy to take back her gift, it seemed ungrateful and ill-bred, and she thought she would try to stand it, but she hardly knew how she could, for a whole year. So it went on and on, and it was Christmas on St. Valentine's Day, and Washington's Birthday just the same as any day, and it didn't skip even the First of April, though everything was counterfeit that day, and that was some *little* relief.

After a while, coal and potatoes began to be awfully scarce, so many had been wrapped up in tissue paper to fool papas and mammas with. Turkeys got to be about a thousand dollars apiece—

"Papa!"

"Well, what?"

"You're beginning to fib."

"Well, *two* thousand, then."

And they got to passing off almost anything for turkeys,—half-grown hummingbirds, and even rocs out of the "Arabian Nights,"—the real turkeys were so scarce. And cranberries—well, they asked a diamond apiece for cranberries. All the woods and orchards were cut down for Christmas-trees, and where the woods and orchards used to be, it looked just like a stubble-field, with the stumps. After a while they had to make Christmas-trees out of rags, and stuff them with bran, like old-fashioned dolls;

but there were plenty of rags, because people got so poor, buying presents for one another, that they couldn't get any new clothes, and they just wore their old ones to tatters. They got so poor that everybody had to go to the poor-house, except the confectioners, and the fancy storekeepers, and the picture-booksellers, and the expressmen; and *they* all got so rich and proud that they would hardly wait upon a person when he came to buy; it was perfectly shameful!

Well, after it had gone on about three or four months, the little girl, whenever she came into the room in the morning and saw those great ugly lumpy stockings dangling at the fire-place, and the disgusting presents around everywhere, used to just sit down and burst out crying. In six months she was perfectly exhausted; she couldn't even cry any more; she just lay on the lounge and rolled her eyes and panted. About the beginning of October she took to sitting down on dolls, wherever she found them,— French dolls, or any kind,—she hated the sight of them so; and by Thanksgiving she was crazy, and just slammed her presents across the room.

By that time people didn't carry presents around nicely any more. They flung them over the fence, or through the window, or anything; and, instead of running their tongues out and taking great pains to write "For dear Papa," or "Mamma," or "Brother," or "Sister," or "Susie," or "Sammie," or "Billie," or "Bobby," or "Jimmie," or "Jennie," or whoever it was, and troubling to get the spelling right, and then signing their names, and "Xmas, 188—," they used to write in the gift-books, "Take it, you horrid old thing!" and then go and bang it against the front door. Nearly everybody had built barns to hold their presents, but pretty soon the barns overflowed, and then they used to let them lie out in the rain, or anywhere. Sometimes the police used to come and tell them to shovel their presents off the sidewalk, or they would arrest them.

"I thought you said everybody had gone to the poor-house," interrupted the little girl.

"They did go, at first," said her papa; "but after a while the poor-houses got so full that they had to send the people back to their own houses. They tried to cry, when they got back, but they couldn't make the least sound."

"Why couldn't they?"

"Because they had lost their voices, saying 'Merry Christmas' so much. Did I tell you how it was on the Fourth of July?"

"No; how was it?" And the little girl nestled closer, in expectation of something uncommon.

———

Well, the night before, the boys stayed up to celebrate, as they always do, and fell asleep before twelve o'clock, as usual, expecting to be wakened by the bells and cannon. But it was nearly eight o'clock before the first boy in the United States woke up, and then he found out what the trouble was. As soon as he could get his clothes on, he ran out of the house and smashed a big cannon-torpedo down on the pavement; but it didn't make any more noise than a damp wad of paper, and, after he tried about twenty or thirty more, he began to pick them up and look at them. Every single torpedo was a big raisin! Then he just streaked it upstairs, and examined his fire-crackers and toy-pistol and two-dollar collection of fireworks, and found that they were nothing but sugar and candy painted up to look like fireworks! Before ten o'clock, every boy in the United States found out that his Fourth of July things had turned into Christmas things; and then they just sat down and cried,—they were so mad. There are about twenty million boys in the United States, and so you can imagine what a noise they made. Some men got together before night, with a little powder that hadn't turned into purple sugar yet, and they said they would fire off *one* cannon, any way. But the cannon burst into a thousand pieces, for it was nothing but rock-candy, and some of the men nearly got killed. The Fourth of July orations all turned into Christmas carols, and when anybody tried to read the Declaration, instead of saying, "When in the course of human events it becomes necessary," he was sure to sing, "God rest you, merry gentlemen." It was perfectly awful.

The little girl drew a deep sigh of satisfaction.

"And how was it at Thanksgiving?" she asked.

Her papa hesitated. "Well, I'm almost afraid to tell you. I'm afraid you'll think it's wicked."

"Well, tell, any way," said the little girl.

Well, before it came Thanksgiving, it had leaked out who had caused all these Christmases. The little girl had suffered so much that she had talked about it in her sleep; and after that, hardly anybody would play with her. People just perfectly despised her, because if it had not been for her greediness, it wouldn't have happened; and now, when it came Thanksgiving, and she wanted them to go to church, and have squash-pie and turkey, and show their gratitude, they said that all the turkeys had been eaten up for her old Christmas dinners, and if she would stop the Christmases, they would see about the gratitude. Wasn't it dreadful? And the very next day the little girl began to send letters to the Christmas Fairy, and then telegrams, to stop it. But it didn't do any good; and then she got to calling at the Fairy's house, but the girl that came to the door always said "Not at home," or "Engaged," or "At dinner," or something like that; and so it went on till it came to the old once-a-year Christmas Eve. The little girl fell asleep, and when she woke up in the morning—

"She found it was all nothing but a dream," suggested the little girl.

"No, indeed!" said her papa. "It was all every bit true!"

"Well, what *did* she find out then?"

"Why, that it wasn't Christmas at last, and wasn't ever going to be, any more. Now it's time for breakfast."

The little girl held her papa fast around the neck.

"You sha'n't go if you're going to leave it *so!*"

"How do you want it left?"

"Christmas once a year."

"All right," said her papa; and he went on again.

Well, there was the greatest rejoicing all over the country, and it extended clear up into Canada. The people met together everywhere, and kissed and cried for joy. The city carts went around and gathered up all the candy and raisins and nuts, and dumped them into the river; and it made the fish perfectly sick; and the whole United States, as far out as Alaska, was one blaze of bonfires, where the children were burning up their gift-books and presents of all kinds. They had the greatest *time!*

The little girl went to thank the old Fairy because she had stopped its being Christmas, and she said she hoped she would keep her promise, and see that Christmas never, never came again. Then the Fairy frowned, and asked her if she was sure she knew what she meant; and the little girl asked her, why not? and the old Fairy said that now she was behaving just as greedily as ever, and she'd better look out. This made the little girl think it all over carefully again, and she said she would be willing to have it Christmas about once in a thousand years; and then she said a hundred, and then she said ten, and at last she got down to one. Then the Fairy said that was the good old way that had pleased people ever since Christmas began, and she was agreed. Then the little girl said, "What're your shoes made of?" And the Fairy said, "Leather." And the little girl said, "Bargain's done forever," and skipped off, and hippity-hopped the whole way home, she was so glad.

"How will that do?" asked the papa.

"First-rate!" said the little girl; but she hated to have the story stop, and was rather sober. However, her mamma put her head in at the door, and asked her papa:

"Are you never coming to breakfast? What have you been telling that child?"

"Oh, just a moral tale."

The little girl caught him around the neck again.

"*We* know! Don't you tell *what*, Papa! Don't you tell *what!*"

From the Garden of a Friend

MARY AGNES TINCKER

Carl Petersen was one of the innumerable company of artists who paint pretty pictures for a living, and Mimi was his wife. They were Danes by parentage, but had lived so long in Rome that there was very little Dane left in them, except the honor and simplicity of character one so frequently finds in that people.

They were about as poor as they could comfortably be, this young couple. Carl painted from morning till night, and sold his pictures to Spilorchia, the dealer, who paid for them ten per cent of the price they ultimately brought. Carl knew that he got only ten per cent, but it was better to be sure of so much than to wait for more from purchasers who might never come. What can a poor artist do when people *will* go to the dealers instead of the studios to buy?

But Carl had a plan of escape from this servitude. He meant to lay by a little money, bit by bit, till he should be able to keep back one picture from Spilorchia, and place it instead in the window of a friendly book-seller. He might have to wait a good while; but then he would have ten times as much. And one step made in advance, the second must follow.

The Petersens lived in one of those Roman para-dises which you reach by passing through a Roman purgatory, if that can be called a purgatory which soils instead of cleansing. You cross to Trastevere, pass through several dingy streets, enter a dingier one, that is narrow and dark as well, pass a gloomy *portone* into a green and dripping court, go up a wide stair that smells of garlic and is sometimes infested by dirty children,—up and up to the top. There is an anteroom which has possibilities. Disgust gives place to doubt. There is an ineffably dingy kitchen, which nevertheless calls forth an exclamation of delight from an artist; for, going to the window, you see through wide coincident rifts of many a succeeding line of roofs an exquisite airy vista of mountain, villa, and grove.

Carl had advertised for a studio with two or three rooms attached, and on their first visit to the locality the young couple began as we have, leaving the stu-dio for the last. They were anxious, for they had been house-hunting for a whole month, and were nearly worn out. Besides, time was money to them.

The last door opened. They caught their breath, stepped in, and gave one glance; then turned and rushed into each other's arms. Eureka!

The chamber was palatial in size, and beautifully proportioned; but the glory of it was what came in from outside. Three windows looking toward the northeast gave them the whole of Rome, the Alban and Sabine mountains, and a flood of light. They would have a full view of the sunrise, too; and up to ten o'clock three oblique lines of sunshine moved across their floor.

This room was both studio and salon. Mimi had her work-table at one window, the dining-table stood before another, and Carl's easel was set by the third. They did everything there but cook and sleep, and the place was charming, if bare. Little by little they were covering the rough walls with pictures of all sorts, cut from illustrated papers and magazines, and at intervals Carl painted a slender panel of deep blue, or dull gold, or soft green. His few artistic properties were scattered about. There was a screen or two, a carved chair, and a beautiful oaken chest, very old and carved in palm-leaves. A graceful wicker basket hung over this chest, against one of Carl's blue panels. Mimi cherished this basket, for it had been sent to her on her wedding-day, full of white camellias and blue violets.

Besides the apartment, they had also a garden, only one story below, against the hill-side. A little flight of stairs led to it from the studio. In this garden they had found a treasure,—a young mandarin orange-tree in the first year of its blooming. It was so white with blossoms that it seemed to be fainting under the weight of them. Mimi carefully pinched them all off but one.

"The tree isn't strong enough to bear," she said, "and these blossoms will perfume the studio." She carried them up in her apron, and poured the sweet white drift into her wicker basket on the wall.

The one blossom she had spared faded off in time, and left a green bullet. The bullet grew, and became a ball two inches in diameter. How they watched that little one, having no child of their own! How they guarded it from every possible harm! It was shielded from the wind, covered from hail and heavy rain; and woe to the spider which should spin its web there, or the lizard led by curiosity to whisk up the large brown vase that held their treasure!

The tree grew in the light of their eyes as well as in the sunshine, and seemed to take pride in its own achievement, holding out the laden twig as who should say, "Do you see this child of mine? I also have produced an orange, O my sisters multitudinous of Sorrento and Seville!"

The mandarin turned yellow gradually. At Christmas there were only a tiny cloud and a thread of green. But Mimi was impatient. When Carl sat down to his Christmas dinner, there lay upon his napkin a fragrant golden ball, with a pointed green leaf standing out at either side, wing-like, as if the thing had flown there.

"If it turns out to be dry or sour, I shall feel betrayed," Mimi said. "I couldn't wait any longer to know. Let's try it before we eat."

Carl gave the fruit a scientific pinch, as a cat takes her kittens up by the neck. "It will at least be juicy," he said. "The skin doesn't come off too easily."

The orange was carefully divided, as an orange ought to be, according to the manner of its putting together, and Carl leaned across the table and put one section between the two rows of pearly teeth his wife opened to receive it. Then, while she waited with immovable jaws and lips drawn back, a second section disappeared under his blonde mustache. Looking anxiously into each other's faces, they closed their teeth at the same instant, like two small wine-presses; and at the same instant a sparkling satisfaction foamed up into the eyes of both. The mandarin was a success!

"U-u-m-m-m!" growled Mimi, inarticulately and low, like a cat over a mouse. "It is the king of mandarins!" she cried, when her tongue was free. "It is the Emperor of China himself. How can we wait a whole year for another crop!"

They had to wait, however; and when blossom-time came round again, they left thirty of the finest flowers, the tree having grown stout and matronly. At Christmas thirty globes of pure gold hung amid the dark green foliage.

"I have exchanged fifteen of them for a chicken," Mimi said to her husband on the morning of December 24th. "You know, Carl, we can afford neither to eat nor to give them away, after the extra expenses we have had."

These extra expenses were for a dress coat and a silk dress with a train, or, as Mimi called them for short, a *rondine* and a *strascico*. The young people had some fine friends, who did not choose that they should remain in obscurity, and they were invited out occasionally. Aside from the pleasure they found in society, they knew that it might help Carl in his art to meet such people; and therefore, with tremulous hearts, they had ventured not only to spend their little savings, but to incur a small debt, in order to make themselves presentable. Nor was this all. They had still further diminished their present means by keeping back one of Carl's pictures from the dealer, and setting it in the bookseller's window instead.

This adventurous picture was nothing less than a portrait of their mandarin orange-tree as it had been the year before. It was the same, yet not the same. It was the tree as love saw it.

There was the high, dark gray wall, with an undulating line of green Janiculum above it, and above that a band of pure azure. Below, on a jagged table of ancient masonry that had once been a wall, stood the large brown vase. The slender, supple tree leaned all one way toward the single orange that hung heavily at the tip of its foremost twig, and all the leaves seemed to be twisting their stems about in order to see it. There were still a few faint green lines upon its yellow ripeness; and, studying, one might see that they hinted forth the picture's name,—Il Primogenito. In the wall above was set a torn umbrella, with bunches of long grass carefully stopping the holes. A blue cup full of water stood beside the vase, and a painter's brush, still tinged with blue, was stuck, handle down, where it had loosened the earth about the tree. Around the vase, making a half circle from the wall, was a rough protective barrier, composed of fragments of antique sculpture, heads, arms, hands, half-seen faces, a shoulder pushing out, a strip of egg-moulding as white as milk, a bit of stone-fluting, the curling tip of an acanthus leaf. Lastly, the picture was flooded with sunshine.

If Carl was ever to be famous, it would be for painting sunshine.

They had hopes of this picture, and of their new friends. Only the week before, at a musicale given by the Signora Cremona, they had made the acquaintance of the famous English poetess, Madama Landon, and the great lady had praised one of Carl's pictures which she had seen at the house of a friend. Who knew but she might wish to see others, to buy one, or at least to praise them to others?

The Primogenito unsold, then, Mimi had exchanged half of her oranges for their Christmas roast. "And I have been thinking, Carl," she said, "that we might send the other half to the Cremonas as an acknowledgment of their kindness to us. We have dined there twice, and there was the musicale. We could send them in my basket, and they will make a very pretty show."

They went to work at once. The basket was lined with moss, and over that Mimi laid a little open-wrought napkin, laboriously made by her own fingers by drawing threads out of linen. Each mandarin was cut with a stem and a leaf or two, and artistically placed.

"How beautiful!" sighed Mimi. "And there are

just enough. One more would be a bump, and one less a dent."

A note was written on their last sheet of fine paper; the basket was covered with white tissue-paper, and tied with blue ribbons preserved from their wedding presents.

When Carl went out with the basket, Mimi followed him to the stairs, and looked after him with tears in her eyes.

"It's like sending one's own children out into the world," she thought. "Dear little creatures! They have never had anything but love and praising here."

And so the basket of mandarins began its travels; its grand tour, in fact.

It reached the Signora Cremona in safety.

"How pretty!" said the lady. "But we have fruit for to-day, and to-morrow we dine out. I will send the basket to Mrs. James, with our regrets for her breakfast to-morrow."

A note was written. The Signora Cremona was *so* sorry that a previous engagement would prevent their breakfasting with Mrs. James the next day, and begged her to accept a basket of mandarin oranges, which she thought would be fine, as they were from a friend's garden.

Mrs. James and her sister were just having their after-breakfast coffee and cigarettes when the present was brought in.

"The Cremonas cannot come," Mrs. James said, reading the note. "And see what a lovely basket of mandarins! If we had not bought and settled everything for to-morrow, I would set this in the middle of the table, just as it is. Oh! I'll tell you what we can do,—send it with a note to Monsignore Appetitoso. He might hear of our breakfast, you know, and feel slighted. Poor soul! I shouldn't want to offend him. He is very useful."

The note was written, the blue ribbons were tied for the third time, and the young tourists set out anew on their travels.

Monsignore Appetitoso was a *jubilato a mezza paga;* that is, having passed a certain age, he was dispensed from the duties of his office with a pension of half its salary. Besides this, the pay being small, the Pope had assigned him a free apartment in the canonicate of Santa Veronica del Fazzoletto, a palace that was nearly vacant, the canons preferring to reside outside. Here the old gentleman lived very comfortably, though without luxury; going out to dinner when he was invited, getting an afternoon cup of tea and slice of cake in some lady's drawing-room now and then, and dreaming over the happy days, long past, when he was *delegato*, and rounded his dinner off with ices, candies, and vin santo, instead of roasted chestnuts and a biscuit.

Monsignore dined at one o'clock, and was just

eating a *biscottino* with his glass of Marsala, after the soup, boiled beef and greens, stewed pigeons and roasted chestnuts, which had formed the repast, when Mrs. James's present arrived.

(We make haste to add, lest scrupulous souls should be scandalized at a priest's eating meat on a vigil, that Monsignore was dispensed from both fasting and abstinence on account of his sixty-eight years and a disease of the stomach. Some of his laughing brethren averred that the disease was a constant voracious appetite; but that is not our affair.)

The basket was uncovered with eagerness, and, settling himself more comfortably in his chair, Monsignore prepared to devour its whole contents then and there. But as he smilingly lifted off the topmost orange, a thought arrested him.

He had just heard—the news came in with the roasted chestnuts—that the rector of the College of Converted Zulus had been taken seriously ill that morning, and therefore could not have the honor of dining with Cardinal Inghilterra the next evening.

Now Monsignore had felt hurt at not receiving an invitation to this dinner. He loved the cardinal as only a poor gourmand can love a rich one, and had served him to the extent of his power. Who knows, he thought, but I may be asked to fill the rector's place? There was every probability of it, if only that pushing Monsignore Barili did not thrust himself in.

Would not the cardinal be touched by the amiable piety of a man who should send him a basket of fruit after having been excluded from his dinner-table? He, Monsignore, was not expected to know anything about the rector of the Zulus' opportune seizure, or at least not so quickly.

He put the orange carefully back into its place, and, after ringing his bell, tied the blue ribbons again,—their fourth tying, as the creases in them began to hint.

"Giacomo," he said, when his man appeared, "run as fast as you can with this to Cardinal Inghilterra, and ask permission to see him. Make the proper compliments, and try to find out if Monsignore Barili has been there to-day."

Cardinal Inghilterra lunched when Monsignore dined, and he was still at table when Giacomo was graciously permitted to present himself. Poor Monsignore was useful to others beside Mrs. James, and the cardinal used him a good deal, and treated him with good-natured, condescending familiarity.

He sat in a room like a green tent, with a window full of sunshine and a garden behind him. Before him on the table was a cup of coffee, into which he was just dropping a lump of sugar from the tips of his white dimpled fingers. At his right hand was a liquor stand, and a gilded glass rosily full of "Perfetto Amore," one of the new Turin liquors that are trying to oust French ones from the market. An open note, the agonized regrets of the rector of the Zulus, lay at his left hand.

As Giacomo entered, and received a nod of recognition and a sign to wait, the cardinal was listening to his majordomo, who, full of reverential anxiety, was communicating to his Eminence the possibility that fish might not be forthcoming for to-morrow's dinner. A storm had driven back the fishes of the west coast the night before, and the wind there was still contrary. There was not even a minnow in the market to-day; and the dealers had promised more than they expected to receive. The cook had prayed, bribed, and threatened, but the event still remained doubtful.

The cardinal listened with tranquillity, sipping his coffee. He did not believe in impossibilities—for himself.

"There is a telegraph in Rome," he remarked, as if communicating an item of news. "And there is"—he sipped his coffee—"a telegraph at Civita Vecchia"—another sip—"and at Porto d'Anzio"—sip—"and at Ancona"—sip—"and at various other sea, and therefore fish, ports around the coast of Italy;" and he finished his coffee, and set the cup aside.

"Certainly, Eminenza!" the man struck in. "But I could not incur the expense without a special permission. If I send three telegrams to make sure of one, I may have to pay for three baskets of fishes; and besides, the price"—

"You can discuss that with the cook," interrupted his master, and, waving him away, beckoned Giacomo to advance.

"Monsignore is very good," he said after listening to the man's errand. "Tell him that I am infinitely obliged. And"—he hesitated, and glanced at the letter beside him. He saw through Monsignore's little pious ruse perfectly; but, as we have said, he was good-natured. "Wait in the anteroom a moment," he added. "See if Antonio is there, and send him to me."

Giacomo bowed himself out backward, and Antonio bowed himself in forward. He was a man of such a villainous solemnity of aspect that, had one encountered him in heaven even, one would have recognized him as the confidential servant of a priest. Face cleanly shaven, eyes downcast, mouth firmly closed, neck advanced as if to lay its head on the block (for virtue's sake, *s' intende*), and what mocking young Italy calls an expression of *Gesù mio* made Antonio one of the cream of his kind.

"Cover these mandarins with the best roses that you can find in the garden," the cardinal said, "and take them, with my compliments, to the Signora Landon. Throw away the wraps; they are soiled. And you need not let Giacomo see you."

Exit Antonio in funereal silence.

About the same time two ladies were examining a picture set up frameless on a table in a little salon in Hotel Bristol.

"Isn't it charming?" said one of them. "I bought it this morning, and I am going to send it home to Tom. I can't keep it for myself, because the sunshine of it freckles me. Tom will be delighted with it, it is so Italian. I know the artist. He and his wife were at La Cremona's musicale last week. Such a nice little couple!—like two birds."

Enter Antonio.

"Oh! was it you, Antonio?" cried the lady, turning. "I thought it was my shoemaker. How is his Eminence?"

Antonio, with the air of taking his last leave of his dearest friend, delivered his message.

"How perfectly lovely!" was the response. "Will you come and look at these mandarins, Lady Mary? See how well they are arranged! *Mandarini* smothered in roses! They need not blush before strawberries and cream. It is a poem. Eminenza's fruit is worthy to have grown on my painted orange-tree. Stay a moment, Antonio, while I write my thanks."

The quill went scrawling over a sheet of cream-colored paper, that had initials and a crest occupying all the left side; a prompt white hand slapped the blotting-book over those large characters, folded, inclosed, and directed the note, and sealed it with a ring worn on the writer's thumb.

Antonio received this missive as though it were his death-warrant, but with a sudden convulsion of face as he felt the generous breadth of a five-franc piece under it. He had nearly smiled.

"The cardinal has such good taste!" the poetess said, smilingly contemplating his gift, when Antonio had faded away. "But, unfortunately, I never eat oranges. They make me bilious. Oh! I know what I will do. I can send them to the artist who painted that picture. It will be a pleasant way of announcing to him that his picture is sold. The bookseller told me that he had already been in this morning to see if any one had looked at it, and seemed very sad. Jeannette can carry the basket over with a note to-morrow morning. There is no time this afternoon. Will you please touch the bell-knob at your elbow, Mary?"

A servant appeared.

"Bring me a vase with water for these roses," Mrs. Landon said. "And send my maid to me."

The next day Mimi and Carl had their dinner at noon. It was a poorer dinner than they had ever before eaten on a *festa* day, for there was nothing to follow their chicken but four *soldi* worth of cheese and their coffee. To be sure, there isn't much sense in eating cheese when you have no fruit; but, as Mimi said, their hearts had been so full of the mandarins that may be their stomachs might have felt the influence. Besides, cheese gives a certain air.

Their cheerfulness was a little forced to-day. Carl had been painting since daybreak, and was tired, and his wife was not feeling well.

"Did you say that this was a chicken?" he asked, probing the fowl before him.

"Why, yes, dear, and a nice plump one, too," replied Mimi, trying to make the best of everything. "Didn't I pay fifteen golden mandarins fresh from the mint for it? Did you think that it was a goose?"

"No," said Carl, laboriously cutting, "I didn't think that it was a goose; but—err—seems to me that it has—err—a good deal of—err—character for a chicken."

"You don't mean to say that it's tough!" Mimi faltered, trying to keep back the tears that made a sudden rush for her eyes.

Carl's reply was checked by the sound of their door-bell, sharply rung.

"A beggar!" said Mimi, and started up hastily, glad to hide her face, and snatching a piece of bread as she went.

"I oughtn't to have let her know that it is tough, poor Mimi!" thought Carl.

In two minutes she came back radiant.

"See! a present and a note from Madama Landon!" she cried, holding out a basket swathed in tissue-paper, and elaborately tied with a silken cord.

"Her maid brought it. It is fruit, as sure as you live. God is good! How nice it is to be remembered, and have something come in,—just in the nick of time, too! That dear lady! I knew she had a good heart, she is so bright-eyed and has so much color. She blushes if she stirs. I always noticed—Why, Carl, the handle of this basket is just like ours!"

"Of course there are plenty in the world like it," remarked Carl, watching with great interest the careful undoing of the blue, softly twisted cords.

"It is heavenly to get just such a one back," said Mimi, picking carefully, with an impatient tremor, at the knots. "It makes this seem a sort of second wedding-day, doesn't it, dear?"

The last cover off, the two stared for one moment in silence at their gift, then at each other, then at their gift again. Their faces had grown very blank. Then Mimi, with a finger and thumb, lifted out by the stem one mandarin after another, setting them in a row on the table. There were fifteen.

"I didn't need this to prove it," she said in a hushed voice, picking the napkin out of the basket. "I know the looks of those mandarins as well as I know yours. I could go out now and set each one on its own twig on the tree."

Another blank silence; then Mimi burst into a

laugh: "Don't you see, Carl? La Cremona must have sent them to her, they were so pretty; and she has sent them to us, without ever suspecting. Isn't it comical, and delightful? Oh, little prodigals, welcome home again!"

They bethought themselves to read the note. The lady had written:—

Dear Signor Petersen,—Allow me to offer you some mandarins which are worthy to have grown on your own tree, which, by the way, is now my tree. I have bought your Primogenito, and am so much pleased with it that I would like to have a companion picture, when you have time to favor me with one. With compliments to your charming wife, and a *buona festa* to both,

Yours sincerely, Clare Landon.

P.S. I send you the basket just as it was sent to me by a cardinal. C.L.

"A cardinal!"

No matter! Let the mystery go, since it had brought a miracle of joy. Mimi was weeping with delight.

"Give me the two very largest," she said, "and I will carry them down to those two children on the ground floor. How wicked I have been to hate them, even if they do dirty the stairs and throw stones at me! I will kiss them, Carl, since I cannot kiss God!"

"We mustn't utter the word mandarins to La Cremona," Carl said.

But the very next time he met the Signora Cremona she thanked him with graceful cordiality for his present. "They were delicious," she said.

Carl bowed with perfect gravity.

And then he saw her blush slightly, as she hastened away from him to meet her friend, Mrs. James, who was coming across from the Spanish steps to speak to her.

"I want to thank you for that lovely fruit," Mrs. James said, with effusion. "It was the finest I have had this year; so fresh, and honey-sweet!"

The lady had excellent authority for her praises; for Monsignore Appetitoso had called on her that very morning to make his compliments on her gift. "Your mandarins arrived just in time for my dinner," he said, smacking his lips, as if he still had the taste of them in his mouth.

Mrs. James professed herself honored in having been allowed to contribute to Monsignore's Christmas dinner. "I thought the mandarins would be fine," she said. "They were sent me from the garden of a friend."

"Oh! it was the day before. I dined with his Eminence, Cardinal Inghilterra, last evening," Monsignore replied complacently. "And I thought that you might like to see the *menu*," drawing a carefully

folded paper from his pocket, and a white satin ribbon from the paper.

With a simultaneous "Oh!" Mrs. James and her
sister seized the dainty gold-lettered trifle, and
bumped their heads together in the eagerness with
which they bent over it to see what a cardinal would
give his friends for dinner.

"I hope that your Eminence enjoyed the little basket of fruit I took the liberty to send yesterday,"
Monsignore had said the evening before, in a
momentary pause in the talk about the table. "It was
from a friend's garden, and I thought it choice."

"It was most excellent!" was the gracious answer.
"I have never eaten better."

And here the odor of truffles stole into Monsignore's nostrils from a dish waiting at his left
elbow. Oh, how he loved that man sitting opposite
him, glorious in scarlet and diamonds, and still more
glorious as the dispenser of such bounties! His Eminence would have been proclaimed Pope on the
instant, if Monsignore Appetitoso had had the
power. Oh, how he loved him! What! Château
Yquem? He would die for that man—that god! And
then to have directly before his plate an exquisite
dish of Spillman's best candies, and to know that
what he did not eat then he could carry away in a
bonbonière!

Poor Monsignore had to wink hard more than

once during dinner to keep from crying outright with rapture and gratitude. When they arrived at the liquors, tears were, in fact, running down his cheeks. But as all the reverend company were by this time in a more or less beaming condition, no one observed his emotion.

"Eminence," said Mrs. Landon, the first time he visited her after Christmas, "I knew, of course, that you are intimate with the saints; but I was not aware that the pagan divinities also serve you. You must be on the best of terms with the Hesperides. Nowhere but in their orchards could have been mingled the fire and honey of your delicious mandarins."

His Eminence bowed smilingly.

"I am happy to know that you found them to your taste," he said, in his superb, deliberate way. "They were, in fact, from—err—the garden of a friend."

The Christmas Club

A Ghost Story

EDWARD EGGLESTON

T he Dickens!"

That was just what Charley Vanderhuyn said that Christmas Eve, and as a faithful historian I give the exact words. It sounded like swearing, though why we should regard it profane to make free with the devil's name, or even his Nickname, I never could see. Can you? Besides, there was some ambiguity about Charley's use of the word under the circumstances, and he himself couldn't tell whether his exclamation had reference to the Author of Evils or only to the Author of Novels. The circumstances were calculated to suggest equally thoughts of the Great Teller of Stories and of the Great Storyteller, and I have a mind to amuse you at this Christmas season by telling you the circumstances, and letting you decide, if you can, which Dickens it was that Charles Vanderhuyn intended.

Charley Vanderhuyn was one of those young men that could grow nowhere on this Continent except in New York. He had none of the severe dignity that belongs to a young man of wealth who has passed his life in sight of long rows of red brick houses, with clean door steps and white wooden shutters. Something of the venerableness of Independence Hall, the dignity of Girard College, and the air of financial importance that belongs to the Mint, gets into the blood of a Philadelphian. Charley had none of that. Neither did he have that air of profound thought, that Adams-Hancock-Quincy-Webster-Emerson-Sumner look that is the inevitable mark of Beacon Street. When you see such a young man you know that he has grown part of Faneuil Hall, and the Common, and the Pond, and the Historic Elm. He has lived where the very trees are learned, and carry their Latin names about with them. Charley had none of the "vim" and dash that belongs to a Westerner. He was of the metropolis—metropolitan. He had good blood in him, else he could never have founded the Christmas Club, for you cannot get more out of a man than there is in his blood. Charley Vanderhuyn bore a good old Dutch name— I have heard that the Van der Huyns were a famous and noble family—his Dutch blood was mingled with other good strains, and the whole was mellowed into generousness and geniality in generations of prosperous ancestors; for the richest and choicest fruit (and the rankest weeds, as well!) can only be produced in the sunlight. And a very choice fruit of a very choice stock was and is our Charley Vanderhuyn. That everybody knows who knows him now, and that we all felt who knew him earlier, in the days of the Hasheesh Club.

You remember the Hasheesh Club, doubtless. In its day it numbered the choicest spirits in New York, and the very center of all of them was this same Charley Vanderhuyn, whose face, the boys used to say, was like the British Empire—for on it the sun never set. His unflagging spirits, his keen love for society, his quick sympathy with everybody, his fine appreciation of every man's good points, whatever they might be, made Charley a prince wherever he went. I said he was the center of the circle of young men about the Hasheesh Club ten years ago, and so he was, though, to tell the truth, he was then but about twenty-one years of age. They had a great time at the Club, I remember, when he came of age, and came into possession of his patrimony—a trifle of half a million I believe. He gave a dinner, and there was such a time as the Hasheesh Club never saw before nor since. I fear there was over-much wine-drinking, and I am sure there was a fearful amount of punch drunk. Charley never drank to excess, never lost his self-control for a moment under any temptation. But there was many another young man of different temperament, to whom the rooms of the Club were what candles are to moths. One poor fellow, who always burnt his wings, was a blue-eyed golden-haired young magazine writer of that day. We all thought of his ability and promise— his name was John Perdue, but you will doubtless remember him by his *nom de plume* of "Baron Bertram." Poor fellow! he loved Charley passionately, and always drank himself drunk at the Club. He wasted all he had and all he made, his clothes grew shabby, he borrowed of Charley, who was always open-handed, until his pride would allow him to borrow no more. He had just married, too, and he was so ashamed of his own wreck that he completed his ruin by drinking to forget it. I am not writing a story with a temperance moral; temperance tales are always stupid, and always useless. The world is brimfull of walking morals on that subject, and if one will not read the lesson of the life of his next-door neighbor, what use of bringing Lazarus from the dead to warn him of a perdition that glares at him out of the eyes of so many men.

I only mentioned John Perdue—poor golden haired "Baron Bertram"—because he had something to do with the circumstances which led

Charley Vanderhuyn to use that ambiguous interjection about "the Dickens!" Perdue, as I said, dropped away from the Hasheesh Club, lost his employment as literary editor of the *Luminary*, fell out of good society, and at last earned barely enough to keep him and his wife and his child in bread, and to supply himself with whiskey, by writing sensation stories for the "penny dreadfuls." We all suspected that he would not have received half so much for his articles had they been paid for on their merits, or at the standard price for hack writing. But Charley Vanderhuyn had something to do with it. He sent Henry Vail—he always sent Henry Vail on his missions of mercy—to find out where Perdue sold his articles, and I have no doubt the price of each article was doubled, at Vanderhuyn's expense.

And that mention of Henry Vail reminds me that I cannot tell this story rightly unless I let you know who he was. A distant relation of Charley's, I believe. He was a studious fellow from the country, and quite awkward in company. The contrast between him and Charley was marked. Vanderhuyn was absolutely *au fait* in all the usages of society; he knew by instinct how a thing ought to be done, and his example was law. He had a genius for it, everybody said. Vail was afraid of his shadow, did not know just what was proper to do in any new circumstances. His manners hung about him loosely—

Vanderhuyn's were part of himself. When Vail came to the Hasheesh Club for the first time, it was on the occasion of Charley's majority dinner. Vail consulted Vanderhuyn about his costume, and was told that he must wear evening dress; and never having seen anything but provincial society, he went with perfect assurance to a tailor's and ordered a new frock coat and a white vest. When he saw that the other gentlemen present wore dress coats, and that most of them had black vests, he was in some consternation. He even debated whether he should not go out and hire a dress coat for the evening. He drew Charley aside, and asked him why he did not tell him that those sparrow-tail things had come into fashion again!

But he never took kindly to the club-life; he soon saw that however harmless it might be to some men, it was destruction to others. After attending a few times, Henry Vail, who was something of a Puritan, and much of a philanthropist, declared his opposition to what he called an English dissipation.

Henry Vail was a scholarly fellow, of real genius, and studied for the ministry; but he had original notions, and about the time he was to have taken deacon's orders in the Episcopal Church he drew back. He said that orders would do for some men, but he did not intend to build a wall between himself and his fellows. He could do more by remaining a man of like passions with other men than he could by casing himself in a clerical "strait-jacket," as he called it. Having a little income of his own, he set up on his own account, in the dingiest part of that dingy street called Huckleberry Street—the name, with all its suggestions of fresh fields and pure air and liberty, is a dreary mockery. Just where Greenfield Court—the blackest and dingiest of New York alleys—runs out of Huckleberry Street, he set up shop, to use his own expression. He was a kind of independent lay clergyman, ministering to the physical and spiritual wants of his neighbors, climbing to garrets and penetrating to cellars, now talking to a woman who owned a candy and gingerbread stall, and now helping to bury a drunken sailor. Such a life for a scholar! But he always declared that digging out Greek and Hebrew roots was not half so fascinating a work as digging out human souls from the filth of Huckleberry Street.

Of course he did not want for money to carry on his operations. Charley Vanderhuyn's investments brought large returns, and Charley knew how to give. When Vail would begin a pathetic story, Vanderhuyn would draw out his check-book, and say, "How much shall it be, Harry?—never mind the story. It's handy to have you to give away my money for me. I should never take the trouble to see that it went to the people that needed. One dollar given by you is worth ten that I bestow on Tom, Dick and Harry, so I prefer to let Tom and Dick go without, and give it all to Harry." In fact Vanderhuyn had been the prey of so many impostors that he adopted the plan of sending all of his applicants to Vail, with a note to him, which generally ran thus, "Please investigate." The tramps soon ceased to bother him, and then he took to entrusting to Vail each month a sum equal to what he had been in the habit of giving away loosely.

It was about the first of December, four years ago, that Harry Vail, grown younger and fresher in two years of toil among the poor—glorified he seemed by the tenderness of his sympathies and the nobleness of his aims—it was four years ago that Harry came into Charley Vanderhuyn's rooms for his regular monthly allotment. Vail generally came in the evening, and Charley generally managed to be disengaged for that evening. The two old friends whose paths diverged so widely were fond of one another's company, and Vail declared that he needed one evening in the month with Vanderhuyn; he liked to carry away some of Charley's sunshine to the darkness of Huckleberry Street and Greenfield Court. And Charley said that Harry brought more sunlight than he took. I believe he was right. Charley, like all men who live without a purpose, was growing less refined and charming than he had been, his cheeks were just a trifle graver than those of the young Charley had been. But he talked magnificently as ever. Vail said that he himself was an explorer in a barbarous desert, and that Charles Vanderhuyn was the one civilized man he could meet.

It is a curious thing that Vail had never urged Charley to a different life from the self-indulgent one that he led, but it was a peculiarity of Henry's that he was slow to attack a man directly. I have heard that it was one great secret of his success among the poor, that he would meet an intemperate man twenty times, perhaps, before he attacked his vice. Then, when the man had ceased to stand guard, Vail would suddenly find an entrance to him by an unwatched gate. It was remarkable, too, that when he did seize on a man he never for an instant relaxed his grasp. I have often looked at his aquiline nose, and wondered if it were not an index to this eagle-like swoop at the right moment, and this unwavering firmness of hold.

On this evening, about the first of December, four years ago, he sat in Charley's cozy bed-room and listened to Vanderhuyn's stories of a life antipodal to the life he was accustomed to see—for the antipodes do not live round the world, but round the first street corner—he listened and laughed at the graphic and eloquent and grotesque pictures that Charley drew for him till nearly midnight, and then got ready to go back to his home, among the noisy saloons of Huckleberry Street. Charley drew out his check-book, and wrote and tore off the check, and handed it to Vail.

"I want more, Charley, this time," said Vail in his quiet, earnest way, with gray eyes fixed on his friend's blue ones.

"Got more widows without coal than usual, eh, old fellow? How much shall it be? Double? Ask anything. I can't refuse the half of my fortune to such a good angel as you are, Vail. I don't spend any money that pays so well as what I give you. I go to the clubs and to parties. I sit at the opera and listen to Signora Scracchioli, and say to myself, 'Well, there's Vail using my money to help some poor devil in trouble.' I tell you I get a comfortable conscience by an easy system of commutation. Here, exchange with me, this is for double the amount, and I am glad you mentioned it."

"But I want more than that this time," and Vail fixed his eyes on Charley in a way that made the latter feel just a little ill at ease, a sensation very new to him.

"Well, how much, Harry? Don't be afraid to ask. I told you you should have half my kingdom, old fellow?" And Vanderhuyn took his pen, and began to date another check.

"But Charley, I am almost afraid to ask; I want

more than half you have—I want something worth more than all you have."

"Why, you make me curious. Never saw you in that vein before, Vail," and Charley twisted a piece of paper, lighted it in the gas-jet, and held it gracefully in his fingers while he set his cigar going, hoping to hide his restlessness under the wistful gaze of his friend by this occupation of his attention.

But however nervous Henry Vail might be in the performance of little acts that were mere matters of convention, there was no lack of quiet self-possession in matters that called out his earnestness of spirit. And now he sat gazing steadily at Charley until the cigar had been gracefully lighted, the bit of paper tossed on the grate, and until Charley had watched his cigar a moment. When the latter reluctantly brought his eyes back into range with the dead-earnest ones that had never ceased to look on him with that strange wistful expression, then Henry Vail proceeded.

"I want *you*, Charley."

Charley laughed heartily now. "Me? What a missionary *I* would make! Kid-glove gospeller I'd be called in the first three days. What a superb Sunday-school teacher I'd make! Why, Henry Vail, you know better. There's just one thing in this world I have a talent for—and that's society. I'm a man of the world in my very fiber. But as for following in your illustrious footsteps—I wish I could be so good a man, but you see I'm not built in that way. I'm a man of the world."

"That's just what I want," said Henry Vail, looking with the same tender, wistful look into his friend's eyes. "If I'd wanted a missionary I shouldn't have come to you. If I'd wanted a Sunday-school teacher, I could have found twenty better; and for tract distributing and Bible-reading, you couldn't do either if you'd try. What I want for Huckleberry Street more than I want anything else, is a man of the world. You are a man of the world,—of the whole world. I have seen a restaurant waiter stop and gape and listen to your talk. I have seen a coal-heaver delighted with your manners when you paid him. Charley, you're the most magnificent man of the world I ever saw. Must a man of the world be useless? I tell you I want you for God and Huckleberry Street, and I mean to have you some day, old fellow;" and the perfect assurance with which he said this, and the settled conviction of final success that was visible in his quiet gray eyes, fascinated Charley Vanderhuyn, and he felt spell-bound, like the wedding guest by the "Ancient Mariner."

"I tell you what, Henry," he said presently, "I've got no call. I'm an Epicurean. I say to you in the words of an American poet:—

'Take the current of your nature, make it
stagnant if you will:

Dam it up to drudge forever at the service
of your will.

Mine the rapture and the freedom of the
torrent on the hill!

I shall wander o'er the meadows where the
fairest blossoms call:

Though the ledges seize and fling me
headlong from the rocky wall,

I shall leave a rainbow hanging o'er the
ruins of my fall.'"

"Charley, I don't want to preach," said Vail; "but
you know that this doctrine of mere selfish floating
on the current of impulse, which your traveler poet
teaches is devilish laziness, and devilish laziness
always tends to something worse. You may live such
a life, and quote such poetry, but you don't believe
that a man should flow on like a purposeless river.
The lines you quoted bear the mark of a restless
desire to apologize to conscience for a fearful waste
of power and possibility. No," he said, rising, "I
don't want that check. This one will do; but you
won't forget that God and Huckleberry Street want
you, and they will have you, too, noble-hearted fellow. Good night! God bless you!" and he shook
Charley's hand and went out into the night to seek

his home in Huckleberry Street. And the genial Charley never saw his brave friend again. Yes, he did, too. Or did he?

II.

The month of December four years ago was a month of much festivity in the metropolis. Charley was wanted nearly every night to grace some gathering or other, and Charley was too obliging to refuse to go where he was wanted,—that is, when he was wanted in Fifth Avenue or Thirty-fourth Street. As for Huckleberry Street and Greenfield Court they were fast fading out of Charley's mind. He knew that Henry Vail would introduce the subject when he came for his January check, and he expected some annoyance from the discussion of the question—annoyance, because there was something in his own breast that answered to Vail's appeal. Charley was more than an Epicurean. To eat and drink, to laugh and talk, and die, was not enough for such a soul. He mentally compared himself to Felix, and said that Vail wouldn't let him forget his duty, anyhow. But for the present it was too delightful to him to honor the entertainment given by the Honorable Mr. So-and-so and lady; it was pleasant to be assured by Mrs. Forty-Millions that her party would fail but for his presence. And then he had just achieved the end of his ambition. He was President of the Hasheesh Club. He took his seat at the head of the table on Christmas Eve.

Now, patient reader, we draw near to the time when Charley uttered the exclamation set down at the head of this story. Bear with my roundabout way of telling a little longer. It is Christmas-tide anyway, why should we hurry ourselves through this happy season?

Just as Charley went into the door of the Club-House—you remember the Hasheesh Club-House was in Madison Avenue then—just as Charley entered, he met the burly form and genial face of the eminent Dr. Van Doser, who said, "Well, Vander-huyn, how's your cousin Vail?"—"Is he sick?" asked Charley, struck with a foreboding that made him tremble.

"Sick? Didn't you know? Well, that's just like Vail. He was taken with small-pox two weeks ago, and I wanted to take the risk of penalties and not report his case, but he said if I didn't he would do it him-self; that sanitary regulations requiring small-pox patients to go to a hospital were necessary, and that it became one in his position to set a good example to Huckleberry Street. So I was compelled to report him, and let him go to the Island. And he hasn't let you know? For fear you would try to communicate with him probably, and thus expose yourself to infection. Extraordinary man that Vail. I never saw his like," and with that the Doctor turned to speak to some gentlemen who had just come in.

And so Charley's Christmas Eve dinner at the Hasheesh Club was spoiled. There are two inconvenient things in this world—a conscience and a tender heart—and Charley Vanderhuyn was plagued with both. While going through with the toasts, his mind was busy with poor Henry Vail suffering in a small-pox hospital. In his graceful response to the sentiment, "The President of the Hasheesh Club," he alluded to the retiring president, and made some witty remark—I forget what—about his being a denizen of Lexington Avenue; but in saying Lexington Avenue he came near slipping into Huckleberry Street, and in fact he did get the first syllable out before he checked himself. He was horrified afterwards to think how near he had come, later in the evening, to addressing the company as "Gentlemen of the Smallpox Hospital."

Charley drank more wine and punch than usual. Those who sat near him looked at one another significantly, in a way that implied their belief that Vanderhuyn was too much elated over his election. Little did they know that at that moment the presidency of the famous Hasheesh Club appeared to Charley the veriest bawble in the world. If he had not known how futile would be any attempt to gain an entrance to the small-pox hospital he would have excused himself, and started for the Island on the instant.

But it was one o'clock before Charley got away. Out of the brilliantly lighted rooms he walked, stunned with grief, and a little heavy with the wine and punch he had drunk, for in his pre-occupation of mind he had forgotten to be as cautious as usual. Following an impulse, he took a car and went directly down town, and then made his way to Huckleberry Street. He stopped at a saloon door and asked if they could tell him were Mr. Vail's rooms were.

"The blissed man as wint about like a saint! Shure and I can," said the boozy Irishman. "Its right fer-ninst where yer afther stanin, up the stairs on the corner of Granefield Coort—over there, bedad."

Seeing a light in the rooms indicated by the man, Charley crossed over, passed through a sorrowful-looking crowd at the door, and went up the stairs. He found the negro woman who kept the rooms for Vail, standing talking to an Irishwoman. Both the women were deeply pitted with small-pox.

He inquired if they could tell him how Mr. Vail was.

"Oh, honey, he's done dead sence three o'clock," said the black woman, sitting down in a chair, and beginning to wipe her eyes on her apron. "This Misses Mcgroarty's jist done tole me this minute."

The Irishwoman came round in front of Mr. Vanderhuyn, and looked inquisitively at him a moment, and then said, "Faix, mister, and is yer name Charley?"

"Why do you ask?" said Vanderhuyn.

"Because I thought, mebbe, you might be after him, the gentleman. It's me husband Pat Mcgroarty as is a nurruss in the horsepital, and a good one as iver ye seed, and it's Pat as has been a tellin me about that blissed saint of a man, as how in his delairyum he kept a talkin to Charley all the time, and Pat said as he seemed to have something on his mind he wanted to say to Charley. An' whin I see yer face, sich a gintleman's face as ye've got, too, I says shure that must be Charley."

"What did he say?" asked Vanderhuyn.

"Shure and Pat said it wasn't much he could gether, for he was in a awful delairyum ye know, but he would keep a sayin,' 'Charley, Charley, God and Huckleberry Street want you.' Pat says he'd say it so awful as would make him shiver, that God and Huckleberry Street wanted Charley. Shure it must a bin the delairyum, you know, that made him mix up things loike, and put God and Huckleberry Street together, when its more loike the divil would seem more proper to go with Huckleberry Street, ye know. But if yer name's Charley, and yer loike the loike's of him as is dead, shure Huckleberry Street is after wantin' of you, bad enough."

"My name's Charley, but I'm not a bit like him, though, I'm sorry to say, my good woman. Tell your husband to come and see me—there's my number."

Charley went out, and the men at the door whispered, "that must be the rich man as give him all the money." He took the last car up-town, and he who had been two hours before in that brilliant company at the Hasheesh was now one of ten people riding in a street car. Of his fellow-passengers six were drunken men and two were low women of the town; one of them had no bonnet and lacked a penny of enough to pay her fare, but the conductor mercifully let her ride, remarking to Vanderhuyn, who stood on the platform, that "the poor devil had a hard life anyhow." Said I not a minute ago, that the antipodes live, not around the world, but around the street corner? Antipodes ride in the same street car.

As the car was passing Mott Street, a passenger, half drunk, came out, turned his haggard face a moment towards the face of Charley Vanderhuyn, and then with an exclamation of startled recognition, leaped from the car and hurried away in the darkness. It was not till the car had gone three blocks farther that Vanderhuyn guessed, from the golden hair, that this was Perdue, the brilliant "Baron Bertram" of the early days of the Hasheesh Club.

When Charley got back to his luxurious apartments, he was possessed with a superstitious feeling.

He took up the paper-weight that Henry Vail had held in his hand the very last night he was in this parlor, and he thought the whole conversation over as he smoked his cigar, fearing to put out his light.

"Confound the man that invented ghost-stories for a Christmas amusement," he said, as he remembered Old Scrooge and Tiny Tim. "Well, I'm not Old Scrooge anyhow, if I'm not as good as poor Henry Vail."

I do not know whether it was the reaction from the punch he had drunk, or the sudden shock of Vail's death, or the troubled conscience, or both, when he got into bed he found himself shaking with nervousness.

He had been asleep an hour perhaps, when he heard a genuine Irish voice say, "Faix mister, and is yer name Charley?"

He started up,—looked around the room. He had made so much concession to his nervous feeling that he had not turned the gas quite out, as was his custom. The dim duskiness made him shudder, he expected to see the Huckleberry Street Irishwoman looking at him. But he shook off his terror a little, uttered another malediction on the man that invented Christmas ghost-stories, concluded that his illusion must have come from his lying on his left side, turned over, and reflected that by so doing he would relieve his heart and stomach from the weight of his liver, repeated this physiological reflection in a soothing way two or three times, dropped off into a quiet snooze, and almost immediately found himself sitting bolt upright in bed, shaking with a chill-terror, sure that the Irish voice had again asked the question, "Faix, mister, and is your name Charley?" He had a feeling, though his back was toward the table, that some one sat at the table. Charley was no coward, but it took him a minute or two to shake off his terror, and regain enough self-control to look around.

For a moment he saw, or thought he saw, a form sitting at the table, then it disappeared, and then, after a good while, Charley got himself composed to sleep again, this time with his head well bolstered, to reduce the circulation in the brain, as he reflected.

He did not get to sleep, however, for before he became unconscious the Irish voice from just above the carved head-board spoke out so clear now, that there could be no mistake, "Faix, mister, and is yer name Charley?" It was then that he rose up in bed and uttered the exclamation which I set down in the first line of this story. Charley Vanderhuyn could not tell whether he meant Charles Dickens or Nick. Perhaps you can. Indeed, it doesn't seem to matter much after all.

III.

A narrative of this sort, like a French sermon, divides itself into three parts. I have now got through the preliminary tanglements of the history of the founding of the Christmas Club, and I hope to be able to tell the remainder of the story with as few digressions as possible, for even at Christmastide a body doesn't want his stories to stretch out to eternity, even if they are ghostly.

Charley Vanderhuyn said "The Dickens," and though his meaning was indefinite, he really meant it, whatever it might be. He looked up at the ornamental figure carved on the rich head-board of his bed, as if he suspected that the head-board of English walnut had spoken in Irish. He looked at the head-board intently a long time, partly because the Irish voice had come from that direction, and partly because he was afraid to look round toward the table. He *knew*, just as well before he looked around as he did afterwards, what he should see. He saw it before he looked round by some other vision than that of his eyes, and that was what made him shiver so. He knew that the persistent gray eyes were upon him, that they would never move until he looked round. *He could feel the look before he saw it.*

At last he turned slowly. Sure enough, in that very chair by the table sat the Presence, the Ghost—the—

it was Henry Vail; or was it? There, in the dim light, was the aquiline nose like an eagle's beak, there were the steady unwavering gray eyes, with that same earnest wistful look fastened on Vanderhuyn; the features were Vail's, but the face was plowed and pitted fearfully as with the smallpox. All this Charley saw, and saw through the ghost and beyond—the carving on the rosewood dressing-case was quite as visible through the unsubstantial apparition as before. Charley was not ordinarily superstitious, and he quickly reasoned that his excited imagination had confounded the features of Harry Vail's face with the pock-marked visage of the Huckleberry Street Irishwoman. So he shook himself, rubbed his eyes and looked again. The apparition this time was much more distinct, and it lifted the paper-weight, as Henry had three weeks before. Charley was so sure that it was Henry Vail himself that he began to get up to shake hands with his friend, but the perfect transparency of the apparition checked him, and he hid his face in his hands a moment, in a terror that he could no longer conceal from himself.

"What do you want?" he said at last, lifting his eyes.

"I want you, Charley!" said the ghost.

Now I hardly know how to describe to you the manner in which the ghost replied. It was not speech, nor any attempt at speech. You have seen a mesmerist or biologist, or whatever-you-call-himist, communicate with a man under his spell without speech. He looks at him, *wills* that a distinct impression shall be made on his victim, and the poor fellow does or says as the master-spirit wishes him. By some such subtle influence the ghost, without the intervention of sound or the sense of hearing, conveyed this reply to Charley. There was no doubt about the reply. It was far more distinct than speech, an impression made directly upon the consciousness.

Charley arose and dressed himself under some sort of fascination. His own will had abdicated; the tender, eager, wistful eyes of Vail held him fast, and he did not feel either inclination or power to resist. The eyes directed him to one article of clothing, and then to another, until he found himself muffled to the ears for a night walk.

"Where are we going?" asked Charley, huskily.

"To Huckleberry Street," answered the eyes, without a sound, and in a minute more the two were passing down the silent streets. They met several policemen and private watchmen, but Vanderhuyn observed that no one took notice either of him or the ghost. The feet of the watchmen made a grinding noise in the crisp snow, but Charley was horrified to find that his own tread and that of his companion made no sound whatever as their feet fell upon the icy sidewalks. Was he then out of the body also? This silence and this loss of the power of choice made him doubtful, indeed, whether he were dead or alive.

In Huckleberry Street they went first to a large saloon, where a set of roysterers were having a Christmas-eve spree preparatory to a Christmas-morning headache. Charley could not imagine why the ghost had brought him here, to be smothered with the smell of this villainous tobacco, for to nothing was Charley more sensitive than the smell of a poor cigar or a cheap pipe. He thought if he should have to stay here long he would like to distribute a box of his best brand among these smokers, so as to give the room the odor of the Hasheesh Club. At first it seemed a Babel of voices; there were men of several different nationalities talking in three or four languages. Six men were standing at the long counter drinking—one German, two Irishmen, a Portuguese sailor, a white American, and a black one. The spirit of Vail seemed to be looking for somebody; it peered round from table to table, where men slammed down the cards so as to make as much noise as possible. Nobody paid the least attention to the two strangers, and at last it flashed upon Vanderhuyn that he and Vail were both invisible to the throng around them.

The Presence stopped in front of a table where

two young men sat. They were playing euchre, and they were drinking. It is an old adage that truth is told in wine, and with some men sense comes with whiskey.

"I say, Joe," said one, "blamed ef it'taint too bad. You and me spendin' our time this way. The ole woman's mos' broke 'r heart over me t'day. Sh' said I ought be the s'port of her ole dage,'stid 'f boozin' roun' thish yer way. 'S so! Tell you, Joe,'s so! Blam'd 'f 'taint. Hey? W'at y' say? Hey?"

"Of course 'tis, Ben," growled the other, "we all know that. But what's a feller goin' to do for company? Go on, it's your deal."

"Who kyeers fer th' deal? I d—ont. Now, Joe, I says, t—to th' ole lady, y' see, I says, a young man can't live up a dingy stairs on th' top floor al'ays, and never git no comp'ny. Can't do it. I don't want t' 'rink much, but I c—ome here to git comp'ny. Comp'ny drinks, and I git drunk 'f—fore I know—'fore you—pshaw! deal yerself'f you want t' play."

After a while he put the cards down again, and began:

"What think I done wunst? He, he! Went to th' Young Men's Chrissen Soshiashen. Ole lady, you know, coaxed. He! he! You bet! Prayer meetin', Bible class, or somethi'n. All slick young fellers 'th side whiskers. Talked pious, an' so genteel, you know. I went there fer comp'ny! Didn go no more. Druther git drunk at the 'free-and-easy' ever' night, by George,'n to be a slick kind 'f feller 'th side-whiskers a lisnin' t' myself make purty speeches 'n a prayer Bible class meetin' or such, you know. Hey? w'at ye say? Hey? 'S comp'ny a feller wants and 's company a fellers got t' have, by cracky. Hey? W'at ye say. Hey, Joe?"

"Blam'd 'f't aint," said Joe.

"That's w'at them rich fellers goes to the club fer? Hey? wat ye say, Joe? Hey?"

"Yes, of course."

"Wish I had a club! Bettern this place to go to. Vail, he used to do a fellow good. If he'd a lived he'd a pulled me out this yer, would, you know. He got's eyes onto me, and they say when he got's eyes onto feller never let go, you know. Done me good. Made me 'shamed. Does feller good t' be 'shamed, Joe. Don't it? Hey? W'at you say?"

"Yes," said Joe.

"But w'en a feller's lonesome, a young feller, I mean; he's got to have company if he has to go down to Davy Joneses, and play seven up with Ole Nick. Hey, Joe? W'at you say? Hey?"

"I s'pose so," said Joe; "but come, deal, old fellow; don't go to preachin."

I have heard Charley say that he never heard anything half so distinctly in his life as he felt what the apparition said to him when their eyes met at that moment.

"God and Huckleberry Street want you, Charley."

Charley looked away restively, and then caught the eyes of the ghost again, and this time the ghost said—

"And they're going to have you, too."

I have heard Charley tell of several other visits they made that night; but, as I said before, even a Christmas yarn and a ghost story must not spin itself out, like Banquo's line, to the crack of doom. However true or authentic a story may be—and you can easily verify this by asking any member of the Christmas Club in Huckleberry Street—however true a yarn may be, it must not be so long that it can never be wound up.

The very last of the wretched places they looked in upon was a bare room in a third story. There was a woman sitting on a box in one corner, holding a sick child. A man with golden hair was pacing the floor.

"There's that devil again!" he said, pointing to the blank wall. "Now he's gone. You see, Carrie, I could quit if I had anybody to help me. O! I heard to-night that Charley Vanderhuyn had been elected president of the Hasheesh. And I saw him an hour ago on a Second Avenue car. I wish Charley would come and talk to me. He'd give me money, but 'taint money. I could make money if I could let whiskey alone. I used to love to hear Charley talk better than to live. I believe it was the ruin of me. But he don't seem to care for a fellow when his clothes get shabby. See there!" and he picked up a piece of wood, and threw it at the wall, startling his wife and making the child cry. "I hit him, that time. I wished I could hear Charley Vanderhuyn talk once more. His talk is enough to drive devils away any time. Great God! what an awful Christmas this is!"

Charley wanted to begin to talk on the spot, but when he found that poor "Baron Bertram" could neither see him nor hear a word he spoke, he had a fearful sense of being a disembodied spirit. The ghost looked wistfully at him, and said, "God and Huckleberry Street want *you*, Charley."

Charley was very loath to leave Perdue and his wife in this condition; he would have loved dearly to while away the dreary night for them, but he could not speak to them, and the eyes of the ghost bade him follow, and the two went swiftly back to Charley's rooms again.

Then the apparition sat down by the table, and fastened its sad and wistful eyes upon the soul of Charley Vanderhuyn. Not a word did it speak. But the look, the old tender, earnest look of Henry Vail drew Charley's heart into his eyes, and made him weep. There Vail sat, still and wistful, until Charley, roused by all that he had seen, resolved to do what he could for Huckleberry Street. He made no communication of his purpose to the ghost. He meant to keep it close in his own breast. But no sooner had he formed the purpose than a smile—the old familiar smile—came across the face of Vail, the hideous scars of his loathsome disease disappeared, and the face began to shine, while a faint aureole appeared about his head. And Vanderhuyn became conscious that the room was full of other mysterious beings; they were radiant, and yet something about them seemed to indicate that they were glorified children from Huckleberry Street. And to his regret Vail ceased now to regard his friend any more, but looked about him at the Huckleberry Street angels, who seemed to be pulling him away. He and they vanished slowly, and on the wall there shone some faint luminous letters, which Vanderhuyn tried to read, but the light of the Christmas dawn disturbed his vision, and he was only able to see the latter part, and even that was not clear to his eyes, but he partly read and partly remembered the words, "When ye fail on earth they may receive ye into everlasting habitations."

He rang for his servant, had the fire replenished, opened his desk and began to write letters. First he resigned the presidency of the Hasheesh Club. Next he begged that Mrs. Rear-Admiral Albatross would excuse him from her Christmas dinner. Unforeseen circumstances, and the death of an intimate friend, were his apologies. Then he sent his regrets, and declined all the invitations to holiday parties. He cancelled his engagements to make New Year's calls in company with Bird, the painter. Then he had breakfast, ordered his carriage, and drove to Huckleberry Street. On the way down he debated what he should do. He couldn't follow in Vail's footsteps. He was not a missionary. He went first and found out Perdue, who had been fighting off a threatened attack of tremens all night, relieved the necessities of his family, and took the golden-haired fellow into his carriage. He ordered the driver to drive the whole length of Huckleberry Street slowly.

"Perdue, what can I do down here? Vail always said that I could do something if I would try?"

"Why, Charley, start a club. That's what these fellows need. How I would like to hear you talk again."

I V.

How provoking this is! I thought I should get through with three parts. But Christmas is a time when a man cannot avoid a tendency to long stories. One cannot quite control one's self in a time of mirth, and here my history has grown until I will have to put in a mansard roof to accommodate it. For in all these three parts I have told you about everything but what my title promised. If you ever went through Huckleberry Street—of course you never did go through such a street except by accident, since you are neither poor, vicious, nor benevolent, and only the poor, the vicious, and the benevolent ever go there intentionally—but if you ever happened to go there by chance of late years, you have seen the Christmas Club building. For on that very morning with poor "Baron Bertram" in the carriage, Charley resolved to found a club in Huckleberry Street. And what house so good as the one in which Henry Vail had lived?

So he drove up to the house on the corner of Greenfield Court, and began to examine it. It was an old-fashioned house; and in its time, when the old families inhabited the down-town streets, it had been an aristocratic mansion. The lower floor was occupied by a butcher's shop, and in the front room, in which some old families had once entertained their guests, cheap roasts were being dispensed to the keepers of low boarding-houses. The antique fireplace and the ancient mantel-piece were forced to keep company with meat-blocks and butchers' cleavers. Above this were Henry Vail's rooms, where the old chamber had been carefully restored; and above these the third story and attic were crowded with tenants. But everywhere the house had traces of its former gentility.

"Good!" said Charley; "Vail preserved his taste for the antique to the last."

"Perdue, what do you think of this for a club-house?"

"Just the thing if you can get it. Ten chances to one it belongs to some saloon-keeper who wouldn't rent it for purposes of civilization."

"O! I'll get it. Such men are always susceptible to the influence of money, and I'm sure this is the spot, or Vail wouldn't have chosen it."

And with that Charley and the delighted Perdue drove to the house of Charley's business agent, the same who had been his father's manager.

"Mr. Johnston," said Charley, "I don't like to ask you to work on Christmas, but I want you to find out to-day, if you can, who owns No. 164 Huckleberry Street."

"Do you mean the house Mr. Vail lived in?"

"Yes, that's it. Look it up for me if you can."

"Oh! that's not hard, the house belongs to you."

"To me! I didn't know I had anything there."

"Yes, that house was your grandfather's, and your mother lived there in her childhood, and your father wouldn't sell it. It brought good rent, and I have never tortured you about it."

"And you let Harry pay me rent."

"Well, sir, he asked me not to mention to you that

he was in your house. He liked to pay his own way. Strange man that Mr. Vail. I heard from another tenant last night that he was dead."

"Perdue," said Charley, "I wish you would go down there to-day, and find out what each tenant in that house will sell his lease for, and give possession immediately. Give them a note to Johnston stating the amount, and I want Johnston to give them fifty per cent over the amount agreed on. I must be on good terms with Huckleberry Street."

Johnston wondered what whim Charley had in his head. "Baron Bertram" completed his negotiations for the leases of the tenants, and then went off and drank Charley's health in so many saloons that he went home entirely drunk, and the next morning was ashamed to see Vanderhuyn. But Charley never even looked a disapproval at him. He had learned from Vail how easy it is for reformers to throw their influence on the wrong side in such a life-and-death struggle as that of Perdue's. In the year that followed he had to forgive him many more than seven times. But Perdue grew stronger in the sunlight of Vanderhuyn's steady friendship.

They had a great time opening the Club on New Year's Eve. There was a banquet, not quite in Delmonico's style, nor quite so fine as those at the Hasheesh. But still it was a grand affair to the dilapidated wrecks that Charley gathered about him. Charley was president, and Vail's portrait hung over the mantel-piece, with this inscription beneath: "The Founder of the Club." Most of Charley's fine paintings were here, and the rooms were indeed brilliant. And if lemonade, and root beer, and good strong coffee could have made people drunk, there would not have been one sober man there. But Ben delighted "the old lady" by going home sober, owning it was better than the free-and-easy, and his friends all agreed with him. To Charley, as he looked round on them, this was a far grander moment than when, one week before, he had presided over the gay company at the Hasheesh. Here were good cheer, laughter, funny stories, and a New Year's Eve worth the having. The gray eyes of the portrait over the antique mantelpiece seemed happy and satisfied.

"Gentlemen," said Charley, "I rise to propose the memory of our founder," and he proceeded to set forth the virtues of Henry Vail. If there had been a reporter present he could have inserted in parenthesis, at several places in Charley's speech, the words, "great applause;" and if he had reported its effect exactly, would have, at several other places, inserted the words "great sensation," which, in reporter's phrase, expresses any great emotion, especially one which makes an audience weep. In conclusion,

Charley lifted his glass of lemonade, and said: "To the memory of Henry Vail, the Founder of the Christmas Club."

"Christmas," said Baron Bertram, "a good name. For this man," pointing to Charley, "receiveth sinners and eateth with them" (applause).

I have done. Dear friends, a Merry Christmas to you all!

Vanka

ANTON CHEKHOV
(Translated by Constance Garnett)

Vanka Zhukov, a boy of nine, who had been for three months apprenticed to Alyahin the shoemaker, was sitting up on Christmas Eve. Waiting till his master and mistress and their workmen had gone to the midnight service, he took out of his master's cupboard a bottle of ink and a pen with a rusty nib, and, spreading out a crumpled sheet of paper in front of him, began writing. Before forming the first letter he several times looked round fearfully at the door and the windows, stole a glance at the dark ikon, on both sides of which stretched shelves full of lasts, and heaved a broken sigh. The paper lay on the bench while he knelt before it.

"Dear grandfather, Konstantin Makaritch," he wrote, "I am writing you a letter. I wish you a happy Christmas, and all blessings from God Almighty. I have neither father nor mother, you are the only one left me."

Vanka raised his eyes to the dark ikon on which the light of his candle was reflected, and vividly recalled his grandfather, Konstantin Makaritch, who was night watchman to a family called Zhivarev. He was a thin but extraordinarily nimble and lively little old man of sixty-five, with an everlastingly laughing face and drunken eyes. By day he slept in the servants' kitchen, or made jokes with the cooks; at night, wrapped in an ample sheepskin, he walked round the grounds and tapped with his little mallet. Old Kashtanka and Eel, so-called on account of his dark colour and his long body like a weasel's, followed him with hanging heads. This Eel was exceptionally polite and affectionate, and looked with equal kindness on strangers and his own masters, but had not a very good reputation. Under his politeness and meekness was hidden the most Jesuitical cunning. No one knew better how to creep up on occasion and snap at one's legs, to slip into the storeroom, or steal a hen from a peasant. His hind legs had been nearly pulled off more than once, twice he had been hanged, every week he was thrashed till he was half dead, but he always revived.

At this moment grandfather was, no doubt, standing at the gate, screwing up his eyes at the red windows of the church, stamping with his high felt boots, and joking with the servants. His little mallet was hanging on his belt. He was clasping his hands, shrugging with the cold, and, with an aged chuckle, pinching first the housemaid, then the cook.

"How about a pinch of snuff?" he was saying, offering the women his snuff-box.

The women would take a sniff and sneeze. Grandfather would be indescribably delighted, go off into a merry chuckle, and cry:

"Tear it off, it has frozen on!"

They give the dogs a sniff of snuff too. Kashtanka sneezes, wriggles her head, and walks away offended. Eel does not sneeze, from politeness, but wags his tail. And the weather is glorious. The air is still, fresh, and transparent. The night is dark, but one can see the whole village with its white roofs and coils of smoke coming from the chimneys, the trees silvered with hoar frost, the snowdrifts. The whole sky spangled with gay twinkling stars, and the Milky Way is as distinct as though it had been washed and rubbed with snow for a holiday. . . .

Vanka sighed, dipped his pen, and went on writing:

"And yesterday I had a wigging. The master pulled me out into the yard by my hair, and whacked me with a boot-stretcher because I accidentally fell asleep while I was rocking their brat in the cradle. And a week ago the mistress told me to clean a herring, and I began from the tail end, and she took the

herring and thrust its head in my face. The workmen laugh at me and send me to the tavern for
vodka, and tell me to steal the master's cucumbers
for them, and the master beats me with anything that
comes to hand. And there is nothing to eat. In the
morning they give me bread, for dinner, porridge,
and in the evening, bread again; but as for tea, or
soup, the master and mistress gobble it all up themselves. And I am put to sleep in the passage, and
when their wretched brat cries I get no sleep at all,
but have to rock the cradle. Dear grandfather, show
the divine mercy, take me away from here, home to
the village. It's more than I can bear. I bow down to
your feet, and will pray to God for you for ever, take
me away from here or I shall die."

Vanka's mouth worked, he rubbed his eyes with
his black fist, and gave a sob.

"I will powder your snuff for you," he went on. "I
will pray for you, and if I do anything you can thrash
me like Sidor's goat. And if you think I've no job,
then I will beg the steward for Christ's sake to let me
clean his boots, or I'll go for a shepherd-boy instead
of Fedka. Dear grandfather, it is more than I can
bear, it's simply no life at all. I wanted to run away to
the village, but I have no boots, and I am afraid of
the frost. When I grow up big I will take care of you
for this, and not let anyone annoy you, and when

you die I will pray for the rest of your soul, just as for my mammy's.

"Moscow is a big town. It's all gentlemen's houses, and there are lots of horses, but there are no sheep, and the dogs are not spiteful. The lads here don't go out with the star, and they don't let anyone go into the choir, and once I saw in a shop window fishing-hooks for sale, fitted ready with the line and for all sorts of fish, awfully good ones, there was even one hook that would hold a forty-pound sheatfish. And I have seen shops where there are guns of all sorts, after the pattern of the master's guns at home, so that I shouldn't wonder if they are a hundred roubles each. . . . And in the butchers' shops there are grouse and woodcocks and fish and hares, but the shopmen don't say where they shoot them.

"Dear grandfather, when they have the Christmas tree at the big house, get me a gilt walnut, and put it away in the green trunk. Ask the young lady Olga Ignatyevna, say it's for Vanka."

Vanka gave a tremulous sigh, and again stared at the window. He remembered how his grandfather always went into the forest to get the Christmas tree for his master's family, and took his grandson with him. It was a merry time! Grandfather made a noise in his throat, the forest crackled with the frost, and looking at them Vanka chortled too. Before chopping down the Christmas tree, grandfather would smoke a pipe, slowly take a pinch of snuff, and laugh at frozen Vanka. . . . The young fir trees, covered with hoar frost, stood motionless, waiting to see which of them was to die. Wherever one looked, a hare flew like an arrow over the snowdrifts. . . . Grandfather could not refrain from shouting: "Hold him, hold him . . . hold him! Ah, the bob-tailed devil!"

When he had cut down the Christmas tree, grandfather used to drag it to the big house, and there set to work to decorate it. . . . The young lady, who was Vanka's favourite, Olga Ignatyevna, was the busiest of all. When Vanka's mother Pelageya was alive, and a servant in the big house, Olga Ignatyevna used to give him goodies, and having nothing better to do, taught him to read and write, to count up to a hundred, and even to dance a quadrille. When Pelageya died, Vanka had been transferred to the servants' kitchen to be with his grandfather, and from the kitchen to the shoemaker's in Moscow.

"Do come, dear grandfather," Vanka went on with his letter. "For Christ's sake, I beg you, take me away. Have pity on an unhappy orphan like me; here everyone knocks me about, and I am fearfully hungry; I can't tell you what misery it is, I am always crying. And the other day the master hit me on the head with a last, so that I fell down. My life is wretched, worse than any dog's. . . . I send greetings to Alyona, one-eyed Yegorka, and the coachman, and don't give my concertina to anyone. I remain, your grandson, Ivan Zhukov. Dear grandfather, do come."

Vanka folded the sheet of writing-paper twice, and put it into an envelope he had bought the day before for a kopeck. . . . After thinking a little, he dipped the pen and wrote the address:

To grandfather in the village.

Then he scratched his head, thought a little, and added: *Konstantin Makaritch.* Glad that he had not been prevented from writing, he put on his cap and, without putting on his little greatcoat, ran out into the street as he was in his shirt. . . .

The shopmen at the butcher's, whom he had questioned the day before, told him that letters were put in post-boxes, and from the boxes were carried about all over the earth in mailcarts with drunken drivers and ringing bells. Vanka ran to the nearest post-box, and thrust the precious letter in the slit. . . .

An hour later, lulled by sweet hopes, he was sound asleep. . . . He dreamed of the stove. On the stove was sitting his grandfather, swinging his bare legs, and reading the letter to the cooks. . . .

By the stove was Eel, wagging his tail.

Reginald's Christmas Revel

SAKI
(H. H. Munro)

They say (said Reginald) that there's nothing sadder than victory except defeat. If you've ever stayed with dull people during what is alleged to be the festive season, you can probably revise that saying. I shall never forget putting in a Christmas at the Babwolds'. Mrs. Babwold is some relation of my father's—a sort of to-be-left-till-called-for cousin—and that was considered sufficient reason for my having to accept her invitation at about the sixth time of asking; though why the sins of the father should be visited by the children—you won't find any notepaper in that drawer; that's where I keep old menus and first-night programmes.

Mrs. Babwold wears a rather solemn personality, and has never been known to smile, even when saying disagreeable things to her friends or making out the Stores list. She takes her pleasures sadly. A state elephant at a Durbar gives one a very similar impression. Her husband gardens in all weathers. When a man goes out in the pouring rain to brush caterpillars off rose trees, I generally imagine his life indoors leaves something to be desired; anyway, it must be very unsettling for the caterpillars.

Of course there were other people there. There was a Major Somebody who had shot things in Lapland, or somewhere of that sort; I forget what they were, but it wasn't for want of reminding. We had them cold with every meal almost, and he was continually giving us details of what they measured from tip to tip, as though he thought we were going to make them warm under-things for the winter. I used to listen to him with a rapt attention that I thought rather suited me, and then one day I quite modestly gave the dimensions of an okapi I had shot in the Lincolnshire fens. The Major turned a beautiful Tyrian scarlet (I remember thinking at the time that I should like my bathroom hung in that colour), and I think that at that moment he almost found it in his heart to dislike me. Mrs. Babwold put on a first-aid-to-the-injured expression, and asked him why he didn't publish a book of his sporting reminiscences; it would be *so* interesting. She didn't remember till afterwards that he had given her two fat volumes on the subject, with his portrait and autograph as a frontispiece and an appendix on the habits of the Arctic mussel.

It was in the evening that we cast aside the cares and distractions of the day and really lived. Cards were thought to be too frivolous and empty a way of passing the time, so most of them played what they called a book game. You went out into the hall—to get an inspiration, I suppose—then you came in again with a muffler tied round your neck and looked silly, and the others were supposed to guess that you were *Wee MacGreegor*. I held out against the inanity as long as I decently could, but at last, in a lapse of good-nature, I consented to masquerade as a book, only I warned them that it would take some time to carry out. They waited for the best part of forty minutes while I went and played wineglass skittles with the page-boy in the pantry; you play it with a champagne cork, you know, and the one who knocks down the most glasses without breaking them wins. I won, with four unbroken out of seven; I think William suffered from over-anxiousness. They were rather mad in the drawing-room at my not having come back, and they weren't a bit pacified when I told them afterwards that I was *At the end of the passage.*

"I never did like Kipling," was Mrs. Babwold's

comment, when the situation dawned upon her. "I couldn't see anything clever in *Earthworms out of Tuscany*—or is that by Darwin?"

Of course these games are very educational, but, personally, I prefer bridge.

On Christmas evening we were supposed to be specially festive in the Old English fashion. The hall was horribly draughty, but it seemed to be the proper place to revel in, and it was decorated with Japanese fans and Chinese lanterns, which gave it a very Old English effect. A young lady with a confidential voice favoured us with a long recitation about a little girl who died or did something equally hackneyed, and then the Major gave us a graphic account of a struggle he had with a wounded bear. I privately wished that the bears would win sometimes on these occasions; at least they wouldn't go vapouring about it afterwards. Before we had time to recover our spirits, we were indulged with some thought-reading by a young man whom one knew instinctively had a good mother and an indifferent tailor—the sort of young man who talks unflaggingly through the thickest soup, and smooths his hair dubiously as though he thought it might hit back. The thought-reading was rather a success; he announced that the hostess was thinking about poetry, and she admitted that her mind was dwelling on one of Austin's odes. Which was near enough. I fancy she had been really wondering whether a scrag-end of mutton and some cold plum-pudding would do for the kitchen dinner next day. As a crowning dissipation, they all sat down to play progressive halma, with milk-chocolate for prizes. I've been carefully brought up, and I don't like to play games of skill for milk-chocolate, so I invented a headache and retired from the scene. I had been preceded a few minutes earlier by Miss Langshan-Smith, a rather formidable lady, who always got up at some uncomfortable hour in the morning, and gave you the impression that she had been in communication with most of the European Governments before breakfast. There was a paper pinned on her door with a signed request that she might be called particularly early on the morrow. Such an opportunity does not come twice in a lifetime. I covered up everything except the signature with another notice, to the effect that before these words should meet the eye she would have ended a misspent life, was sorry for the trouble she was giving, and would like a military funeral. A few minutes later I violently exploded an air-filled paper bag on the landing, and gave a stage moan that could have been heard in the cellars. Then I pursued my original intention and went to bed. The noise those people made in forcing open the good lady's door was positively indecorous; she resisted gallantly, but I believe they searched her for bullets for about a quarter of an hour, as if she had been a historic battlefield.

I hate travelling on Boxing Day, but one must occasionally do things that one dislikes.

Mrs. Podgers' Teapot

LOUISA MAY ALCOTT

"Ah, dear me, dear me, I'm a deal too comfortable!" Judging from appearances, Mrs. Podgers certainly had some cause for that unusual exclamation. To begin with, the room was comfortable. It was tidy, bright, and warm; full of cosy corners and capital contrivances for quiet enjoyment. The chairs seemed to extend their plump arms invitingly; the old-fashioned sofa was so hospitable, that whoever sat down upon it was slow to get up; the pictures, though portraits, did not stare one out of countenance, but surveyed the scene with an air of tranquil enjoyment; and the unshuttered windows allowed the cheery light to shine out into the snowy street through blooming screens of Christmas roses and white chrysanthemums.

The fire was comfortable; for it was neither hidden

in a stove nor imprisoned behind bars, but went rollicking up the wide chimney with a jovial roar. It flickered over the supper-table as if curious to discover what savory viands were concealed under the shining covers. It touched up the old portraits till they seemed to wink; it covered the walls with comical shadows, as if the portly chairs had set their arms akimbo and were dancing a jig; it flashed out into the street with a voiceless greeting to every passer-by; it kindled mimic fires in the brass andirons and the teapot simmering on the hob, and, best of all, it shone its brightest on Mrs. Podgers, as if conscious that it couldn't do a better thing.

Mrs. Podgers was comfortable as she sat there, buxom, blooming, and brisk, in spite of her forty years and her widow's cap. Her black gown was illuminated to such an extent that it couldn't look sombre; her cap had given up trying to be prim long ago, and cherry ribbons wouldn't have made it more becoming as it set off her crisp black hair, and met in a coquettish bow under her plump chin; her white apron encircled her trim waist, as if conscious of its advantages; and the mourning-pin upon her bosom actually seemed to twinkle with satisfaction at the enviable post it occupied.

The sleek cat, purring on the hearth, was comfortable, so was the agreeable fragrance of muffins that pervaded the air, so was the drowsy tick of the clock in the corner; and if anything was needed to give a finishing touch to the general comfort of the scene, the figure pausing in the doorway supplied the want most successfully.

Heroes are always expected to be young and comely, also fierce, melancholy, or at least what novel-readers call "interesting"; but I am forced to own that my present hero was none of these. Half the real beauty, virtue, and romance of the world gets put into humble souls, hidden in plain bodies. Mr. Jerusalem Turner was an example of this; and, at the risk of shocking my sentimental readers, I must frankly state that he was fifty, stout, and bald, also that he used bad grammar, had a double chin, and was only the Co. in a prosperous grocery store. A hale and hearty old gentleman, with cheerful brown eyes, a ruddy countenance, and curly gray hair sticking up all round his head, with an air of energy and independence that was pleasant to behold. There he stood, beaming upon the unconscious Mrs. Podgers, softly rubbing his hands, and smiling to himself with the air of a man enjoying the chief satisfaction of his life, as he was.

"Ah, dear me, dear me, I'm a deal too comfortable," sighed Mrs. Podgers, addressing the teapot.

"Not a bit, mum, not a bit."

In walked the gentleman, and up rose the lady, saying, with a start and an aspect of relief,—

"Bless me, I didn't hear you! I began to think you were never coming to your tea, Mr. 'Rusalem."

Everybody called him Mr. 'Rusalem, and many people were ignorant that he had any other name. He liked it, for it began with the children, and the little voices had endeared it to him, not to mention the sound of it from Mrs. Podgers' lips for ten years.

"I know I'm late, mum, but I really couldn't help it. To-night's a busy time, and the lads are just good for nothing with their jokes and spirits, so I stayed to steady 'em, and do a little job that turned up unexpected."

"Sit right down and have your tea while you can, then. I've kept it warm for you, and the muffins are done lovely."

Mrs. Podgers bustled about with an alacrity that seemed to give an added relish to the supper; and when her companion was served, she sat smiling at him with her hand on the teapot, ready to replenish his cup before he could ask for it.

"Have things been fretting of you, mum? You looked down-hearted as I came in, and that ain't accordin' to the time of year, which is merry," said Mr. 'Rusalem, stirring his tea with a sense of solid satisfaction that would have sweetened a far less palatable draught.

"It's the teapot; I don't know what's got into it to-night; but, as I was waiting for you, it set me thinking of one thing and another, till I declare I felt as if it had up and spoke to me, showing me how I wasn't grateful enough for my blessings, but a deal more comfortable than I deserved."

While speaking, Mrs. Podgers' eyes rested on an inscription which encircled the corpulent little silver teapot: *"To our Benefactor.—They who give to the poor lend to the Lord."* Now one wouldn't think there was anything in the speech or the inscription to disturb Mr 'Rusalem; but there seemed to be, for he fidgeted in his chair, dropped his fork, and glanced at the teapot with a very odd expression. It was a capital little teapot, solid, bright as hands could make it, and ornamented with a robust young cherub perched upon the lid, regardless of the warmth of his seat. With her eyes still fixed upon it, Mrs. Podgers continued meditatively,—

"You know how fond I am of the teapot for poor Podgers' sake. I really feel quite superstitious about it; and when thoughts come to me, as I sit watching it, I have faith in them, because they always remind me of the past."

Here, after vain efforts to restrain himself, Mr. 'Rusalem broke into a sudden laugh, so hearty and infectious that Mrs. Podgers couldn't help smiling, even while she shook her head at him.

"I beg pardon, mum, it's hysterical; I'll never do it again," panted Mr. 'Rusalem, as he got his breath, and went soberly on with his supper.

It was a singular fact that whenever the teapot was particularly alluded to he always behaved in this incomprehensible manner,—laughed, begged pardon, said it was hysterical, and promised never to do it again. It used to trouble Mrs. Podgers very much, but she had grown used to it; and having been obliged to overlook many oddities in the departed Podgers, she easily forgave 'Rusalem his only one. After the laugh there was a pause, during which Mrs. Podgers sat absently polishing up the silver cherub, with the memory of the little son who died two Christmases ago lying heavy at her heart, and Mr. 'Rusalem seemed to be turning something over in his mind as he watched a bit of butter sink luxuriously into the warm bosom of a muffin. Once or twice he paused as if listening, several times he stole a look at Mrs. Podgers, and presently said, in a somewhat anxious tone,—

"You was saying just now that you was a deal too comfortable, mum; would you wish to be made uncomfortable in order to realize your blessings?"

"Yes, I should. I'm getting lazy, selfish, and forgetful of other folks. You leave me nothing to do, and make everything so easy for me that I'm growing young and giddy again. Now that isn't as it should be,'Rusalem."

"It meets my views exactly, mum. You've had your hard times, your worryments and cares, and now it's right to take your rest."

"Then why don't you take yours? I'm sure you've earned it drudging thirty years in the store, with more extra work than holidays for your share."

"Oh well, mum, it's different with me, you know. Business is amusing; and I'm so used to it I shouldn't know myself if I was out of the store for good."

"Well, I hope you are saving up something against the time when business won't be amusing. You are so generous, I'm afraid you forget you can't work for other people all your days."

"Yes, mum, I've put by a little sum in a safe bank that pays good interest, and when I'm past work I'll fall back and enjoy it."

To judge from the cheerful content of the old gentleman's face he was enjoying it already, as he looked about him with the air of a man who had made a capital investment, and was in the receipt of generous dividends. Seeing Mrs. Podgers' bright eye fixed upon him, as if she suspected something, and would have the truth out of him in two minutes, he recalled the conversation to the point from which it had wandered.

"If you would like to try how a little misery suits you, mum, I can accommodate you if you'll step upstairs."

"Good gracious, what do you mean? Who's up there? Why didn't you tell me before?" cried Mrs. Podgers, in a flutter of interest, curiosity, and surprise, as he knew she would be.

"You see, mum, I was doubtful how you'd like it. I did it without stopping to think, and then I was afraid you'd consider it a liberty."

Mr. 'Rusalem spoke with some hesitation; but Mrs. Podgers didn't wait to hear him, for she was already at the door, lamp in hand, and would have been off had she known where to go, "up-stairs" being a somewhat vague expression. The old gentleman led the way to the room he had occupied for thirty years, in spite of Mrs. Podgers' frequent offers of a better and brighter one. He was attached to it, small and dark as it was, for the joys and sorrows of more than half his life had come to him in that little room, and somehow when he was there it brightened up amazingly. Mrs. Podgers looked well about her, but saw nothing new, and her conductor said, as he paused beside the bed,—

"Let me tell you how I found it before I show it. You see, mum, I had to step down the street just at dark, and passing the windows I give a glance in, as I've a bad habit of doing when the lamps is lighted

and you a setting there alone. Well, mum, what did I
see outside but a ragged little chap a flattening his
nose against the glass, and staring in with all his eyes.
I didn't blame him much for it, and on I goes without a word. When I came back I see him a lying
close to the wall, and mistrusting that he was up to
some game that might give you a scare, I speaks to
him: he don't answer; I touches him: he don't stir;
then I picks him up, and seeing that he's gone in a fit
or a faint, I makes for the store with a will. He come
to rapid; and finding that he was most froze and
starved, I fed and warmed and fixed him a trifle, and
then tucked him away here, for he's got no folks to
worry for him, and was too used up to go out again
to-night. That's the story, mum; and now I'll produce the little chap if I can find him."

With that Mr. 'Rusalem began to grope about the
bed, chuckling, yes somewhat anxious, for not a vestige of an occupant appeared, till a dive downward
produced a sudden agitation of the clothes, a squeak,
and the unexpected appearance out at the foot of the
bed of a singular figure, that dodged into a corner,
with one arm up, as if to ward off a blow, while a
sleepy little voice exclaimed beseechingly, "I'm up,
I'm up, don't hit me!"

"Lord love the child, who'd think of doing that!
Wake up, Joe, and see your friends," said Mr.
'Rusalem, advancing cautiously.

At the sound of his voice down went the arm, and Mrs. Podgers saw a boy of nine or ten, arrayed in a flannel garment that evidently belonged to Mr. 'Rusalem, for though none too long it was immensely broad, and the voluminous sleeves were pinned up, showing a pair of wasted arms, chapped with cold and mottled with bruises. A large blue sock still covered one foot, the other was bound up as if hurt. A tall cotton nightcap, garnished with a red tassel, looked like a big extinguisher on a small candle; and from under it a pair of dark, hollow eyes glanced sharply with a shrewd, suspicious look, that made the little face more pathetic than the marks of suffering, neglect, and abuse, which told the child's story without words. As if quite reassured by 'Rusalem's presence, the boy shuffled out of his corner, saying coolly, as he prepared to climb into his nest again,—

"I thought it was the old one when you grabbed me. Ain't this bed a first-rater, though?"

Mr. 'Rusalem lifted the composed young personage into the middle of the big bed, where he sat bolt upright, surveying the prospect from under the extinguisher with an equanimity that quite took the good lady's breath away. But Mr. 'Rusalem fell back and pointed to him, saying, "There he is, mum," with as much pride and satisfaction as if he had found some rare and valuable treasure; for the little child was very precious in his sight. Mrs. Podgers really didn't know whether to laugh or cry, and settled the matter by plumping down beside the boy, saying cordially, as she took the grimy little hands into her own,—

"He's heartily welcome,'Rusalem. Now tell me all about it, my poor dear, and don't be afraid."

"Ho, I ain't afraid a you nor he. I ain't got nothin' to tell, only my name's Joe and I'm sleepy."

"Who is your mother, and where do you live, deary?" asked Mrs. Podgers, haunted with the idea that some woman must be anxious for the child.

"Ain't got any, we don't have 'em where I lives. The old one takes care a me."

"Who is the old one?"

"Granny. I works for her, and she lets me stay alonger her."

"Bless the dear! what work can such a mite do?"

"Heaps a things. I sifs ashes, picks rags, goes beggin', runs arrants, and sometimes the big fellers lets me call papers. That's fun, only I gets knocked round, and it hurts, you'd better believe."

"Did you come here begging, and, being afraid to ring, stand outside looking in at me enjoying myself, like a selfish creeter as I am?"

"I forgot to ask for the cold vittles a lookin' at warm ones, and thinkin' if they was mine what I'd give the little fellers when I has my tree."

"Your what, child?"

"My Christmas-tree. Look a here, I've got it, and all these to put on it to-morrer."

From under his pillow the boy produced a small branch of hemlock, dropped from some tree on its passage to a gayer festival than little Joe's; also an old handkerchief which contained his treasures,—only a few odds and ends picked up in the streets: a gnarly apple, half-a-dozen nuts, two or three dingy bon-bons, gleaned from the sweepings of some store, and a bit of cheese, which last possession he evidently prized highly.

"That's for the old one; she likes it, and I kep it for her,—cause she don't hit so hard when I fetch her goodies. You don't mind, do you?" he said, looking inquiringly at Mr. 'Rusalem, who blew his nose like a trumpet, and patted the big nightcap with a fatherly gesture more satisfactory than words.

"What have you kept for yourself, dear?" asked Mrs. Podgers, with an irrepressible sniff, as she looked at the poor little presents, and remembered that they "didn't have mothers" where the child lived.

"Oh, I had my treat alonger him," said the boy, nodding toward 'Rusalem, and adding enthusiasti-cally, "Wasn't that prime! It was real Christmasy a settin' by the fire, eating lots and not bein' hit."

Here Mrs. Podgers broke down; and, taking the

boy in her arms, sobbed over him as if she had found her lost Neddy in this sad shape. The little lad regarded her demonstration with some uneasiness at first, but there is a magic about a genuine woman that wins its way everywhere, and soon the outcast nestled to her, feeling that this wonderful night was getting more "Christmasy" every minute.

Mrs. Podgers was herself again directly; and seeing that the child's eyelids were heavy with weakness and weariness, she made him comfortable among the pillows, and began to sing the lullaby that used to hush her little son to sleep. Mr. 'Rusalem took something from his drawer, and was stealing away, when the child opened his eyes and started up, calling out as he nodded, till the tassel danced on his preposterous cap,—

"I say! good night, good night!"

Looking much gratified, Mr. 'Rusalem returned, shook the little hand extended to him, kissed the grateful face, and went away to sit on the stairs with tear after tear dropping off the end of his nose, as he listened to the voice that, after two years of silence, sung the air this simple soul thought the loveliest in the world. At first, it was more sob than song, but soon the soothing music flowed on unbroken, and the wondering child, for the first time within his memory, fell asleep in the sweet shelter of a woman's arms.

When Mrs. Podgers came out, she found Mr. 'Rusalem intent on stuffing another parcel into a long gray stocking already full to overflowing.

"For the little chap, mum. He let fall that he'd never done this sort of thing in his life, and as he hadn't any stockings of his own, poor dear, I took the liberty of lending him one of mine," explained Mr. 'Rusalem, surveying the knobby article with evident regret that it wasn't bigger.

Mrs. Podgers said nothing, but looked from the stocking to the fatherly old gentleman who held it; and it is my private belief, that if Mrs. Podgers had obeyed the impulse of her heart, she would have forgotten decorum, and kissed him on the spot. She didn't, however, but went briskly into her own room, whence she presently returned with red eyes, and a pile of small garments in her hands. Having nearly exhausted his pincushion in trying to suspend the heavy stocking, Mr. 'Rusalem had just succeeded as she appeared. He saw what she carried, watched her arrange the little shirt, jacket and trousers, the half-worn shoes and tidy socks, beside the bed, with motherly care, and stand looking at the unconscious child, with an expression which caused Mr. 'Rusalem to dart down stairs, and compose himself by rubbing his hair erect, and shaking his fist in the painted face of the late Podgers.

An hour or two later the store was closed, the

room cleared, Mrs. Podgers in her arm-chair on one side of the hearth, with her knitting in her hand, Mr. 'Rusalem in his arm-chair on the other side, with his newspaper on his knee, both looking so cosy and comfortable that any one would have pronounced them a Darby and Joan on the spot. Ah, but they weren't, you see, and that spoilt the illusion, to one party at least. Both were rather silent, both looked thoughtfully at the fire, and the fire gave them both excellent counsel, as it seldom fails to do when it finds any kindred warmth and brightness in the hearts and souls of those who study it. Mrs. Podgers kindled first, and broke out suddenly with a nod of great determination.

" 'Rusalem, I'm going to keep that boy if it's possible!"

"You shall, mum, whether it's possible or not," he answered, nodding back at her with equal decision.

"I don't know why I never thought of such a thing before. There's a many children suffering for mothers, and heaven knows I'm wearying for some little child to fill my Neddy's place. I wonder if you didn't think of this when you took that boy in; it would be just like you!"

Mr. 'Rusalem shook his head, but looked so guilty, that Mrs. Podgers was satisfied, called him "a thoughtful dear," within herself, and kindled still more.

"Between you, and Joe, and the teapot, I've got another idea into my stupid head, and I know you won't laugh at it. That loving little soul has tried to get a tree for some poor babies who have no one to think of them but him, and even remembered the old one, who must be a wretch to hit that child, and hit hard, too, I know by the looks of his arms. Well, I've a great longing to go and give him a tree,—a right good one, like those Neddy used to have; to get in the 'little fellers' he tells of, give them a good din-ner, and then a regular Christmas frolic. Can't it be done?"

"Nothing could be easier, mum;" and Mr. 'Rusalem, who had been taking counsel with the fire till he quite glowed with warmth and emotion, nodded, smiled, and rubbed his hands, as if Mrs. Podgers had invited him to a Lord Mayor's feast, or some equally gorgeous jollification.

"I suppose it's the day, and thinking of how it came to be, that makes me feel as if I wanted to help everybody, and makes this Christmas so bright and happy that I never can forget it," continued the good woman, with a heartiness that made her honest face quite beautiful to behold.

If Mrs. Podgers had only known what was going on under the capacious waistcoat opposite, she would have held her tongue; for the more charitable, earnest, and tender-hearted she grew, the harder it

became for Mr. 'Rusalem to restrain the declaration
which had been hovering on his lips ever since old
Podgers died. As the comely relict sat there talking
in that genial way, and glowing with good-will to all
mankind, it was too much for Mr. 'Rusalem; and
finding it impossible to resist the desire to know his
fate, he yielded to it, gave a porpentous hem, and said
abruptly,—

"Well, mum, have I done it?"

"Done what?" asked Mrs. P., going on with her
work.

"Made you uncomfortable, according to promise."

"Oh dear, no, you've made me very happy, and
will have to try again," she answered, laughing.

"I will, mum."

As he spoke Mr. 'Rusalem drew his chair nearer,
leaned forward, and looking straight at her, said
deliberately, though his voice shook a little,—

"Mrs. Podgers, I love you hearty; would you have
any objections to marrying of me?"

Not a word said Mrs. Podgers; but her knitting
dropped out of her hand, and she looked as uncomfortable as she could desire.

"I thought that would do it," muttered Mr.
'Rusalem, but went on steadily, though his ruddy
face got paler and paler, his voice huskier and
huskier, and his heart fuller and fuller every word he
attempted.

"You see, mum, I have took the liberty of loving you ever since you came, more than ten years ago. I was eager to make it known long before this, but Podgers spoke first and then it was no use. It come hard for a time, but I learned to give you up, though I couldn't learn not to love you, being as it was impossible. Since Podgers died I've turned it over in my mind frequent, but felt as if I was too old, and rough, and poor every way to ask so much. Lately, the wish has growed too strong for me, and to-night it won't be put down. If you want a trial, mum, I should be that I'll warrant, for do my best, I could never be all I'm wishful of being for your sake. Would you give it name, and if not agreeable, we'll let it drop, mum, we'll let it drop."

If it hadn't been for the teapot, Mrs. Podgers would have said Yes at once. The word was on her lips, but as she looked up the fire flashed brightly on the teapot (which always occupied the place of honor on the sideboard, for Mrs. P. was intensely proud of it), and she stopped to think, for it reminded her of something. In order to explain this, we must keep Mr. 'Rusalem waiting for his answer a minute.

Rather more than ten years ago, old Podgers happening to want a housekeeper, invited a poor relation to fill that post in his bachelor establishment. He never would have thought of marrying her, though the young woman was both notable and handsome, if he hadn't discovered that his partner loved her. Whereupon the perverse old fellow immediately proposed, lest he should lose his house-keeper, and was accepted from motives of gratitude. Mrs. Podgers was a dutiful wife, but not a very happy one, for the world said that Mr. P. was a hard, miserly man, and his wife was forced to believe the world in the right, till the teapot changed her opinion. There happened to be much suffering among the poor one year, owing to the burning of the mills, and contributions were solicited for their relief. Old Podgers, though a rich man, refused to give a penny, but it was afterwards discovered that his private charities exceeded many more ostentatious ones, and the word "miserly" was changed to "peculiar." When times grew prosperous again, the workmen, whose families had been so quietly served, clubbed together, got the teapot, and left it at Mr. Podgers' door one Christmas Eve. But the old gentleman never saw it; his dinner had been too much for him, and apoplexy took him off that very afternoon.

In the midst of her grief Mrs. Podgers was surprised, touched and troubled by this revelation, for she had known nothing of the affair till the teapot came. Womanlike, she felt great remorse for what now seemed like blindness and ingratitude; she fancied she owed him some atonement, and remembering how often he had expressed a hope that she wouldn't marry again after he was gone, she resolved to gratify him. The buxom widow had had many opportunities of putting off her weeds, but she had refused all offers without regret till now. The teapot reminded her of Podgers and her vow; and though her heart rebelled, she thought it her duty to check the answer that sprung to her lips, and slowly, but decidedly, replied,—

"I'm truly grateful to you,'Rusalem, but I couldn't do it. Don't think you'd ever be a trial, for you're the last man to be that to any woman. It's a feeling I have that it wouldn't be kind to Podgers. I can't forget how much I owe him, how much I wronged him, and how much I can please him by staying as I am, for his frequent words were, 'Keep the property together, and don't marry, Jane.'"

"Very well, mum, then we'll let it drop, and fall back into the old ways. Don't fret yourself about it, I shall bear up, and—" there Mr. 'Rusalem's voice gave out, and he sat frowning at the fire, bent on bearing up manfully, though it was very hard to find that Podgers dead as well as Podgers living was to keep from him the happiness he had waited for so long. His altered face and broken voice were almost too much for Mrs. P., and she found it necessary to confirm her resolution by telling it. Laying one hand on his shoulder, she pointed to the teapot with the other, saying gently,—

"The day that came and I found out how good he was, too late to beg his pardon and love him for it, I said to myself, 'I'll be true to Podgers till I die, because that's all I can do now to show my repentance and respect.' But for that feeling and that promise I couldn't say No to you,'Rusalem, for you've been my best friend all these years, and I'll be yours all my life, though I can't be anything else, my dear."

For the first time since its arrival, the mention of the teapot did not produce the accustomed demonstration from Mr. 'Rusalem. On the contrary, he looked at it with a momentary expression of indignation and disgust, strongly suggestive of an insane desire to cast the precious relic on the floor and trample on it. If any such temptation did assail him, he promptly curbed it, and looked about the room with a forlorn air, that made Mrs. Podgers hate herself, as he meekly answered,—

"I'm obliged to you, mum; the feeling does you honor. Don't mind me, it's rather a blow, but I'll be up again directly."

He retired behind his paper as he spoke, and Mrs. Podgers spoilt her knitting in respectful silence, till Mr. 'Rusalem began to read aloud as usual, to assure her that in spite of the blow he *was* up again.

In the gray dawn the worthy gentleman was roused from his slumbers, by a strange voice whispering shrilly in his ear,—

"I say, there's two of em. Ain't it jolly?"

Starting up, he beheld a comical little goblin standing at his bedside, with a rapturous expression of countenance, and a pair of long gray stockings in its hands. Both were heaping full, but one was evidently meant for Mr. 'Rusalem, for every wish, whim and fancy of his had been guessed, and gratified in a way that touched him to the heart. If it were not indecorous to invade the privacy of a gentleman's apartment, I could describe how there were two boys in the big bed that morning; how the old boy revelled in the treasures of his stocking as heartily as the young one; how they laughed and exclaimed, pulled each others nightcaps off, and had a regular pillow fight; how little Joe was got into his new clothes, and strutted like a small peacock in them; how Mr. 'Rusalem made himself splendid in his Sunday best, and spent ten good minutes in tying the fine cravat somebody had hemmed for him. But lest it should be thought improper, I will merely say, that nowhere in the city did the sun shine on happier faces than these two showed Mrs. Podgers, as Mr. 'Rusalem came in with Joe on his shoulder, both wishing her a merry Christmas, as heartily as if this were the first the world had ever seen.

Mrs. Podgers was as brisk and blithe as they, though she must have sat up one-half the night making presents for them, and laid awake the other half making plans for the day. As soon as she had hugged Joe, toasted him red, and heaped his plate with everything on the table, she told them the order of performances.

"As soon as ever you can't eat any more you must order home the tree, 'Rusalem, and then go with Joe to invite the party, while I see to dinner, and dress up the pine as well as I can in such a hurry."

"Yes, mum," answered Mr. 'Rusalem with alacrity; though how she was going to do her part was not clear to him. But he believed her capable of working any miracle within the power of mortal woman; and having plans of his own, he soon trudged away with Joe prancing at his side, so like the lost Neddy, in the little cap and coat, that Mrs. Podgers forgot her party to stand watching them down the crowded street, with eyes that saw very dimly when they looked away again.

Never mind how she did it, the miracle was wrought, for Mrs. Podgers and her maid Betsey fell to work with a will, and when women set their hearts on anything it is a known fact that they seldom fail to accomplish it. By noon everything was ready, the tree waiting in the best parlor, the dinner smoking on the table, and Mrs. Podgers at the window to catch the first glimpse of her coming guests. A last thought struck her as she stood waiting. There was but one high chair in the house, and the big ones would be doubtless too low for the little people. Bent on making them as comfortable as her motherly heart could desire, she set about mending the matter by bringing out from Podgers' bookcase several fat old ledgers, and arranging them in the chairs. While busily dusting one of these it slipped from her hands, and as it fell a paper fluttered from among the leaves. She picked it up, looked at it, dropped her duster, and became absorbed. It was a small sheet filled with figures, and here and there short memoranda,—not an interesting looking document in the least; but Mrs. Podgers stood like a statue till she had read it several times; then she caught her breath, clapped her hands, laughed and cried together, and put the climax to her extraordinary behavior by running across the room and embracing the astonished little teapot.

How long she would have gone on in this wild manner it is impossible to say, had not the the jingle of bells, and a shrill, small cheer announced that the party had arrived. Whisking the mysterious paper into her pocket, and dressing her agitated countenance in smiles, she hastened to open the door before chilly fingers could find the bell.

Such a merry load as that was! Such happy faces

looking out from under the faded hoods and caps! Such a hearty "Hurrah for Mrs. Podgers!" greeted her straight from the grateful hearts that loved her the instant she appeared! And what a perfect Santa Claus Mr. 'Rusalem made, with his sleigh full of bundles as well as children, his face full of sunshine, his arms full of babies, whom he held up that they too might clap their little hands, while he hurrahed with all his might. I really don't think reindeers, or the immemorial white beard and fur cap, could have improved the picture; and the neighbors were of my opinion, I suspect.

It was good to see Mrs. Podgers welcome them all in a way that gave the shyest courage, made the poorest forget patched jackets or ragged gowns, and caused them all to feel that this indeed was merry Christmas. It was better still to see Mrs. Podgers preside over the table, dealing out turkey and pudding with such a bounteous hand, that the small feasters often paused, in sheer astonishment, at the abundance before them, and then fell to again with renewed energy, as if they feared to wake up presently and find the whole a dream. It was best of all to see Mrs. Podgers gather them about her afterwards, hearing their little stories, learning their many wants, and winning their young hearts by such gentle wiles that they soon regarded her as some beautiful, benignant fairy, who had led them from a cold, dark world into the land of innocent delights they had imagined, longed for, yet never hoped to find.

Then came the tree, hung thick with bonbons, fruit and toys, gay mittens and tippets, comfortable socks and hoods, and, lower down, more substantial but less showy gifts; for Mrs. Podgers had nearly exhausted the Dorcas basket that fortunately chanced to be with her just then. There was no time for candles, but, as if he understood the matter and was bent on supplying all deficiencies, the sun shone gloriously on the little tree, and made it doubly splendid in the children's eyes.

It would have touched the hardest heart to watch the poor little creatures, as they trooped in and stood about the wonderful tree. Some seemed ready to go wild with delight, some folded their hands and sighed with solemn satisfaction, others looked as if bewildered by such unwonted and unexpected good fortune; and when Mr. 'Rusalem told them how this fruitful tree had sprung up from their loving play-mate's broken bough, little Joe hid his face in Mrs. Podgers' gown, and could find no vent for his great happiness but tears. It was not a large tree, but it took a long while to strip it; and even when the last gilded nut was gone the children still lingered about it, as if they regarded it with affection as a generous bene-factor, and were loath to leave it.

Next they had a splendid round of games. I don't

know what will be thought of the worthy souls, but Mr. 'Rusalem and Mrs. Podgers played with all their might. Perhaps the reason why he gave himself up so freely to the spirit of the hour was, that his disappointment was very heavy; and, according to his simple philosophy, it was wiser to soothe his wounded heart and cheer his sad spirit with the sweet society of little children, than to curse fate and reproach a woman. What was Mrs. Podgers' reason it is impossible to tell, but she behaved as if some secret satisfaction filled her heart so full that she was glad to let it bubble over in this harmless fashion. Both tried to be children again, and both succeeded capitally, though now and then their hearts got the better of them. When Mr. 'Rusalem was blinded he tossed all the little lads up to the ceiling when he caught them, kissed all the little girls, and, that no one might feel slighted, kissed Mrs. Podgers also. When they played "Open the gates," and the two grown people stood hand in hand while the mirthful troops marched under the tall arch, Mrs. Podgers never once looked Mr. 'Rusalem in the face, but blushed and kept her eyes on the ground, as if she was a bashful girl playing games with some boyish sweetheart. The children saw nothing of all this, and, bless their innocent little hearts! they wouldn't have understood it if they had; but it was perfectly evident that the gray-headed gentleman and the mature matron had forgotten all about their years, and were in their teens again; for true love is gifted with immortal youth.

When weary with romping, they gathered round the fire, and Mr. 'Rusalem told fairy tales, as if his dull ledgers had preserved these childish romances like flowers between their leaves, and kept them fresh in spite of time. Mrs. Podgers sung to them, and made them sing with her, till passers-by smiled and lingered as the childish voices reached them, and, looking through the screen of roses, they caught glimpses of the happy little group singing in the ruddy circle of that Christmas fire.

It was a very humble festival, but with these poor guests came also Love and Charity, Innocence and Joy,—the strong, sweet spirits who bless and beautify the world; and though eclipsed by many more splendid celebrations, I think the day was the better and the blither for Mrs. Podgers' little party.

When it was all over,—the grateful farewells and riotous cheers as the children were carried home, the twilight raptures of Joe, and the long lullaby before he could extinguish himself enough to go to sleep, the congratulations and clearing up,—then Mr. 'Rusalem and Mrs. Podgers sat down to tea. But no sooner were they alone together than Mrs. P. fell into a curious flutter, and did the oddest things. She gave Mr. 'Rusalem warm water instead of tea, passed the slop-bowl when he asked for the sugar-basin, burnt her fingers, laid her handkerchief on the tray, and tried to put her fork in her pocket, and went on in such a way that Mr. 'Rusalem began to fear the day had been too much for her.

"You're tired, mum," he said presently, hearing her sigh.

"Not a bit," she answered briskly, opening the teapot to add more water, but seemed to forget her purpose, and sat looking into its steamy depths as if in search of something. If it was courage, she certainly found it, for all of a sudden she handed the mysterious paper to Mr. 'Rusalem, saying solemnly,—

"Read that, and tell me if it's true."

He took it readily, put on his glasses, and bent to examine it, but gave a start that caused the spectacles to fly off his nose, as he exclaimed,—

"Lord bless me, he said he'd burnt it!"

"Then it is true? Don't deny it, 'Rusalem; it's no use, for I've caught you at last!" and in her excitement Mrs. Podgers slapped down the teapot-lid as if she had got him inside.

"I assure you, mum, he promised to burn it. He made me write down the sums, and so on, to satisfy him that I hadn't took more'n my share of the profits. It was my own; and though he called me a fool he let me do as I liked, but I never thought it would come up again like this, mum."

"Of course you didn't, for it was left in one of the old ledgers we had down for the dears to sit on. I found it, I read it, and I understood it in a minute. It was you who helped the mill-people, and then hid behind Podgers because you didn't want to be thanked. When he died, and the teapot came, you saw how proud I was of it,—how I took comfort in thinking he did the kind things; and for my sake you never told the truth, not even last night, when a word would have done so much. Oh, 'Rusalem, how could you deceive me all these years?"

If Mr. 'Rusalem had desired to answer he would have had no chance; for Mrs. Podgers was too much in earnest to let any one speak but herself, and hurried on, fearing that her emotion would get the better of her before she had had her say.

"It was like you, but it wasn't right, for you've robbed yourself of the love and honor that was your due; you've let people praise Podgers when he didn't deserve it; you've seen me take pride in this because I thought he'd earned it; and you've only laughed at it all as if it was a fine joke to do generous things and never take the credit of 'em. Now I know what bank you've laid up your hard earnings in, and what a blessed interest you'll get by and by. Truly they who give to the poor lend to the Lord,—and you don't need to have the good words written on silver, for you keep 'em always in your heart."

Mrs. Podgers stopped a minute for breath, and felt that she was going very fast; for 'Rusalem sat looking at her with so much humility, love, and longing in his honest face, that she knew it would be all up with her directly.

"You saw how I grieved for Neddy, and gave me this motherless boy to fill his place; you knew I wanted some one to make the house seem like home again, and you offered me the lovingest heart that ever was. You found I wasn't satisfied to lead such a selfish life, and you showed me how beautiful Charity could make it; you taught me to find my duty waiting for me at my own door; and, putting by your own trouble, you've helped to make this day the happiest Christmas of my life."

If it hadn't been for the teapot Mrs. Podgers would have given out here; but her hand was still on it, and something in the touch gave her steadiness for one more burst.

"I loved the little teapot for Podgers' sake; now I love it a hundred times more for yours, because you've brought its lesson home to me in a way I never can forget, and have been my benefactor as well as theirs, who shall soon know you as well as I do. 'Rusalem, there's only one way in which I can thank you for all this, and I do it with my whole heart. Last night you asked me for something, and I thought I couldn't give it to you. Now I'm sure I can, and if you still want it why—"

Mrs. Podgers never finished that sentence; for, with an impetuosity surprising in one of his age and figure, Mr. 'Rusalem sprang out of his chair and took her in his arms, saying tenderly, in a voice almost inaudible, between a conflicting choke and chuckle,—

"My dear! my dear! God bless you!"

The Story of the Goblins Who Stole a Sexton

CHARLES DICKENS

I n an old Abbey town, down in this part of the country, a long, long while ago—so long, that the story must be a true one, because our great grandfathers implicitly believed it—there officiated as sexton and grave-digger in the churchyard, one Gabriel Grub. It by no means follows that because a man is a sexton, and constantly surrounded by emblems of mortality, therefore he should be a morose and melancholy man; your undertakers are the merriest fellows in the world, and I once had the honour of being on intimate terms with a mute, who in private life, and off duty, was as comical and jocose a little fellow as ever chirped out a devil-may-care song, without a hitch in his memory, or drained off a good stiff glass of grog without stopping for breath. But notwithstanding these precedents to the contrary, Gabriel Grub was an ill-conditioned, cross-grained, surly fellow—a morose and lonely man, who consorted with nobody but himself, and an old wicker bottle which fitted into his large deep waistcoat pocket; and who eyed each merry face as it passed him by, with such a deep scowl of malice and ill-humour, as it was difficult to meet without feeling something the worse for.

"A little before twilight one Christmas eve, Gabriel shouldered his spade, lighted his lantern, and betook himself towards the old churchyard, for he had got a grave to finish by next morning, and feeling very low he thought it might raise his spirits perhaps, if he went on with his work at once. As he wended his way up the ancient street, he saw the cheerful light of the blazing fires gleam through the old casements, and heard the loud laugh and the cheerful shouts of those who were assembled around them; he marked the bustling preparations for next day's good cheer, and smelt the numerous savoury odours consequent thereupon, as they steamed up from the kitchen windows in clouds. All this was gall and wormwood to the heart of Gabriel Grub; and as groups of children bounded out of the houses, tripped across the road, and were met, before they could knock at the opposite door, by half a dozen curly-headed little rascals who crowded round them as they flocked up-stairs to spend the evening in their Christmas games, Gabriel smiled grimly, and clutched the handle of his spade with a firmer grasp, as he thought of measles, scarlet-fever, thrush, whooping-cough, and a good many other sources of consolation beside.

"In this happy frame of mind, Gabriel strode along, returning a short sullen growl to the good-humoured greetings of such of his neighbours as now and then passed him, until he turned into the dark lane which led to the churchyard. Now Gabriel had been looking forward to reaching the dark lane, because it was, generally speaking, a nice gloomy mournful place, into which the towns-people did not much care to go, except in broad day-light, and when the sun was shining; consequently he was not a little indignant to hear a young urchin roaring out some jolly song about a merry Christmas, in this very sanctuary, which had been called Coffin Lane ever since the days of the old abbey, and the time of the shaven-headed monks. As Gabriel walked on, and the voice drew nearer, he found it proceeded from a small boy, who was hurrying along, to join one of the little parties in the old street, and who, partly to keep himself company, and partly to pre-pare himself for the occasion, was shouting out the song at the highest pitch of his lungs. So Gabriel waited till the boy came up, and then dodged him into a corner, and rapped him over the head with his lantern five or six times, just to teach him to modulate his voice. And as the boy hurried away with his hand to his head, singing quite a different sort of tune, Gabriel Grub chuckled very heartily to himself, and entered the churchyard, locking the gate behind him.

"He took off his coat, set down his lantern, and getting into the unfinished grave, worked at it for an hour or so, with right good will. But the earth was hardened with the frost, and it was no easy matter to break it up, and shovel it out; and although there was a moon, it was a very young one, and shed little light upon the grave, which was in the shadow of the church. At any other time, these obstacles would have made Gabriel Grub very moody and miserable, but he was so well pleased with having stopped the small boy's singing, that he took little heed of the scanty progress he had made, and looked down into the grave when he had finished work for the night, with grim satisfaction, murmuring as he gathered up his things—

'Brave lodgings for one, brave lodgings for one,
A few feet of cold earth, when life is done;
A stone at the head, a stone at the feet,

A rich, juicy meal for the worms to eat;
Rank grass over head, and damp clay around,
Brave lodgings for one, these, in holy ground!

"'Ho! ho!' laughed Gabriel Grub, as he sat himself down on a flat tombstone which was a favourite resting place of his; and drew forth his wicker bottle. 'A coffin at Christmas—a Christmas Box. Ho! ho! ho!'

"'Ho! ho! ho!' repeated a voice which sounded close behind him.

"Gabriel paused in some alarm, in the act of raising the wicker bottle to his lips, and looked round. The bottom of the oldest grave about him, was not more still and quiet, than the churchyard in the pale moonlight. The cold hoar-frost glistened on the tombstones, and sparkled like rows of gems among the stone carvings of the old church. The snow lay hard and crisp upon the ground, and spread over the thickly-strewn mounds of earth so white and smooth a cover that it seemed as if corpses lay there, hidden only by their winding sheets. Not the faintest rustle broke the profound tranquillity of the solemn scene. Sound itself appeared to be frozen up, all was so cold and still.

"'It was the echoes,' said Gabriel Grub, raising the bottle to his lips again.

" 'It was *not*,' said a deep voice.

"Gabriel started up, and stood rooted to the spot with astonishment and terror; for his eyes rested on a form which made his blood run cold.

"Seated on an upright tombstone, close to him, was a strange unearthly figure, whom Gabriel felt at once, was no being of this world. His long fantastic legs, which might have reached the ground, were cocked up, and crossed after a quaint, fantastic fashion; his sinewy arms were bare, and his hands rested on his knees. On his short round body he wore a close covering, ornamented with small slashes; and a short cloak dangled at his back; the collar was cut into curious peaks, which served the goblin in lieu of ruff or neckerchief; and his shoes curled up at the toes into long points. On his head he wore a broad-brimmed sugar-loaf hat, garnished with a single feather. The hat was covered with the white frost, and the goblin looked as if he had sat on the same tombstone very comfortably, for two or three hundred years. He was sitting perfectly still; his tongue was put out, as if in derision; and he was grinning at Gabriel Grub with such a grin as only a goblin could call up.

" 'It was *not* the echoes,' said the goblin.

"Gabriel Grub was paralysed, and could make no reply.

" 'What do you here on Christmas eve?' said the goblin sternly.

" 'I came to dig a grave, Sir,' stammered Gabriel Grub.

" 'What man wanders among graves and church-yards on such a night as this?' said the goblin.

" 'Gabriel Grub! Gabriel Grub!' screamed a wild chorus of voices that seemed to fill the churchyard. Gabriel looked fearfully round—nothing was to be seen.

" 'What have you got in that bottle?' said the goblin.

" 'Hollands, Sir,' replied the sexton, trembling more than ever; for he had bought it of the smug-glers, and he thought that perhaps his questioner might be in the excise department of the goblins.

" 'Who drinks Hollands alone, and in a church-yard, on such a night as this?' said the goblin.

" 'Gabriel Grub! Gabriel Grub!' exclaimed the wild voices again.

"The goblin leered maliciously at the terrified sexton, and then raising his voice, exclaimed—

" 'And who, then, is our fair and lawful prize?'

"To this inquiry the invisible chorus replied, in a strain that sounded like the voices of many choris-ters singing to the mighty swell of the old church organ—a strain that seemed borne to the sexton's ears upon a gentle wind, and to die away as its soft breath passed onward—but the burden of the reply was still the same, 'Gabriel Grub! Gabriel Grub!'

"The goblin grinned a broader grin than before, as he said, 'Well, Gabriel, what do you say to this?'

"The sexton gasped for breath.

"'What do you think of this, Gabriel?' said the goblin, kicking up his feet in the air on either side the tombstone, and looking at the turned-up points with as much complacency as if he had been contemplating the most fashionable pair of Wellingtons in all Bond Street.

"'It's—it's—very curious, Sir,' replied the sexton, half dead with fright, 'very curious, and very pretty, but I think I'll go back and finish my work, Sir, if you please.'

"'Work!' said the goblin, 'what work?'

"'The grave, Sir, making the grave,' stammered the sexton.

"'Oh, the grave, eh?' said the goblin. 'Who makes graves at a time when all other men are merry, and takes a pleasure in it?'

"Again the mysterious voices replied, 'Gabriel Grub! Gabriel Grub!'

"'I'm afraid my friends want you, Gabriel,' said the goblin, thrusting his tongue further into his cheek than ever—and a most astonishing tongue it was—'I'm afraid my friends want you, Gabriel,' said the goblin.

"'Under favour, Sir,' replied the horror-struck

sexton, 'I don't think they can, Sir; they don't know me, Sir; I don't think the gentlemen have ever seen me, Sir.'

" 'Oh yes they have,' replied the goblin; 'we know the man with the sulky face and the grim scowl, that came down the street to-night, throwing his evil looks at the children, and grasping his burying spade the tighter. We know the man that struck the boy in the envious malice of his heart, because the boy could be merry, and he could not. We know him, we know him.'

"Here the goblin gave a loud shrill laugh, that the echoes returned twenty fold, and throwing his legs up in the air, stood upon his head, or rather upon the very point of his sugar-loaf hat, on the narrow edge of the tombstone, from whence he threw a summerset with extraordinary agility, right to the sexton's feet, at which he planted himself in the attitude in which tailors generally sit upon the shop-board.

" 'I—I—am afraid I must leave you, Sir,' said the sexton, making an effort to move.

" 'Leave us!' said the goblin, 'Gabriel Grub going to leave us. Ho! ho! ho!'

"As the goblin laughed, the sexton observed for one instant a brilliant illumination within the windows of the church, as if the whole building were lighted up; it disappeared, the organ pealed forth a lively air, and whole troops of goblins, the very counterpart of the first one, poured into the church-yard, and began playing at leap-frog with the tomb-stones, never stopping for an instant to take breath, but overing the highest among them, one after the other, with the most marvellous dexterity. The first goblin was a most astonishing leaper, and none of the others could come near him; even in the extrem-ity of his terror the sexton could not help observing, that while his friends were content to leap over the common-sized gravestones, the first one took the family vaults, iron railings and all, with as much ease as if they had been so many street posts.

"At last the game reached to a most exciting pitch; the organ played quicker and quicker, and the goblins leaped faster and faster, coiling themselves up, rolling head over heels upon the ground, and bounding over the tombstones like foot-balls. The sexton's brain whirled round with the rapidity of the motion he beheld, and his legs reeled beneath him, as the spirits flew before his eyes, when the goblin king, suddenly darting towards him, laid his hand upon his collar, and sank with him through the earth.

"When Gabriel Grub had had time to fetch his breath, which the rapidity of his descent had for the moment taken away, he found himself in what appeared to be a large cavern, surrounded on all sides by crowds of goblins, ugly and grim; in the centre of the room, on an elevated seat, was stationed his friend of the churchyard; and close beside him stood Gabriel Grub himself, without the power of motion.

" 'Cold to-night,' said the king of the goblins, 'very cold. A glass of something warm, here.'

"At this command, half a dozen officious goblins, with a perpetual smile upon their faces, whom Gabriel Grub imagined to be courtiers, on that account, hastily disappeared, and presently returned with a goblet of liquid fire, which they presented to the king.

" 'Ah!' said the goblin, whose cheeks and throat were quite transparent, as he tossed down the flame, 'this warms one, indeed: bring a bumper of the same, for Mr. Grub.'

"It was in vain for the unfortunate sexton to protest that he was not in the habit of taking any-thing warm at night; for one of the goblins held him while another poured the blazing liquid down his throat, and the whole assembly screeched with laughter as he coughed and choked, and wiped away the tears which gushed plentifully from his eyes, after swallowing the burning draught.

" 'And now,' said the king, fantastically poking the taper corner of his sugar-loaf hat into the sexton's eye, and thereby occasioning him the most exquisite pain—'And now, show the man of misery and gloom a few of the pictures from our own great storehouse.'

"As the goblin said this, a thick cloud which obscured the further end of the cavern, rolled gradually away, and disclosed, apparently at a great distance, a small and scantily furnished, but neat and clean apartment. A crowd of little children were gathered round a bright fire, clinging to their mother's gown, and gamboling round her chair. The mother occasionally rose, and drew aside the window-curtain as if to look for some expected object; a frugal meal was ready spread upon the table, and an elbow chair was placed near the fire. A knock was heard at the door: the mother opened it, and the children crowded round her, and clapped their hands for joy, as their father entered. He was wet and weary, and shook the snow from his garments, as the children crowded round him, and seizing his cloak, hat, stick, and gloves, with busy zeal, ran with them from the room. Then as he sat down to his meal before the fire, the children climbed about his knee, and the mother sat by his side, and all seemed happiness and comfort.

"But a change came upon the view, almost imperceptibly. The scene was altered to a small bed-room, where the fairest and youngest child lay dying; the roses had fled from his cheek, and the light from his eye; and even as the sexton looked upon him with an interest he had never felt or known before, he died. His young brothers and sisters crowded round his little bed, and seized his tiny hand, so cold and heavy; but they shrunk back from its touch and looked with awe on his infant face; for calm and tranquil as it was, and sleeping in rest and peace as the beautiful child seemed to be, they saw that he was dead, and they knew that he was an angel looking down upon, and blessing them, from a bright and happy Heaven.

"Again the light cloud passed across the picture, and again the subject changed. The father and mother were old and helpless now, and the number of those about them was diminished more than half; but content and cheerfulness sat on every face, and beamed in every eye, as they crowded round the fireside, and told and listened to old stories of earlier and bygone days. Slowly and peacefully the father sank into the grave, and, soon after, the sharer of all his cares and troubles followed him to a place of rest and peace. The few, who yet survived them, knelt by their tomb, and watered the green turf which covered it with their tears; then rose and turned away, sadly and mournfully, but not with bitter cries, or despairing lamentations, for they knew that they should one day meet again; and once more they mixed with the busy world, and their content and

CLASSIC CHRISTMAS STORIES

cheerfulness were restored. The cloud settled upon the picture, and concealed it from the sexton's view.

" 'What do you think of *that*?' said the goblin, turning his large face towards Gabriel Grub.

"Gabriel murmured out something about its being very pretty, and looked somewhat ashamed, as the goblin bent his fiery eyes upon him.

" '*You* a miserable man!' said the goblin, in a tone of excessive contempt. 'You!' He appeared disposed to add more, but indignation choked his utterance, so he lifted up one of his very pliable legs, and flourishing it above his head a little, to insure his aim, administered a good sound kick to Gabriel Grub; immediately after which, all the goblins in waiting crowded round the wretched sexton, and kicked him without mercy, according to the established and invariable custom of courtiers upon earth, who kick whom royalty kicks, and hug whom royalty hugs.

" 'Show him some more,' said the king of the goblins.

"At these words the cloud was again dispelled, and a rich and beautiful landscape was disclosed to view—there is just such another to this day, within half a mile of the old abbey town. The sun shone from out the clear blue sky, the water sparkled beneath his rays, and the trees looked greener, and the flowers more gay, beneath his cheering influence.

The water rippled on, with a pleasant sound, the trees rustled in the light wind that murmured among their leaves, the birds sang upon the boughs, and the lark carolled on high her welcome to the morning. Yes, it was morning, the bright, balmy morning of summer; the minutest leaf, the smallest blade of grass, was instinct with life. The ant crept forth to her daily toil, the butterfly fluttered and basked in the warm rays of the sun; myriads of insects spread their transparent wings, and revelled in their brief but happy existence. Man walked forth, elated with the scene; and all was brightness and splendour.

" 'You a miserable man!' said the king of the goblins, in a more contemptuous tone than before. And again the king of the goblins gave his leg a flourish; again it descended on the shoulders of the sexton; and again the attendant goblins imitated the example of their chief.

"Many a time the cloud went and came, and many a lesson it taught to Gabriel Grub, who although his shoulders smarted with pain from the frequent applications of the goblin's feet thereunto, looked on with an interest which nothing could diminish. He saw that men who worked hard, and earned their scanty bread with lives of labour, were cheerful and happy; and that to the most ignorant, the sweet face of nature was a never-failing source of cheerfulness and joy. He saw those who had been delicately nurtured, and tenderly brought up, cheerful under privations, and superior to suffering that would have crushed many of a rougher grain, because they bore within their own bosoms the materials of happiness, contentment, and peace. He saw that women, the tenderest and most fragile of all God's creatures, were the oftenest superior to sorrow, adversity, and distress; and he saw that it was because they bore in their own hearts an inexhaustible well-spring of affection and devotedness. Above all, he saw that men like himself, who snarled at the mirth and cheerfulness of others, were the foulest weeds on the fair surface of the earth; and setting all the good of the world against the evil, he came to the conclusion that it was a very decent and respectable world after all. No sooner had he formed it, than the cloud which had closed over the last picture, seemed to settle on his senses, and lull him to repose. One by one, the goblins faded from his sight, and as the last one disappeared, he sunk to sleep.

"The day had broken when Gabriel Grub awoke, and found himself lying at full length on the flat grave-stone in the churchyard, with the wicker bottle lying empty by his side, and his coat, spade, and lantern, all well whitened by the last night's frost, scattered on the ground. The stone on which he had first seen the goblin seated, stood bolt upright before him, and the grave at which he had worked, the night before, was not far off. At first he began to doubt the reality of his adventures, but the acute pain in his shoulders when he attempted to rise, assured him that the kicking of the goblins was certainly not ideal. He was staggered again, by observing no traces of footsteps in the snow on which the goblins had played leap-frog with the gravestones, but he speedily accounted for this circumstance when he remembered that, being spirits, they would leave no visible impression behind them. So Gabriel Grub got on his feet as well as he could, for the pain in his back; and brushing the frost off his coat, put it on, and turned his face towards the town.

"But he was an altered man, and he could not bear the thought of returning to a place where his repentance would be scoffed at, and his reformation disbelieved. He hesitated for a few moments; and then turned away to wander where he might, and seek his bread elsewhere.

"The lantern, the spade, and the wicker bottle, were found that day in the churchyard. There were a great many speculations about the sexton's fate at first, but it was speedily determined that he had been carried away by the goblins; and there were not wanting some very credible witnesses who had distinctly seen him whisked through the air on the back of a chestnut horse blind of one eye, with the hind quarters of a lion, and the tail of a bear. At length all this was devoutly believed; and the new sexton used to exhibit to the curious, for a trifling emolument, a good-sized piece of the church weathercock which had been accidentally kicked off by the aforesaid horse in his aerial flight, and picked up by himself in the churchyard, a year or two afterwards.

"Unfortunately these stories were somewhat disturbed by the unlooked-for re-appearance of Gabriel Grub himself, some ten years afterwards, a ragged, contented, rheumatic old man. He told his story to the clergyman, and also to the mayor; and in course of time it began to be received as a matter of history, in which form it has continued down to this very day. The believers in the weathercock tale, having misplaced their confidence once, were not easily prevailed upon to part with it again, so they looked as wise as they could, shrugged their shoulders, touched their foreheads, and murmured something about Gabriel Grub's having drunk all the Hollands, and then fallen asleep on the flat tombstone; and they affected to explain what he supposed he had witnessed in the goblin's cavern, by saying that he had seen the world, and grown wiser. But this opinion, which was by no means a popular one at any time, gradually died off; and be the matter how it may, as Gabriel Grub was afflicted with rheumatism to the end of his days, this story has at least one moral, if it teach no better one—and that is, that if a man turns sulky and drinks by himself at Christmas time, he may make up his mind to be not a bit the better for it, let the spirits be ever so good, or let them be even as many degrees beyond proof, as those which Gabriel Grub saw in the goblin's cavern."

The Christmas Shadrach

FRANK R. STOCKTON

Whenever I make a Christmas present I like it to mean something, not necessarily my sentiments toward the person to whom I give it, but sometimes an expression of what I should like that person to do or to be. In the early part of a certain winter not very long ago I found myself in a position of perplexity and anxious concern regarding a Christmas present which I wished to make.

The state of the case was this. There was a young lady, the daughter of a neighbor and old friend of my father, who had been gradually assuming relations toward me which were not only unsatisfactory to me, but were becoming more and more so. Her name was Mildred Bronce. She was between twenty and twenty-five years of age, and as fine a woman in every way as one would be likely to meet in a lifetime. She was handsome, of a tender and generous disposition, a fine intelligence, and a thoroughly well-stocked mind. We had known each other for a long time, and when fourteen or fifteen Mildred had been my favorite companion. She was a little younger than I, and I liked her better than any boy I knew. Our friendship had continued through the years, but of late there had been a change in it; Mildred had become very fond of me, and her fondness seemed to have in it certain elements which annoyed me.

As a girl to make love to no one could be better than Mildred Bronce; but I had never made love to her,—at least not earnestly,—and I did not wish that any permanent condition of loving should be established between us. Mildred did not seem to share this opinion, for every day it became plainer to me that she looked upon me as a lover, and that she was perfectly willing to return my affection.

But I had other ideas upon the subject. Into the rural town in which my family passed the greater part of the year there had recently come a young lady, Miss Janet Clinton, to whom my soul went out of my own option. In some respects, perhaps, she was not the equal of Mildred, but she was very pretty, she was small, she had a lovely mouth, was apparently of a clinging nature, and her dark eyes looked into mine with a tingling effect that no other eyes had ever produced. I was in love with her because I wished to be, and the consciousness of this fact caused me a proud satisfaction. This affair was not the result of circumstances, but of my own free will.

I wished to retain Mildred's friendship, I wished to make her happy; and with this latter intent in view I wished very much that she should not disappoint herself in her anticipations of the future.

Each year it had been my habit to make Mildred a Christmas present, and I was now looking for something to give her which would please her and suit my purpose.

When a man wishes to select a present for a lady which, while it assures her of his kind feeling toward her, will at the same time indicate that not only has he no matrimonial inclinations in her direction, but that it would be entirely unwise for her to have any such inclinations in his direction; that no matter with what degree of fondness her heart is disposed to turn toward him, his heart does not turn toward her, and that, in spite of all sentiments induced by long association and the natural fitness of things, she need never expect to be to him anything more than a sister, he has, indeed, a difficult task before him. But such was the task which I set for myself.

Day after day I wandered through the shops. I looked at odd pieces of jewelry and bric-a-brac, and at many a quaint relic or bit of art work which seemed to have a meaning, but nothing had the meaning I wanted. As to books, I found none which satisfied me; not one which was adapted to produce the exact impression that I desired.

One afternoon I was in a little basement shop kept by a fellow in a long overcoat, who, so far as I was able to judge, bought curiosities but never sold any. For some minutes I had been looking at a beautifully decorated saucer of rare workmanship for which there was no cup to match, and for which the proprietor informed me no cup could now be found or manufactured. There were some points in the significance of an article of this sort, given as a present to a lady, which fitted to my purpose, but it would signify too much: I did not wish to suggest to Mildred that she need never expect to find a cup. It would be better, in fact, if I gave her anything of this kind, to send her a cup and saucer entirely unsuited to each other, and which could not, under any conditions, be used together.

I put down the saucer, and continued my search among the dusty shelves and cases.

"How would you like a paper-weight?" the shopkeeper asked. "Here is something a little odd," handing me a piece of dark-colored mineral nearly as big as my fist, flat on the under side and of a pleasing irregularity above. Around the bottom was a

band of arabesque work in some dingy metal, probably German silver. I smiled as I took it.

"This is not good enough for a Christmas present," I said. "I want something odd, but it must have
some value."

"Well," said the man, "that has no real value, but
there is a peculiarity about it which interested me
when I heard of it, and so I bought it. This mineral
is a piece of what the iron-workers call shadrach. It
is a portion of the iron or iron ore which passes
through the smelting-furnaces without being
affected by the great heat, and so they have given it
the name of one of the Hebrew youths who was cast
into the fiery furnace by Nebuchadnezzar, and who
came out unhurt. Some people think there is a sort
of magical quality about this shadrach, and that it
can give out to human beings something of its
power to keep their minds cool when they are in
danger of being overheated. The old gentleman
who had this made was subject to fits of anger, and
he thought this piece of shadrach helped to keep
him from giving way to them. Occasionally he used
to leave it in the house of a hot-tempered neighbor,
believing that the testy individual would be cooled
down for a time, without knowing how the change
had been brought about. I bought a lot of things of
the old gentleman's widow, and this among them. I
thought I might try it some time, but I never have."

I held the shadrach in my hand, ideas concerning it rapidly flitting through my mind. Why would not this be a capital thing to give to Mildred? If it should, indeed, possess the quality ascribed to it; if it should be able to cool her liking for me, what better present could I give her? I did not hesitate long.

"I will buy this," I said; "but the ornamentation must be of a better sort. It is now too cheap- and tawdry-looking."

"I can attend to that for you," said the shopkeeper. "I can have it set in a band of gold or silver filigree-work like this, if you choose."

I agreed to this proposition, but ordered the band to be made of silver, the cool tone of that metal being more appropriate to the characteristics of the gift than the warmer hues of gold.

When I gave my Christmas present to Mildred she was pleased with it; its oddity struck her fancy.

"I don't believe anybody ever had such a paper-weight as that," she said, as she thanked me. "What is it made of?"

I told her, and explained what shadrach was; but I did not speak of its presumed influence over human beings, which, after all, might be nothing but the wildest fancy. I did not feel altogether at my ease, as I added that it was merely a trifle, a thing of no value except as a reminder of the season.

"The fact that it is a present from you gives it

value," she said, as she smilingly raised her eyes to mine.

I left her house—we were all living in the city then—with a troubled conscience. What a deception I was practising upon this noble girl, who, if she did not already love me, was plainly on the point of doing so. She had received my present as if it indicated a warmth of feeling on my part, when, in fact, it was the result of a desire for a cooler feeling on her part.

But I called my reason to my aid, and I showed myself that what I had given Mildred—if it should prove to possess any virtue at all—was, indeed, a most valuable boon. It was something which would prevent the waste of her affections, the wreck of her hopes. No kindness could be truer, no regard for her happiness more sincere, than the motives which prompted me to give her the shadrach.

I did not soon again see Mildred, but now as often as possible I visited Janet. She always received me with a charming cordiality, and if this should develop into warmer sentiments I was not the man to wish to cool them. In many ways Janet seemed much better suited to me than Mildred. One of the greatest charms of this beautiful girl was a tender trustfulness, as if I were a being on whom she could lean and to whom she could look up. I liked this; it was very different from Mildred's manner: with the latter I had always been well satisfied if I felt myself standing on the same plane.

The weeks and months passed on, and again we were all in the country; and here I saw Mildred often. Our homes were not far apart, and our families were very intimate. With my opportunities for frequent observation I could not doubt that a change had come over her. She was always friendly when we met, and seemed as glad to see me as she was to see any other member of my family, but she was not the Mildred I used to know. It was plain that my existence did not make the same impression on her that it once made. She did not seem to consider it important whether I came or went; whether I was in the room or not; whether I joined a party or stayed away. All this had been very different. I knew well that Mildred had been used to consider my presence as a matter of much importance, and I now felt sure that my Christmas shadrach was doing its work. Mildred was cooling toward me. Her affection, or, to put it more modestly, her tendency to affection, was gently congealing into friendship. This was highly gratifying to my moral nature, for every day I was doing my best to warm the soul of Janet. Whether or not I succeeded in this I could not be sure. Janet was as tender and trustful and charming as ever, but no more so than she had been months before.

Sometimes I thought she was waiting for an indication of an increased warmth of feeling on my part before she allowed the temperature of her own sentiments to rise. But for one reason and another I delayed the solution of this problem. Janet was very fond of company, and although we saw a great deal of each other, we were not often alone. If we two had more frequently walked, driven, or rowed together, as Mildred and I used to do, I think Miss Clinton would soon have had every opportunity of making up her mind about the fervor of my passion.

The summer weeks passed on, and there was no change in the things which now principally concerned me, except that Mildred seemed to be growing more and more indifferent to me. From having seemed to care no more for me than for her other friends, she now seemed to care less for me than for most people. I do not mean that she showed a dislike, but she treated me with a sort of indifference which I did not fancy at all. This sort of thing had gone too far, and there was no knowing how much further it would go. It was plain enough that the shadrach was overdoing the business.

I was now in a state of much mental disquietude. Greatly as I desired to win the love of Janet, it grieved me to think of losing the generous friendship of Mildred—that friendship to which I had been accustomed for the greater part of my life, and on which, as I now discovered, I had grown to depend.

In this state of mind I went to see Mildred. I found her in the library writing. She received me pleasantly, and was sorry her father was not at home, and begged that I would excuse her finishing the note on which she was engaged, because she wished to get it into the post-office before the mail closed. I sat down on the other side of the table, and she finished her note, after which she went out to give it to a servant.

Glancing about me, I saw the shadrach. It was partly under a litter of papers, instead of lying on them. I took it up, and was looking at it when Mildred returned. She sat down and asked me if I had heard of the changes that were to be made in the time-table of the railroad. We talked a little on the subject, and then I spoke of the shadrach, saying carelessly that it might be interesting to analyze the bit of metal; there was a little knob which might be filed off without injuring it in the least.

"You may take it," she said, "and make what experiments you please. I do not use it much; it is unnecessarily heavy for a paper-weight."

From her tone I might have supposed that she had forgotten that I had given it to her. I told her that I would be very glad to borrow the paper-weight for a time, and, putting it into my pocket, I went away, leaving her arranging her disordered papers on the table, and giving quite as much regard to this occupation as she had given to my little visit.

I could not feel sure that the absence of the shadrach would cause any diminution in the coolness of her feelings toward me, but there was reason to believe that it would prevent them from growing cooler. If she should keep that shadrach she might in time grow to hate me. I was very glad that I had taken it from her.

My mind easier on this subject, my heart turned more freely toward Janet, and, going to her house, the next day I was delighted to find her alone. She was as lovely as ever, and as cordial, but she was flushed and evidently annoyed.

"I am in a bad humor to-day" she said, "and I am glad you came to talk to me and quiet me. Dr. Gilbert promised to take me to drive this afternoon, and we were going over to the hills where they find the wild rhododendron. I am told that it is still in blossom up there, and I want some flowers ever so much—I am going to paint them. And besides, I am crazy to drive with his new horses; and now he sends me a note to say that he is engaged."

This communication shocked me, and I began to talk to her about Dr. Gilbert. I soon found that several times she had been driving with this handsome young physician, but never, she said, behind his new horses, nor to the rhododendron hills.

Dr. Hector Gilbert was a fine young fellow, beginning practice in town, and one of my favorite associates. I had never thought of him in connection with Janet, but I could now see that he might make a most dangerous rival. When a young and talented doctor, enthusiastic in his studies, and earnestly desirous of establishing a practice, and who, if his time were not fully occupied, would naturally wish that the neighbors would think that such were the case, deliberately devotes some hours on I know not how many days to driving a young lady into the surrounding country, it may be supposed that he is really in love with her. Moreover, judging from Janet's present mood, this doctor's attentions were not without encouragement.

I went home; I considered the state of affairs; I ran my fingers through my hair; I gazed steadfastly upon the floor. Suddenly I rose. I had had an inspiration; I would give the shadrach to Dr. Gilbert.

I went immediately to the doctor's office, and found him there. He too was not in a very good humor.

"I have had two old ladies here nearly all the afternoon, and they have bored me to death," he said. "I could not get rid of them because I found they had made an appointment with each other to visit me to-day and talk over a hospital plan which I proposed some time ago and which is really very important to me, but I wish they had chosen some other time to come here. What is that thing?"

"That is a bit of shadrach," I said, "made into a paper-weight." And then I proceeded to explain what shadrach is, and what peculiar properties it must possess to resist the power of heat, which melts other metal apparently of the same class; and I added that I thought it might be interesting to analyze a bit of it and discover what fire-proof constituents it possessed.

"I should like to do that," said the doctor, attentively turning over the shadrach in his hand. "Can I take off a piece of it?"

"I will give it to you," said I, "and you can make what use of it you please. If you do analyze it I shall be very glad indeed to hear the results of your investigations."

The doctor demurred a little at taking the paper-weight with such a pretty silver ring around it, but I assured him that the cost of the whole affair was trifling, and I should be gratified if he would take it. He accepted the gift, and was thanking me, when a patient arrived, and I departed.

I really had no right to give away this paper-weight, which, in fact, belonged to Mildred, but there are times when a man must keep his eyes on the chief good, and not think too much about other things. Besides, it was evident that Mildred did not care in the least for the bit of metal, and she had virtually given it to me.

There was another point which I took into consideration. It might be that the shadrach might simply cool Dr. Gilbert's feelings toward me, and that would be neither pleasant nor advantageous. If I could have managed matters so that Janet could have given it to him, it would have been all right. But now all that I could do was to wait and see what would happen. If only the thing would cool the doctor in a general way, that would help. He might then give more thought to his practice and his hospital ladies, and let other people take Janet driving.

About a week after this I met the doctor; he seemed in a hurry, but I stopped him. I had a curiosity to know if he had analyzed the shadrach, and asked him about it.

"No," said he; "I haven't done it. I haven't had time. I knocked off a piece of it, and I will attend to it when I get a chance. Good day."

Of course if the man was busy he could not be expected to give his mind to a trifling matter of that sort, but I thought that he need not have been so curt about it. I stood gazing after him as he walked rapidly down the street. Before I resumed my walk I saw him enter the Clinton house. Things were not going on well. The shadrach had not cooled Dr. Gilbert's feelings toward Janet.

But because the doctor was still warm in his attentions to the girl I loved, I would not in the least relax my attentions to her. I visited her as often as I could find an excuse to do so. There was generally some one else there, but Janet's disposition was of such gracious expansiveness that each one felt obliged to be satisfied with what he got, much as he may have wished for something different.

But one morning Janet surprised me. I met her at Mildred's house, where I had gone to borrow a book of reference. Although I had urged her not to put herself to so much trouble, Mildred was standing on a little ladder looking for the book, because, she said, she knew exactly what I wanted, and she was sure she could find the proper volume better than I could. Janet had been sitting in a window-seat reading, but when I came in she put down her book and devoted herself to conversation with me. I was a little sorry for this, because Mildred was very kindly engaged in doing me a service, and I really wanted to talk to her about the book she was looking for. Mildred showed so much of her old manner this morning that I would have been very sorry to have her think that I did not appreciate her returning interest in me. Therefore, while under other circumstances I would have been delighted to talk to Janet, I did not wish to give her so much of my attention then. But Janet Clinton was a girl who insisted on people attending to her when she wished them to do so, and, having stepped through an open door into the garden, she presently called me to her. Of course I had to go.

"I will not keep you a minute from your fellow student," she said, "but I want to ask a favor of you." And into her dark, uplifted eyes there came a look of tender trustfulness clearer than any I had yet seen there. "Don't *you* want to drive me to the rhodo-dendron hills?" she said. "I suppose the flowers are all gone by this time, but I have never been there, and I should like ever so much to go."

I could not help remarking that I thought Dr. Gilbert was going to take her there.

"Dr. Gilbert, indeed!" she said with a little laugh. "He promised once, and didn't come, and the next day he planned for it it rained. I don't think doctors make very good escorts, anyway, for you can't tell who is going to be sick just as you are about to start on a trip. Besides there is no knowing how much botany I should have to hear, and when I go on a pleasure-drive I don't care very much about studying things. But of course I don't want to trouble you."

"Trouble!" I exclaimed. "It will give me the

greatest delight to take you that drive or any other, and at whatever time you please."

"You are always so good and kind," she said, with her dark eyes again upraised. "And now let us go in and see if Mildred has found the book."

I spoke the truth when I said that Janet's proposition delighted me. To take a long drive with that charming girl, and at the same time to feel that she had chosen me as her companion, was a greater joy than I had yet had reason to expect; but it would have been a more satisfying joy if she had asked me in her own house and not in Mildred's; if she had not allowed the love which I hoped was growing up between her and me to interfere with the revival of the old friendship between Mildred and me.

But when we returned to the library Mildred was sitting at a table with a book before her, opened at the passage I wanted.

"I have just found it," she said with a smile. "Draw up a chair, and we will look over these maps together. I want you to show me how he traveled when he left his ship."

"Well, if you two are going to the pole," said Janet, with her prettiest smile, "I will go back to my novel."

She did not seem in the least to object to my geographical researches with Mildred, and if the latter had even noticed my willingness to desert her at the call of Janet, she did not show it. Apparently she was as much a good comrade as she had ever been. This state of things was gratifying in the highest degree. If I could be loved by Janet and still keep Mildred as my friend, what greater earthly joys could I ask?

The drive with Janet was postponed by wet weather. Day after day it rained, or the skies were heavy, and we both agreed that it must be in the bright sunshine that we would make this excursion. When we should make it, and should be alone together on the rhododendron hill, I intended to open my soul to Janet.

It may seem strange to others, and at the time it also seemed strange to me, but there was another reason besides the rainy weather which prevented my declaration of love to Janet. This was a certain nervous anxiety in regard to my friendship for Mildred. I did not in the least waver in my intention to use the best endeavors to make the one my wife, but at the same time I was oppressed by a certain alarm that in carrying out this project I might act in such a way as to wound the feelings of the other.

This disposition to consider the feelings of Mildred became so strong that I began to think that my own sentiments were in need of control. It was not right that while making love to one woman I should give so much consideration to my relations with another. The idea struck me that in a measure I had shared the fate of those who had thrown the Hebrew youths into the fiery furnace. My heart had not been consumed by the flames, but in throwing the shadrach into what I supposed were Mildred's affections it was quite possible that I had been singed by them. At any rate my conscience told me that under the circumstances my sentiments toward Mildred were too warm; in honestly making love to Janet I ought to forget them entirely.

It might have been a good thing, I told myself, if I had not given away the shadrach, but kept it as a gift from Mildred. Very soon after I reached this conclusion it became evident to me that Mildred was again cooling in my direction as rapidly as the mercury falls after sunset on a September day. This discovery did not make my mercury fall; in fact, it brought it for a time nearly to the boiling-point. I could not imagine what had happened. I almost neglected Janet, so anxious was I to know what had made this change in Mildred.

Weeks passed on, and I discovered nothing, except that Mildred had now become more than indifferent to me. She allowed me to see that my companionship did not give her pleasure.

Janet had her drive to the rhododendron hills, but she took it with Dr. Gilbert and not with me. When I heard of this it pained me, though I could not help admitting that I deserved the punishment; but my surprise was almost as great as my pain, for Janet had recently given me reason to believe that she had a very small opinion of the young doctor. In fact, she had criticized him so severely that I had been obliged to speak in his defense. I now found myself in a most doleful quandary, and there was only one thing of which I could be certain—I needed cooling toward Mildred if I still allowed myself to hope to marry Janet.

One afternoon I was talking to Mr. Bronce in his library, when, glancing toward the table used by his daughter for writing purposes, I was astounded to see, lying on a little pile of letters, the Christmas shadrach. As soon as I could get an opportunity I took it in my hand and eagerly examined it. I had not been mistaken. It was the paper-weight I had given Mildred. There was the silver band around it, and there was the place where a little piece had been knocked off by the doctor. Mildred was not at home, but I determined that I would wait and see her. I would dine with the Bronces; I would spend the evening; I would stay all night; I would not leave the house until I had had this mystery explained. She returned in about half an hour and greeted me in the somewhat stiff manner she had adopted of late; but when she noticed my perturbed expression and saw that I held the shadrach in my hand; she took a seat by the table, where for some time I had been waiting for her, alone.

"I suppose you want to ask me about that paper-weight," she remarked.

"Indeed I do," I replied. "How in the world did you happen to get it again?"

"Again?" she repeated satirically. "You may well say that. I will explain it to you. Some little time ago I called on Janet Clinton, and on her writing-desk I saw that paper-weight. I remembered it perfectly. It was the one you gave me last Christmas and afterward borrowed of me, saying that you wanted to analyze it, or something of the sort. I had never used it very much, and of course was willing that you should take it, and make experiments with it if you wanted to, but I must say that the sight of it on Janet Clinton's desk both shocked and angered me. I asked her where she got it, and she told me a gentleman had given it to her. I did not need to waste any words in inquiring who this gentleman was, but I determined that she should not rest under a mistake in regard to its proper ownership, and told her plainly that the person who had given it to her had previously given it to me; that it was mine, and he had no right to give it to any one else. 'Oh, if that is the case,' she exclaimed, 'take it, I beg of you. I don't care for it, and, what is more, I don't care any more for the man who gave it to me than I do for the thing itself.' So I took it and brought it home with me. Now you know how I happened to have it again."

For a moment I made no answer. Then I asked her how long it had been since she had received the shadrach from Janet Clinton.

"Oh, I don't remember exactly," she said; "it was several weeks ago."

Now I knew everything; all the mysteries of the past were revealed to me. The young doctor, fervid in his desire to please the woman he loved, had given Janet this novel paper-weight. From that moment she had begun to regard his attentions with apathy, and finally—her nature was one which was apt to go to extremes—to dislike him. Mildred repossessed herself of the shadrach, which she took, not as a gift from Janet, but as her rightful property, presented to her by me. And this horrid little object, probably with renewed power, had cooled, almost frozen indeed, the sentiments of that dear girl toward me. Then, too, had the spell been taken from Janet's inclinations, and she had gone to the rhododendron hills with Dr. Gilbert.

One thing was certain. *I* must have that shadrach.

"Mildred," I exclaimed, "will you not give me this paper-weight? Give it to me for my own?"

"What do you want to do with it?" she asked sarcastically. "Analyze it again?"

"Mildred," said I, "I did not give it to Janet. I gave it to Dr. Gilbert, and he must have given it to her. I know I had no right to give it away at all, but I did not believe that you would care; but now I beg that you will let me have it. Let me have it for my own. I assure you solemnly I will never give it away. It has caused trouble enough already."

"I don't exactly understand what you mean by trouble," she said, "but take it if you want it. You are perfectly welcome." And picking up her gloves and hat from the table she left me.

As I walked home my hatred of the wretched piece of metal in my hand increased with every step. I looked at it with disgust when I went to bed that night, and when my glance lighted upon it the next morning I involuntarily shrank from it, as if it had been an evil thing. Over and over again that day I asked myself why I should keep in my possession something which would make my regard for Mildred grow less and less; which would eventually make me care for her not at all? The very thought of not caring for Mildred sent a pang through my heart.

My feelings all prompted me to rid myself of what I looked upon as a calamitous talisman, but my reason interfered. If I still wished to marry Janet it was my duty to welcome indifference to Mildred.

In this mood I went out, to stroll, to think, to

decide; and that I might be ready to act on my decision I put the shadrach into my pocket. Without exactly intending it I walked toward the Bronce place, and soon found myself on the edge of a pretty pond which lay at the foot of the garden. Here, in the shade of a tree, there stood a bench, and on this lay a book, an ivory paper-cutter in its leaves as marker.

I knew that Mildred had left that book on the bench; it was her habit to come to this place to read. As she had not taken the volume with her, it was probable that she intended soon to return. But then the sad thought came to me that if she saw me there she would not return. I picked up the book; I read the pages she had been reading. As I read I felt that I could think the very thoughts that she thought as she read. I was seized with a yearning to be with her, to read with her, to think with her. Never had my soul gone out to Mildred as at that moment, and yet, heavily dangling in my pocket, I carried—I could not bear to think of it. Seized by a sudden impulse, I put down the book; I drew out the shadrach, and, tearing off the silver band, I tossed the vile bit of metal into the pond.

"There!" I cried. "Go out of my possession, out of my sight! You shall work no charm on me. Let nature take its course, and let things happen as they may." Then, relieved from the weight on my heart and the weight in my pocket, I went home.

Nature did take its course, and in less than a fortnight from that day the engagement of Janet and Dr. Gilbert was announced. I had done nothing to prevent this, and the news did not disturb my peace of mind; but my relations with Mildred very much disturbed it. I had hoped that, released from the baleful influence of the shadrach, her friendly feelings toward me would return, and my passion for her had now grown so strong that I waited and watched, as a wrecked mariner waits and watches for the sight of a sail, for a sign that she had so far softened toward me that I might dare to speak to her of my love. But no such sign appeared.

I now seldom visited the Bronce house; no one of that family, once my best friends, seemed to care to see me. Evidently Mildred's feelings toward me had extended themselves to the rest of the household. This was not surprising, for her family had long been accustomed to think as Mildred thought.

One day I met Mr. Bronce at the post-office, and, some other gentlemen coming up, we began to talk of a proposed plan to introduce a system of waterworks into the village, an improvement much desired by many of us.

"So far as I am concerned," said Mr. Bronce, "I

am not now in need of anything of the sort. Since I set up my steam-pump I have supplied my house from the pond at the end of my garden with all the water we can possibly want for every purpose."

"Do you mean," asked one of the gentlemen, "that you get your drinking-water in that way?"

"Certainly," replied Mr. Bronce. "The basin of the pond is kept as clean and in as good order as any reservoir can be, and the water comes from an excellent, rapid-flowing spring. I want nothing better."

A chill ran through me as I listened. The shadrach was in that pond. Every drop of water which Mildred drank, which touched her, was influenced by that demoniacal paperweight, which, without knowing what I was doing, I had thus bestowed upon the whole Bronce family.

When I went home I made diligent search for a stone which might be about the size and weight of the shadrach, and having repaired to a retired spot I practised tossing it as I had tossed the bit of metal into the pond. In each instance I measured the distance which I had thrown the stone, and was at last enabled to make a very fair estimate of the distance to which I had thrown the shadrach when I had buried it under the waters of the pond.

That night there was a half-moon, and between eleven and twelve o'clock, when everybody in our village might be supposed to be in bed and asleep, I

made my way over the fields to the back of the
Bronce place, taking with me a long fish-cord with a
knot in it, showing the average distance to which I
had thrown the practice stone. When I reached the
pond I stood as nearly as possible in the place by the
bench from which I had hurled the shadrach, and to
this spot I pegged one end of the cord. I was attired
in an old tennis suit, and, having removed my shoes
and stockings, I entered the water, holding the roll of
cord in my hand. This I slowly unwound as I
advanced toward the middle of the pond, and when
I reached the knot I stopped, with the water above
my waist.

I had found the bottom of the pond very smooth,
and free from weeds and mud, and I now began feeling about with my bare feet, as I moved from side to
side, describing a small arc; but I discovered nothing
more than an occasional pebble no larger than a
walnut.

Letting out some more of the cord, I advanced a
little farther into the center of the pond, and slowly
described another arc. The water was now nearly up
to my armpits, but it was not cold, though if it had
been I do not think I should have minded it in the
ardor of my search. Suddenly I put my foot on
something hard and as big as my fist, but in an
instant it moved away from under my foot; it must
have been a turtle. This occurrence made me shiver

a little, but I did not swerve from my purpose, and, loosing the string a little more, I went farther into the pond. The water was now nearly up to my chin, and there was something weird, mystical, and awe-inspiring in standing thus in the depths of this silent water, my eyes so near its gently rippling surface, fantastically lighted by the setting moon, and tenanted by nobody knew what cold and slippery creatures. But from side to side I slowly moved, reaching out with my feet in every direction, hoping to touch the thing for which I sought.

Suddenly I set my right foot upon something hard and irregular. Nervously I felt it with my toes. I patted it with my bare sole. It was as big as the shadrach! It felt like the shadrach! In a few moments I was almost convinced that the direful paper-weight was beneath my foot.

Closing my eyes, and holding my breath, I stooped down into the water, and groped on the bottom with my hands. In some way I had moved while stooping, and at first I could find nothing. A sensation of dread came over me as I felt myself in the midst of the dark solemn water,—around me, above me, everywhere,—almost suffocated, and apparently deserted even by the shadrach. But just as I felt that I could hold my breath no longer my fingers touched the thing that had been under my foot, and, clutching it, I rose and thrust my head out of the water. I could do nothing until I had taken two or three long breaths; then, holding up the object in my hand to the light of the expiring moon, I saw that it was like the shadrach; so like, indeed, that I felt that it must be it.

Turning, I made my way out of the water as rapidly as possible, and, dropping on my knees on the ground, I tremblingly lighted the lantern which I had left on the bench, and turned its light on the thing I had found. There must be no mistake; if this was not the shadrach I would go in again. But there was no necessity for reentering the pond; it *was* the shadrach.

With the extinguished lantern in one hand and the lump of mineral evil in the other, I hurried home. My wet clothes were sticky and chilly in the night air. Several times in my haste I stumbled over clods and briers, and my shoes, which I had not taken time to tie, flopped up and down as I ran. But I cared for none of these discomforts; the shadrach was in my power.

Crossing a wide field I heard, not far away, the tramping of hoofs, as of a horseman approaching at full speed. I stopped and looked in the direction of the sound. My eyes had now become so accustomed to the dim light that I could distinguish objects somewhat plainly, and I quickly perceived that the animal that was galloping toward me was a bull. I well knew what bull it was; this was Squire Starling's pasture-field, and that was his great Alderney bull, Ramping Sir John of Ramapo II.

I was well acquainted with that bull, renowned throughout the neighborhood for his savage temper and his noble pedigree—son of Ramping Sir John of Ramapo I., whose sire was the Great Rodolphin, son of Prince Maximus of Granby, one of whose daughters averaged eighteen pounds of butter a week, and who, himself, had killed two men.

The bull, who had not perceived me when I crossed the field before, for I had then made my way with as little noise as possible, was now bent on punishing my intrusion upon his domains, and bellowed as he came on. I was in a position of great danger. With my flopping shoes it was impossible to escape by flight; I must stand and defend myself. I turned and faced the furious creature, who was not twenty feet distant, and then, with all my strength, I hurled the shadrach, which I held in my right hand, directly at his shaggy forehead. My ability to project a missile was considerable, for I had held, with credit, the position of pitcher in a base-ball nine, and as the shadrach struck the bull's head with a great thud he stopped as if he had suddenly run against a wall.

I do not know that actual and violent contact with the physical organism of a recipient accelerates the influence of a shadrach upon the mental organism of said recipient, but I do know that the contact of my projectile with that bull's skull instantly cooled the animal's fury. For a few moments he stood and looked at me, and then his interest in me as a man and trespasser appeared to fade away, and, moving slowly from me, Ramping Sir John of Ramapo II. began to crop the grass.

I did not stop to look for the shadrach; I considered it safely disposed of. So long as Squire Starling used that field for a pasture connoisseurs in mineral fragments would not be apt to wander through it, and when it should be plowed, the shadrach, to ordinary eyes no more than a common stone, would be buried beneath the sod. I awoke the next morning refreshed and happy, and none the worse for my wet walk.

"Now," I said to myself, "nature shall truly have her own way. If the uncanny comes into my life and that of those I love, it shall not be brought in by me."

About a week after this I dined with the Bronce family. They were very cordial, and it seemed to me the most natural thing in the world to be sitting at their table. After dinner Mildred and I walked together in the garden. It was a charming evening, and we sat down on the bench by the edge of the pond. I spoke to her of some passages in the book I had once seen there.

"Oh, have you read that?" she asked with interest.

"I have seen only two pages of it," I said, "and those I read in the volume you left on this bench, with a paper-cutter in it for a marker. I long to read more and talk with you of what I have read."

"Why, then, didn't you wait? You might have known that I would come back."

I did not tell her that I knew that because I was there she would not have come. But before I left the bench I discovered that hereafter, wherever I might be, she was willing to come and to stay.

Early in the next spring Mildred and I were married, and on our wedding-trip we passed through a mining district in the mountains. Here we visited one of the great ironworks, and were both much interested in witnessing the wonderful power of man, air, and fire over the stubborn king of metals.

"What is this substance?" asked Mildred of one of the officials who was conducting us through the works.

"That," said the man, "is what we call shad—"

"My dear," I cried, "we must hurry away this instant or we shall lose the train. Come; quick; there is not a moment for delay." And with a word of thanks to the guide I seized her hand and led her, almost running, into the open air.

Mildred was amazed.

"Never before," she exclaimed, "have I seen you

in such a hurry. I thought the train we decided to take did not leave for at least an hour."

"I have changed my mind," I said, "and think it will be a great deal better for us to take the one which leaves in ten minutes."

Dancing Dan's Christmas

DAMON RUNYON

Now one time it comes on Christmas, and in fact it is the evening before Christmas, and I am in Good Time Charley Bernstein's little speakeasy in West Forty-seventh Street, wishing Charley a Merry Christmas and having a few hot Tom and Jerrys with him.

This hot Tom and Jerry is an old-time drink that is once used by one and all in this country to celebrate Christmas with, and in fact it is once so popular that many people think Christmas is invented only to furnish an excuse for hot Tom and Jerry, although of course this is by no means true.

But anybody will tell you that there is nothing that brings out the true holiday spirit like hot Tom and Jerry, and I hear that since Tom and Jerry goes out of style in the United States, the holiday spirit is never quite the same.

Well, as Good Time Charley and I are expressing our holiday sentiments to each other over our hot Tom and Jerry, and I am trying to think up the poem about the night before Christmas and all through the house, which I know will interest Charley no little, all of a sudden there is a big knock at the front door, and when Charley opens the door, who comes in carrying a large package under one arm but a guy by the name of Dancing Dan.

This Dancing Dan is a good-looking young guy, who always seems well-dressed, and he is called by the name of Dancing Dan because he is a great hand for dancing around and about with dolls in night clubs, and other spots where there is any dancing. In fact, Dan never seems to be doing anything else, although I hear rumors that when he is not dancing he is carrying on in a most illegal manner at one thing and another. But of course you can always hear rumors in this town about anybody, and personally I am rather fond of Dancing Dan as he always seems to be getting a great belt out of life.

Anybody in town will tell you that Dancing Dan is a guy with no Barnaby whatever in him, and in fact he has about as much gizzard as anybody around, although I wish to say I always question his judgment in dancing so much with Miss Muriel

O'Neill, who works in the Half Moon night club. And the reason I question his judgment in this respect is because everybody knows that Miss Muriel O'Neill is a doll who is very well thought of by Heine Schmitz, and Heine Schmitz is not such a guy as will take kindly to anybody dancing more than once and a half with a doll that he thinks well of.

Well, anyway, as Dancing Dan comes in, he weighs up the joint in one quick peek, and then he tosses the package he is carrying into a corner where it goes plunk, as if there is something very heavy in it, and then he steps up to the bar alongside of Charley and me and wishes to know what we are drinking.

Naturally we start boosting hot Tom and Jerry to Dancing Dan, and he says he will take a crack at it with us, and after one crack, Dancing Dan says he will have another crack, and Merry Christmas to us with it, and the first thing anybody knows it is a couple of hours later and we are still having cracks at the hot Tom and Jerry with Dancing Dan, and Dan says he never drinks anything so soothing in his life. In fact, Dancing Dan says he will recommend Tom and Jerry to everybody he knows, only he does not know anybody good enough for Tom and Jerry, except maybe Miss Muriel O'Neill, and she does not drink anything with drugstore rye in it.

Well, several times while we are drinking this Tom and Jerry, customers come to the door of Good

Time Charley's little speakeasy and knock, but by now Charley is commencing to be afraid they will wish Tom and Jerry, too, and he does not feel we will have enough for ourselves, so he hangs out a sign which says "Closed on Account of Christmas," and the only one he will let in is a guy by the name of Ooky, who is nothing but an old rum-dum, and who is going around all week dressed like Santa Claus and carrying a sign advertising Moe Lewinsky's clothing joint around in Sixth Avenue.

This Ooky is still wearing his Santa Claus outfit when Charley lets him in, and the reason Charley permits such a character as Ooky in his joint is because Ooky does the porter work for Charley when he is not Santa Claus for Moe Lewinsky, such as sweeping out, and washing the glasses, and one thing and another.

Well, it is about nine-thirty when Ooky comes in, and his puppies are aching, and he is all petered out generally from walking up and down and here and there with his sign, for any time a guy is Santa Claus for Moe Lewinsky he must earn his dough. In fact, Ooky is so fatigued, and his puppies hurt him so much that Dancing Dan and Good Time Charley and I all feel very sorry for him, and invite him to have a few mugs of hot Tom and Jerry with us, and wish him plenty of Merry Christmas.

But old Ooky is not accustomed to Tom and Jerry and after about the fifth mug he folds up in a chair, and goes right to sleep on us. He is wearing a pretty good Santa Claus make-up, what with a nice red suit trimmed with white cotton, and a wig, and false nose, and long white whiskers, and a big sack stuffed with excelsior on his back, and if I do not know Santa Claus is not apt to be such a guy as will snore loud enough to rattle the windows, I will think Ooky is Santa Claus sure enough.

Well, we forget Ooky and let him sleep, and go on with our hot Tom and Jerry, and in the meantime we try to think up a few songs appropriate to Christmas, and Dancing Dan finally renders My Dad's Dinner Pail in a nice baritone and very loud, while I do first rate with Will You Love Me in December As You Do in May?

About midnight Dancing Dan wishes to see how he looks as Santa Claus.

So Good Time Charley and I help Dancing Dan pull off Ooky's outfit and put it on Dan, and this is easy as Ooky only has this Santa Claus outfit on over his ordinary clothes, and he does not even wake up when we are undressing him of the Santa Claus uniform.

Well, I wish to say I see many a Santa Claus in my time, but I never see a better looking Santa Claus than Dancing Dan, especially after he gets the wig and white whiskers fixed just right, and we put a sofa pillow that Good Time Charley happens to have around the joint for the cat to sleep on down his pants to give Dancing Dan a nice fat stomach such as Santa Claus is bound to have.

"Well," Charley finally says, "it is a great pity we do not know where there are some stockings hung up somewhere, because then," he says, "you can go around and stuff things in these stockings, as I always hear this is the main idea of a Santa Claus. But," Charley says, "I do not suppose anybody in this section has any stockings hung up, or if they have," he says, "the chances are they are so full of holes they will not hold anything. Anyway," Charley says, "even if there are any stockings hung up we do not have anything to stuff in them, although personally," he says, "I will gladly donate a few pints of Scotch."

Well, I am pointing out that we have no reindeer and that a Santa Claus is bound to look like a terrible sap if he goes around without any reindeer, but Charley's remarks seem to give Dancing Dan an idea, for all of a sudden he speaks as follows:

"Why," Dancing Dan says, "I know where a stocking is hung up. It is hung up at Miss Muriel O'Neill's flat over here in West Forty-ninth Street. This stocking is hung up by nobody but a party by the name of Gammer O'Neill, who is Miss Muriel

O'Neill's grandmamma," Dancing Dan says. "Gammer O'Neill is going on ninety-odd," he says, "and Miss Muriel O'Neill tells me she cannot hold out much longer, what with one thing and another, including being a little childish in spots.

"Now," Dancing Dan says, "I remember Miss Muriel O'Neill is telling me just the other night how Gammer O'Neill hangs up her stocking on Christmas Eve all her life, and," he says, "I judge from what Miss Muriel O'Neill says that the old doll always believes Santa Claus will come along some Christmas and fill the stocking full of beautiful gifts. But," Dancing Dan says, "Miss Muriel O'Neill tells me Santa Claus never does this, although Miss Muriel O'Neill personally always takes a few gifts home and pops them into the stocking to make Gammer O'Neill feel better.

"But, of course," Dancing Dan says, "these gifts are nothing much because Miss Muriel O'Neill is very poor, and proud, and also good, and will not take a dime off of anybody and I can lick the guy who says she will.

"Now," Dancing Dan goes on, "it seems that while Gammer O'Neill is very happy to get whatever she finds in her stocking on Christmas morning, she does not understand why Santa Claus is not more liberal, and," he says, "Miss Muriel O'Neill is saying to me that she only wishes she can give Gammer O'Neill one real big Christmas before the old doll puts her checks back in the rack.

"So," Dancing Dan states, "here is a job for us. Miss Muriel O'Neill and her grandmamma live all alone in this flat over in West Forty-ninth Street, and," he says, "at such an hour as this Miss Muriel O'Neill is bound to be working, and the chances are Gammer O'Neill is sound asleep, and we will just hop over there and Santa Claus will fill up her stocking with beautiful gifts."

Well, I say, I do not see where we are going to get any beautiful gifts at this time of night, what with all the stores being closed, unless we dash into an all-night drug store and buy a few bottles of perfume and a bum toilet set as guys always do when they forget about their ever-loving wives until after store hours on Christmas Eve, but Dancing Dan says never mind about this, but let us have a few more Tom and Jerrys first.

So we have a few more Tom and Jerrys, and then Dancing Dan picks up the package he heaves into the corner, and dumps most of the excelsior out of Ooky's Santa Claus sack, and puts the bundle in, and Good Time Charley turns out all the lights, but one, and leaves a bottle of Scotch on the table in front of Ooky for a Christmas gift, and away we go.

Personally, I regret very much leaving the hot Tom

and Jerry, but then I am also very enthusiastic about going along to help Dancing Dan play Santa Claus, while Good Time Charley is practically overjoyed, as it is the first time in his life Charley is ever mixed up in so much holiday spirit.

As we go up Broadway, headed for Forty-ninth Street, Charley and I see many citizens we know and give them a large hello, and wish them Merry Christmas, and some of these citizens shake hands with Santa Claus, not knowing he is nobody but Dancing Dan, although later I understand there is some gossip among these citizens because they claim a Santa Claus with such a breath on him as our Santa Claus has is a little out of line.

And once we are somewhat embarrassed when a lot of little kids going home with their parents from a late Christmas party somewhere gather about Santa Claus with shouts of childish glee, and some of them wish to climb up Santa Claus' legs. Naturally, Santa Claus gets a little peevish, and calls them a few names, and one of the parents comes up and wishes to know what is the idea of Santa Claus using such language, and Santa Claus takes a punch at the parent, all of which is no doubt astonishing to the little kids who have an idea of Santa Claus as a very kindly old guy.

Well, finally we arrive in front of the place where

Dancing Dan says Miss Muriel O'Neill and her grandmamma live, and it is nothing but a tenement house not far back of Madison Square Garden, and furthermore it is a walkup, and at this time there are no lights burning in the joint except a gas jet in the main hall, and by the light of this jet we look at the names on the letter boxes, such as you always find in the hall of these joints, and we see that Miss Muriel O'Neill and her grandmamma live on the fifth floor.

This is the top floor, and personally I do not like the idea of walking up five flights of stairs, and I am willing to let Dancing Dan and Good Time Charley go, but Dancing Dan insists we must all go, and finally I agree because Charley is commencing to argue that the right way for us to do is to get on the roof and let Santa Claus go down a chimney, and is making so much noise I am afraid he will wake somebody up.

So up the stairs we climb and finally we come to a door on the top floor that has a little card in a slot that says O'Neill, so we know we reach our destination. Dancing Dan first tries the knob, and right away the door opens, and we are in a little two or three-room flat, with not much furniture in it, and what furniture there is, is very poor. One single gas jet is burning near a bed in a room just off the one the door opens into, and by this light we see a very old doll is sleeping on the bed, so we judge this is nobody but Gammer O'Neill.

On her face is a large smile, as if she is dreaming of something very pleasant. On a chair at the head of the bed is hung a long black stocking, and it seems to be such a stocking as is often patched and mended, so I can see that what Miss Muriel O'Neill tells Dancing Dan about her grandmamma hanging up her stocking is really true, although up to this time I have my doubts.

Finally Dancing Dan unslings the sack on his back, and takes out his package, and unties this package, and all of a sudden out pops a raft of big diamond bracelets, and diamond rings, and diamond brooches, and diamond necklaces, and I do not know what else in the way of diamonds, and Dancing Dan and I begin stuffing these diamonds into the stocking and Good Time Charley pitches in and helps us.

There are enough diamonds to fill the stocking to the muzzle, and it is no small stocking, at that, and I judge that Gammer O'Neill has a pretty fair set of bunting sticks when she is young. In fact, there are so many diamonds that we have enough left over to make a nice little pile on the chair after we fill the stocking plumb up, leaving a nice diamond-studded vanity case sticking out the top where we figure it will hit Gammer O'Neill's eye when she wakes up.

And it is not until I get out in the fresh air again that all of a sudden I remember seeing large headlines in the afternoon papers about a five-hundred-G's stickup in the afternoon of one of the biggest diamond merchants in Maiden Lane while he is sitting in his office, and I also recall once hearing rumors that Dancing Dan is one of the best lone-hand git-'em-up guys in the world.

Naturally, I commence to wonder if I am in the proper company when I am with Dancing Dan, even if he is Santa Claus. So I leave him on the next corner arguing with Good Time Charley about whether they ought to go and find some more presents somewhere, and look for other stockings to stuff, and I hasten on home and go to bed.

The next day I find I have such a noggin that I do not care to stir around, and in fact I do not stir around much for a couple of weeks.

Then one night I drop around to Good Time Charley's little speakeasy, and ask Charley what is doing.

"Well," Charley says, "many things are doing, and personally," he says, "I'm greatly surprised I do not see you at Gammer O'Neill's wake. You know Gammer O'Neill leaves this wicked old world a couple of days after Christmas," Good Time Charley says, "and," he says, "Miss Muriel O'Neill states that Doc Moggs claims it is at least a day after she is entitled to go, but she is sustained," Charley says, "by great happiness in finding her stocking filled with beautiful gifts on Christmas morning.

"According to Miss Muriel O'Neill," Charley says, "Gammer O'Neill dies practically convinced that there is a Santa Claus, although of course," he says, "Miss Muriel O'Neill does not tell her the real owner of the gifts, an all-right guy by the name of Shapiro leaves the gifts with her after Miss Muriel O'Neill notifies him of the finding of same.

"It seems," Charley says, "this Shapiro is a tenderhearted guy, who is willing to help keep Gammer O'Neill with us a little longer when Doc Moggs says leaving the gifts with her will do it.

"So," Charley says, "everything is quite all right, as the coppers cannot figure anything except that maybe the rascal who takes the gifts from Shapiro gets conscience-stricken, and leaves them the first place he can, and Miss Muriel O'Neill receives a ten-G's reward for finding the gifts and returning them. And," Charley says, "I hear Dancing Dan is in San Francisco and is figuring on reforming and becoming a dancing teacher, so he can marry Miss Muriel O'Neill, and of course," he says, "we all hope and trust she never learn any details of Dancing Dan's career."

Well, it is Christmas Eve a year later that I run into a guy by the name of Shotgun Sam, who is mobbed up with Heine Schmitz in Harlem, and who is a very, very obnoxious character indeed.

"Well, well, well," Shotgun says, "the last time I see you is another Christmas Eve like this, and you are coming out of Good Time Charley's joint, and," he says, "you certainly have your pots on."

"Well, Shotgun," I says, "I am sorry you get such a wrong impression of me, but the truth is," I say, "on the occasion you speak of, I am suffering from a dizzy feeling in my head."

"It is all right with me," Shotgun says. "I have a tip this guy Dancing Dan is in Good Time Charley's the night I see you, and Mockie Morgan, and Gunner Jack and me are casing the joint, because," he says, "Heine Schmitz is all sored up at Dan over some doll, although of course," Shotgun says, "it is all right now, as Heine has another doll.

"Anyway," he says, "we never get to see Dancing Dan. We watch the joint from six-thirty in the evening until daylight Christmas morning, and nobody goes in all night but old Ooky the Santa Claus guy in his Santa Claus makeup, and," Shotgun says, "nobody comes out except you and Good Time Charley and Ooky.

"Well," Shotgun says, "it is a great break for Dancing Dan he never goes in or comes out of Good Time Charley's, at that, because," he says, "we are waiting for him on the second-floor front of the building across the way with some nice little sawed-offs, and are under orders from Heine not to miss."

"Well, Shotgun," I say, "Merry Christmas."

"Well, all right," Shotgun says, "Merry Christmas."

Christmas Storms and Sunshine

ELIZABETH GASKELL

In the town of—(no matter where) there circulated two local newspapers (no matter when). Now the *Flying Post* was long-established and respectable—alias bigoted and Tory; the *Examiner* was spirited and intelligent—alias newfangled and democratic. Every week these newspapers contained articles abusing each other, as cross and peppery as articles could be, and evidently the production of irritated minds, although they seemed to have one stereotyped commencement—"Though the article appearing in our last week's *Post* (or *Examiner*) is below contempt, yet we have been induced," &c. &c.; and every Saturday the Radical shopkeepers shook hands together, and agreed that the *Post* was done for by the slashing, clever *Examiner*; while the

more dignified Tories began by regretting that John-
son should think that low paper, only read by a few
of the vulgar, worth wasting his wit upon; however,
the *Examiner* was at its last gasp.

It was not, though. It lived and flourished; at least
it paid its way, as one of the heroes of my story could
tell. He was chief compositor, or whatever title may
be given to the headman of the mechanical part of a
newspaper. He hardly confined himself to that
department. Once or twice, unknown to the editor,
when the manuscript had fallen short, he had filled
up the vacant space by compositions of his own;
announcements of a forthcoming crop of green peas
in December; a grey thrush having been seen, or a
white hare, or such interesting phenomena; invented
for the occasion, I must confess; but what of that?
His wife always knew when to expect a little specimen of her husband's literary talent by a peculiar
cough, which served as prelude; and, judging from
this encouraging sign, and the high-pitched and
emphatic voice in which he read them, she was
inclined to think, that an "Ode to an early Rosebud," in the corner devoted to original poetry, and a
letter in the correspondence department, signed
"Pro Bono Publico," were her husband's writing,
and to hold up her head accordingly.

I never could find out what it was that occasioned
the Hodgsons to lodge in the same house as the

Jenkinses. Jenkins held the same office in the Tory Paper as Hodgson did in the *Examiner*, and, as I said before, I leave you to give it a name. But Jenkins had a proper sense of his position, and a proper reverence for all in authority, from the king down to the editor and sub-editor. He would as soon have thought of borrowing the king's crown for a nightcap, or the king's sceptre for a walking-stick as he would have thought of filling up any spare corner with any production of his own; and I think it would have even added to his contempt of Hodgson (if that were possible), had he known of the "productions of his brain," as the latter fondly alluded to the paragraphs he inserted, when speaking to his wife.

Jenkins had his wife too. Wives were wanting to finish the completeness of the quarrel which existed one memorable Christmas week, some dozen years ago, between the two neighbours, the two compositors. And with wives, it was a very pretty, a very complete quarrel. To make the opposing parties still more equal, still more well-matched, if the Hodgsons had a baby ("such a baby!—a poor, puny little thing"), Mrs. Jenkins had a cat ("such a cat! a great, nasty, miowling tom-cat, that was always stealing the milk put by for little Angel's supper"). And now, having matched Greek with Greek, I must proceed to the tug of war. It was the day before Christmas; such a cold east wind! such an inky sky! such a blue-black look in people's faces, as they were driven out more than usual, to complete their purchases for the next day's festival.

Before leaving home that morning, Jenkins had given some money to his wife to buy the next day's dinner.

"My dear, I wish for turkey and sausages. It may be a weakness, but I own I am partial to sausages. My deceased mother was. Such tastes are hereditary. As to the sweets—whether plum-pudding or mince-pies—I leave such considerations to you; I only beg you not to mind expense. Christmas comes but once a year."

And again he called out from the bottom of the first flight of stairs, just close to the Hodgsons' door ("such ostentatiousness," as Mrs. Hodgson observed), "You will not forget the sausages, my dear!"

"I should have liked to have had something above common, Mary," said Hodgson, as they too made their plans for the next day; "but I think roast beef must do for us. You see, love, we've a family."

"Only one, Jem! I don't want more than roast beef, though, I'm sure. Before I went to service, mother and me would have thought roast beef a very fine dinner."

"Well, let's settle it, then, roast beef and a plum-pudding; and now, good-bye. Mind and take care of

little Tom. I thought he was a bit hoarse this morning."

And off he went to his work.

Now, it was a good while since Mrs. Jenkins and
Mrs. Hodgson had spoken to each other, although
they were quite as much in possession of the knowledge of events and opinions as though they did.
Mary knew that Mrs. Jenkins despised her for not
having a real lace cap, which Mrs. Jenkins had; and
for having been a servant, which Mrs. Jenkins had
not; and the little occasional pinchings which the
Hodgsons were obliged to resort to, to make both
ends meet, would have been very patiently endured
by Mary, if she had not winced under Mrs. Jenkins's
knowledge of such economy. But she had her
revenge. She had a child, and Mrs. Jenkins had none.
To have had a child, even such a puny baby as little
Tom, Mrs. Jenkins would have worn commonest
caps, and cleaned grates, and drudged her fingers to
the bone. The great unspoken disappointment of
her life soured her temper, and turned her thoughts
inward, and made her morbid and selfish.

"Hang that cat! he's been stealing again! he's
gnawed the cold mutton in his nasty mouth till it's
not fit to set before a Christian; and I've nothing else
for Jem's dinner. But I'll give it him now I've caught
him, that I will!"

So saying, Mary Hodgson caught up her husband's

Sunday cane, and despite pussy's cries and scratches, she gave him such a beating as she hoped might cure him of his thievish propensities; when, lo! and behold, Mrs. Jenkins stood at the door with a face of bitter wrath.

"Aren't you ashamed of yourself, ma'am, to abuse a poor dumb animal, ma'am, as knows no better than to take food when he sees it, ma'am? He only follows the nature which God has given, ma'am; and it's a pity your nature, ma'am, which I've heard is of the stingy saving species, does not make you shut your cupboard door a little closer. There is such a thing as law for brute animals. I'll ask Mr. Jenkins, but I don't think them Radicals has done away with that law yet, for all their Reform Bill, ma'am. My poor precious love of a Tommy, is he hurt? and is his leg broke for taking a mouthful of scraps, as most people would give away to a beggar—if he'd take 'em!" wound up Mrs. Jenkins, casting a contemptuous look on the remnant of a scrag end of mutton.

Mary felt very angry and very guilty. For she really pitied the poor limping animal as he crept up to his mistress, and there lay down to bemoan himself; she wished she had not beaten him so hard, for it certainly was her own careless way of never shutting the cupboard-door that had tempted him to his fault. But the sneer at her little bit of mutton turned her penitence to fresh wrath, and she shut the door in Mrs. Jenkins's face, as she stood caressing her cat in the lobby, with such a bang, that it wakened little Tom, and he began to cry.

Everything was to go wrong with Mary to-day. Now baby was awake, who was to take her husband's dinner to the office? She took the child in her arms and tried to hush him off to sleep again, and as she sung she cried, she could hardly tell why,—a sort of reaction from her violent angry feelings. She wished she had never beaten the poor cat; she wondered if his leg was really broken. What would her mother say if she knew how cross and cruel her little Mary was getting? If she should live to beat her child in one of her angry fits?

It was of no use lullabying while she sobbed so; it must be given up, and she must just carry her baby in her arms, and take him with her to the office, for it was long past dinner-time. So she pared the mutton carefully, although by so doing she reduced the meat to an infinitesimal quantity, and taking the baked potatoes out of the oven, she popped them piping hot into her basket, with the et-cæteras of plate, butter, salt, and knife and fork.

It was, indeed, a bitter wind. She bent against it as she ran, and the flakes of snow were sharp and cutting as ice. Baby cried all the way, though she cuddled him up in her shawl. Then her husband had made his appetite up for a potato-pie, and (literary man as he was) his body got so much the better of his mind, that he looked rather black at the cold mutton. Mary had no appetite for her own dinner when she arrived at home again. So, after she had tried to feed baby, and he had fretfully refused to take his bread and milk, she laid him down as usual on his quilt, surrounded by playthings, while she sided away, and chopped suet for the next day's pudding. Early in the afternoon a parcel came, done up first in brown paper, then in such a white, grass-bleached, sweet-smelling towel, and a note from her dear, dear mother; in which quaint writing she endeavoured to tell her daughter that she was not forgotten at Christmas time; but that, learning that Farmer Burton was killing his pig, she had made interest for some of his famous pork, out of which she had manufactured some sausages, and flavoured them just as Mary used to like when she lived at home.

"Dear, dear mother!" said Mary to herself. "There never was any one like her for remembering other folk. What rare sausages she used to make! Home things have a smack with 'em no bought things can ever have. Set them up with their sausages! I've a notion if Mrs. Jenkins had ever tasted mother's she'd have no fancy for them town-made things Fanny took in just now."

And so she went on thinking about home, till the smiles and the dimples came out again at the remembrance of that pretty cottage, which would look green even now in the depth of winter, with its pyracanthus, and its holly-bushes, and the great Portugal laurel that was her mother's pride. And the back path through the orchard to Farmer Burton's, how well she remembered it! The bushels of unripe apples she had picked up there and distributed among his pigs, till he had scolded her for giving them so much green trash!

She was interrupted—her baby (I call him a baby, because his father and mother did, and because he was so little of his age, but I rather think he was eighteen months old,) had fallen asleep some time before among his playthings; an uneasy, restless sleep; but of which Mary had been thankful, as his morning's nap had been too short, and as she was so busy. But now he began to make such a strange crowing noise, just like a chair drawn heavily and gratingly along a kitchen-floor! His eyes were open, but expressive of nothing but pain.

"Mother's darling!" said Mary, in terror, lifting him up. "Baby, try not to make that noise. Hush,

hush, darling; what hurts him?" But the noise came worse and worse.

"Fanny! Fanny!" Mary called in mortal fright, for her baby was almost black with his gasping breath, and she had no one to ask for aid or sympathy but her landlady's daughter, a little girl of twelve or thirteen, who attended to the house in her mother's absence, as daily cook in gentlemen's families. Fanny was more especially considered the attendant of the upstairs lodgers (who paid for the use of the kitchen, "for Jenkins could not abide the smell of meat cooking"), but just now she was fortunately sitting at her afternoon's work of darning stockings, and hearing Mrs. Hodgson's cry of terror, she ran to her sitting-room, and understood the case at a glance.

"He's got the croup! O Mrs. Hodgson, he'll die as sure as fate. Little brother had it, and he died in no time. The doctor said he could do nothing for him—it had gone too far. He said if we'd put him in a warm bath at first, it might have saved him; but, bless you! he was never half so bad as your baby." Unconsciously there mingled in her statement some of a child's love of producing an effect; but the increasing danger was clear enough.

"Oh, my baby! my baby! Oh, love, love! don't look so ill! I cannot bear it. And my fire so low! There, I was thinking of home, and picking currants, and never minding the fire. O Fanny! what is the fire like in the kitchen? Speak."

"Mother told me to screw it up, and throw some slack on as soon as Mrs. Jenkins had done with it, and so I did. It's very low and black. But, oh, Mrs. Hodgson! let me run for the doctor—I cannot abear to hear him, it's so like little brother."

Through her streaming tears Mary motioned her to go; and trembling, sinking, sick at heart, she laid her boy in his cradle, and ran to fill her kettle.

Mrs. Jenkins, having cooked her husband's snug little dinner, to which he came home; having told him her story of pussy's beating, at which he was justly and dignifiedly (?) indignant, saying it was all of a piece with that abusive *Examiner*; having received the sausages, and turkey, and mince-pies, which her husband had ordered; and cleaned up the room, and prepared everything for tea, and coaxed and duly bemoaned her cat (who had pretty nearly forgotten his beating, but very much enjoyed the petting); having done all these and many other things, Mrs. Jenkins sat down to get up the real lace cap. Every thread was pulled out separately, and carefully stretched: when—what was that? Outside, in the street, a chorus of piping children's voices sang the old carol she had heard a hundred times in the days of her youth—

"As Joseph was a walking he heard an angel
  sing,
'This night shall be born our heavenly King.
He neither shall be born in housen nor in hall,
Nor in the place of Paradise, but in an ox's
  stall.
He neither shall be clothed in purple nor in
  pall,
But all in fair linen, as were babies all:
He neither shall be rocked in silver nor in gold,
But in a wooden cradle that rocks on the
  mould,' " &c.

She got up and went to the window. There, below, stood the group of black little figures, relieved against the snow, which now enveloped everything. "For old sake's sake," as she phrased it, she counted out a halfpenny apiece for the singers, out of the copper bag, and threw them down below.

The room had become chilly while she had been counting out and throwing down her money, so she stirred her already glowing fire, and sat down right before it—but not to stretch her lace; like Mary Hodgson, she began to think over long past days, on softening remembrances of the dead and gone, on words long forgotten, on holy stories heard at her mother's knee.

"I cannot think what's come over me to-night,"

said she, half aloud, recovering herself by the sound of her own voice from her train of thought—"My head goes wandering on them old times. I'm sure more texts have come into my head with thinking on my mother within this last half-hour, than I've thought on for years and years. I hope I'm not going to die. Folks says, thinking too much on the dead betokens we're going to join 'em; I should be loth to go just yet—such a fine turkey as we've got for dinner to-morrow too!"

Knock, knock, knock, at the door, as fast as knuckles could go. And then, as if the comer could not wait, the door was opened, and Mary Hodgson stood there as white as death.

"Mrs. Jenkins!—oh, your kettle is boiling, thank God! Let me have the water for my baby, for the love of God! He's got croup, and is dying!"

Mrs. Jenkins turned on her chair with a wooden, inflexible look on her face, that (between ourselves) her husband knew and dreaded for all his pompous dignity.

"I'm sorry I can't oblige you, ma'am; my kettle is wanted for my husband's tea. Don't be afeared, Tommy, Mrs. Hodgson won't venture to intrude herself where she's not desired. You'd better send for the doctor, ma'am, instead of wasting your time in wringing your hands, ma'am—my kettle is engaged."

Mary clasped her hands together with passionate force, but spoke no word of entreaty to that wooden face—that sharp, determined voice; but, as she turned away, she prayed for strength to bear the coming trial, and strength to forgive Mrs. Jenkins.

Mrs. Jenkins watched her go away meekly, as one who has no hope, and then she turned upon herself as sharply as she ever did on any one else.

"What a brute I am, Lord forgive me! What's my husband's tea to a baby's life? In croup, too, where time is everything. You crabbed old vixen, you!—any one may know you never had a child!"

She was downstairs (kettle in hand) before she had finished her self-upbraiding; and when in Mrs. Hodgson's room, she rejected all thanks (Mary had not the voice for many words), saying, stiffly, "I do it for the poor babby's sake, ma'am, hoping he may live to have mercy to poor dumb beasts, if he does forget to lock his cupboards."

But she did everything, and more than Mary, with her young inexperience, could have thought of. She prepared the warm bath, and tried it with her husband's own thermometer (Mr. Jenkins was as punctual as clockwork in noting down the temperature of every day). She let his mother place her baby in the tub, still preserving the same rigid, affronted aspect, and then she went upstairs without a word. Mary longed to ask her to stay, but dared not; though, when she left the room, the tears chased each other down her cheeks faster than ever. Poor young mother! how she counted the minutes till the doctor should come. But, before he came, down again stalked Mrs. Jenkins, with something in her hand.

"I've seen many of these croup-fits, which, I take it, you've not, ma'am. Mustard plaisters is very sovereign, put on the throat; I've been up and made one, ma'am, and, by your leave, I'll put it on the poor little fellow."

Mary could not speak, but she signed her grateful assent.

It began to smart while they still kept silence; and he looked up to his mother as if seeking courage from her looks to bear the stinging pain; but she was softly crying to see him suffer, and her want of courage reacted upon him, and he began to sob aloud. Instantly Mrs. Jenkins's apron was up, hiding her face: "Peep-bo, baby," said she, as merrily as she could. His little face brightened, and his mother having once got the cue, the two women kept the little fellow amused, until his plaister had taken effect.

"He's better—oh, Mrs. Jenkins, look at his eyes! how different! And he breathes quite softly"—

As Mary spoke thus, the doctor entered. He examined his patient. Baby was really better.

"It has been a sharp attack, but the remedies you

have applied have been worth all the Pharmacopœia an hour later.—I shall send a powder," &c. &c.

Mrs. Jenkins stayed to hear this opinion; and (her heart wonderfully more easy) was going to leave the room, when Mary seized her hand and kissed it; she could not speak her gratitude.

Mrs. Jenkins looked affronted and awkward, and as if she must go upstairs and wash her hand directly.

But, in spite of these sour looks, she came softly down an hour or so afterwards to see how baby was.

The little gentleman slept well after the fright he had given his friends; and on Christmas morning, when Mary awoke and looked at the sweet little pale face lying on her arm, she could hardly realise the danger he had been in.

When she came down (later than usual), she found the household in a commotion. What do you think had happened? Why, pussy had been traitor to his best friend, and eaten up some of Mr. Jenkins's own especial sausages; and gnawed and tumbled the rest so, that they were not fit to be eaten! There were no bounds to that cat's appetite! he would have eaten his own father if he had been tender enough. And now Mrs. Jenkins stormed and cried—"Hang the cat!"

Christmas Day, too! and all the shops shut! "What was turkey without sausages?" gruffly asked Mr. Jenkins.

"O Jem!" whispered Mary, "hearken what a piece of work he's making about sausages—I should like to take Mrs. Jenkins up some of mother's; they're twice as good as bought sausages."

"I see no objection, my dear. Sausages do not involve intimacies, else his politics are what I can no ways respect."

"But, oh, Jem, if you had seen her last night about baby! I'm sure she may scold me for ever, and I'll not answer. I'd even make her cat welcome to the sausages." The tears gathered to Mary's eyes as she kissed her boy.

"Better take 'em upstairs, my dear, and give them to the cat's mistress." And Jem chuckled at his saying.

Mary put them on a plate, but still she loitered.

"What must I say, Jem? I never know."

"Say—I hope you'll accept of these sausages, as my mother—no, that's not grammar;—say what comes uppermost, Mary, it will be sure to be right."

So Mary carried them upstairs and knocked at the door; and when told to "come in," she looked very red, but went up to Mrs. Jenkins, saying, "Please take these. Mother made them." And was away before an answer could be given.

Just as Hodgson was ready to go to church, Mrs. Jenkins came downstairs, and called Fanny. In a minute, the latter entered the Hodgsons' room, and delivered Mr. and Mrs. Jenkins's compliments, and they would be particular glad if Mr. and Mrs. Hodgson would eat their dinner with them.

"And carry baby upstairs in a shawl, be sure," added Mrs. Jenkins's voice in the passage, close to the door, whither she had followed her messenger. There was no discussing the matter, with the certainty of every word being overheard.

Mary looked anxiously at her husband. She remembered his saying he did not approve of Mr. Jenkins's politics.

"Do you think it would do for baby?" asked he.

"Oh, yes," answered she eagerly; "I would wrap him up so warm."

"And I've got our room up to sixty-five already, for all it's so frosty," added the voice outside.

Now, how do you think they settled the matter? The very best way in the world. Mr. and Mrs. Jenkins came down into the Hodgsons' room and dined there. Turkey at the top, roast beef at the bottom, sausages at one side, potatoes at the other. Second course, plum-pudding at the top, and mince-pies at the bottom.

And after dinner, Mrs. Jenkins would have baby on her knee, and he seemed quite to take to her; she declared he was admiring the real lace on her cap, but Mary thought (though she did not say so) that he was pleased by her kind looks and coaxing words.

Then he was wrapped up and carried carefully upstairs to tea, in Mrs. Jenkins's room. And after tea, Mrs. Jenkins, and Mary, and her husband, found out each other's mutual liking for music, and sat singing old glees and catches, till I don't know what o'clock, without one word of politics or newspapers.

Before they parted, Mary had coaxed pussy on to her knee; for Mrs. Jenkins would not part with baby, who was sleeping on her lap.

"When you're busy bring him to me. Do, now, it will be a real favour. I know you must have a deal to do, with another coming; let him come up to me. I'll take the greatest of cares of him; pretty darling, how sweet he looks when he's asleep!"

When the couples were once more alone, the husbands unburdened their minds to their wives.

Mr. Jenkins said to his—"Do you know, Burgess tried to make me believe Hodgson was such a fool as to put paragraphs into the *Examiner* now and then; but I see he knows his place, and has got too much sense to do any such thing."

Hodgson said—"Mary, love, I almost fancy from Jenkins's way of speaking (so much civiler than I expected), he guesses I wrote that 'Pro Bono' and the 'Rosebud,'—at any rate, I've no objection to your naming it, if the subject should come uppermost; I should like him to know I'm a literary man."

Well! I've ended my tale; I hope you don't think it too long; but, before I go, just let me say one thing.

If any of you have any quarrels, or misunderstandings, or coolnesses, or cold shoulders, or shynesses, or tiffs, or miffs, or huffs, with any one else, just make friends before Christmas,—you will be so much merrier if you do.

I ask it of you for the sake of that old angelic song, heard so many years ago by the shepherds, keeping watch by night, on Bethlehem Heights.

The Blue Carbuncle

ARTHUR CONAN DOYLE

I had called upon my friend Sherlock Holmes upon the second morning after Christmas, with the intention of wishing him the compliments of the season. He was lounging upon the sofa in a purple dressing gown, a pipe-rack within his reach upon the right, and a pile of crumpled morning papers, evidently newly studied, near at hand. Beside the couch was a wooden chair, and on the angle of the back hung a very seedy and disreputable hard felt hat, much the worse for wear, and cracked in several places. A lens and a forceps lying upon the seat of the chair suggested that the hat had been suspended in this manner for the purpose of examination.

'You are engaged,' said I; 'perhaps I interrupt you.'

'Not at all. I am glad to have a friend with whom I can discuss my results. The matter is a perfectly trivial one' (he jerked his thumb in the direction of the old hat), 'but there are points in connection with it which are not entirely devoid of interest, and even of instruction.'

I seated myself in his armchair, and warmed my hands before his crackling fire, for a sharp frost had set in, and the windows were thick with the ice crystals. 'I suppose,' I remarked, 'that, homely as it looks, this thing has some deadly story linked on to it—that it is the clue which will guide you in the solution of some mystery, and the punishment of some crime.'

'No, no. No crime,' said Sherlock Holmes, laughing. 'Only one of those whimsical little incidents which will happen when you have four million human beings all jostling each other within the space of a few square miles. Amid the action and reaction of so dense a swarm of humanity, every possible combination of events may be expected to take place, and many a little problem will be presented which may be striking and bizarre without being criminal. We have already had experience of such.'

'So much so,' I remarked, 'that, of the last six cases which I have added to my notes, three have been entirely free of any legal crime.'

'Precisely. You allude to my attempt to recover the Irene Adler papers, to the singular case of Miss Mary

Sutherland, and to the adventure of the man with the twisted lip. Well, I have no doubt that this small matter will fall into the same innocent category. You know Peterson, the commissionaire?'

'Yes.'

'It is to him that this trophy belongs.'

'It is his hat.'

'No, no; he found it. Its owner is unknown. I beg that you will look upon it, not as a battered billy-cock, but as an intellectual problem. And, first, as to how it came here. It arrived upon Christmas morning, in company with a good fat goose; which is, I have no doubt, roasting at this moment in front of Peterson's fire. The facts are these. About four o'clock on Christmas morning, Peterson, who, as you know, is a very honest fellow, was returning from some small jollification, and was making his way homewards down Tottenham Court Road. In front of him he saw, in the gaslight, a tallish man, walking with a slight stagger, and carrying a white goose slung over his shoulder. As he reached the corner of Goodge Street a row broke out between this stranger and a little knot of roughs. One of the latter knocked off the man's hat, on which he raised his stick to defend himself, and, swinging it over his head, smashed the shop window behind him. Peterson had rushed forward to protect the stranger from his assailants, but the man, shocked at having broken the window, and seeing an official-looking person in uniform rushing towards him, dropped his goose, took to his heels and vanished amid the labyrinth of small streets which lie at the back of Tottenham Court Road. The roughs had also fled at the appearance of Peterson, so that he was left in possession of the field of battle, and also of the spoils of victory in the shape of this battered hat and a most unimpeachable Christmas goose.'

'Which surely he restored to their owner?'

'My dear fellow, there lies the problem. It is true that "For Mrs. Henry Baker" was printed upon a small card which was tied to the bird's left leg, and it is also true that the initials "H. B." are legible upon the lining of this hat; but, as there are some thousands of Bakers, and some hundreds of Henry Bakers in this city of ours, it is not easy to restore lost property to any one of them.'

'What, then, did Peterson do?'

'He brought round both hat and goose to me on Christmas morning, knowing that even the smallest problems are of interest to me. The goose we retained until this morning, when there were signs that, in spite of the slight frost, it would be well that it should be eaten without unnecessary delay. Its finder has carried it off, therefore, to fulfil the ultimate destiny of a goose, while I continue to retain the hat of the unknown gentleman who lost his Christmas dinner.'

'Did he not advertise?'

'No.'

'Then, what clue could you have as to his identity?'

'Only as much as we can deduce.'

'From his hat?'

'Precisely.'

'But you are joking. What can you gather from this old battered felt?'

'Here is my lens. You know my methods. What can you gather yourself as to the individuality of the man who has worn this article?'

I took the tattered object in my hands, and turned it over rather ruefully. It was a very ordinary black hat of the usual round shape, hard and much the worse for wear. The lining had been of red silk, but was a good deal discoloured. There was no maker's name; but, as Holmes had remarked, the initials 'H. B.' were scrawled upon one side. It was pierced in the brim for a hat-securer, but the elastic was missing. For the rest, it was cracked, exceedingly dusty, and spotted in several places, although there seemed to have been some attempt to hide the discoloured patches by smearing them with ink.

'I can see nothing,' said I, handing it back to my friend.

'On the contrary, Watson, you can see everything. You fail, however, to reason from what you see. You are too timid in drawing your inferences.'

'Then, pray tell me what it is that you can infer from this hat?'

He picked it up, and gazed at it in the peculiar introspective fashion which was characteristic of him. 'It is perhaps less suggestive than it might have been,' he remarked, 'and yet there are a few inferences which are very distinct, and a few others which represent at least a strong balance of probability. That the man was highly intellectual is of course obvious upon the face of it, and also that he was fairly well-to-do within the last three years, although he has now fallen upon evil days. He had foresight, but has less now than formerly, pointing to a moral retrogression, which, when taken with the decline of his fortunes, seems to indicate some evil influence, probably drink, at work upon him. This may account also for the obvious fact that his wife has ceased to love him.'

'My dear Holmes!'

'He has, however, retained some degree of self-respect,' he continued, disregarding my remonstrance. 'He is a man who leads a sedentary life, goes out little, is out of training entirely, is middle-aged, has grizzled hair which he has had cut within the last few days, and which he anoints with lime-cream.

These are the more patent facts which are to be deduced from his hat. Also, by the way, that it is extremely improbable that he has gas laid on his house.'

'You are certainly joking, Holmes.'

'Not in the least. Is it possible that even now when I give you these results you are unable to see how they are attained?'

'I have no doubt that I am very stupid; but I must confess that I am unable to follow you. For example, how did you deduce that this man was intellectual?'

For answer Holmes clapped the hat upon his head. It came right over the forehead and settled upon the bridge of his nose. 'It is a question of cubic capacity,' said he: 'a man with so large a brain must have something in it.'

'The decline of his fortunes, then?'

'This hat is three years old. These flat brims curled at the edge came in then. It is a hat of the very best quality. Look at the band of ribbed silk, and the excellent lining. If this man could afford to buy so expensive a hat three years ago, and has had no hat since, then he has assuredly gone down in the world.'

'Well, that is clear enough, certainly. But how about the foresight, and the moral retrogression?'

Sherlock Holmes laughed. 'Here is the foresight,'

said he, putting his finger upon the little disc and loop of the hat-securer. 'They are never sold upon hats. If this man ordered one, it is a sign of a certain amount of foresight, since he went out of his way to take this precaution against the wind. But since we see that he has broken the elastic, and has not troubled to replace it, it is obvious that he has less foresight now than formerly, which is a distinct proof of a weakening nature. On the other hand, he has endeavoured to conceal some of these stains upon the felt by daubing them with ink, which is a sign that he has not entirely lost his self-respect.'

'Your reasoning is certainly plausible.'

'The further points, that he is middle-aged, that his hair is grizzled, that it has been recently cut, and that he uses lime-cream, are all to be gathered from a close examination of the lower part of the lining. The lens discloses a large number of hair ends, clean cut by the scissors of the barber. They all appear to be adhesive, and there is a distinct odour of lime-cream. This dust, you will observe, is not the gritty, grey dust of the street, but the fluffy brown dust of the house, showing that it has been hung up indoors most of the time; while the marks of moisture upon the inside are proof positive that the wearer perspired very freely, and could, therefore, hardly be in the best of training.'

'But his wife—you said that she had ceased to love him.'

'This hat has not been brushed for weeks. When I see you, my dear Watson, with a week's accumulation of dust upon your hat, and when your wife allows you to go out in such a state, I shall fear that you also have been unfortunate enough to lose your wife's affection.'

'But he might be a bachelor.'

'Nay, he was bringing home the goose as a peace-offering to his wife. Remember the card upon the bird's leg.'

'You have an answer to everything. But how on earth do you deduce that the gas is not laid on in the house?'

'One tallow stain, or even two, might come by chance; but, when I see no less than five, I think that there can be little doubt that the individual must be brought into frequent contact with burning tallow—walks upstairs at night probably with his hat in one hand and a guttering candle in the other. Anyhow, he never got tallow stains from a gas jet. Are you satisfied?'

'Well, it is very ingenious,' said I, laughing; 'but since, as you said just now, there has been no crime committed, and no harm done save the loss of a goose, all this seems to be rather a waste of energy.'

Sherlock Holmes had opened his mouth to reply, when the door flew open, and Peterson the commissionaire rushed into the apartment with flushed cheeks and the face of a man who is dazed with astonishment.

'The goose, Mr. Holmes! The goose, sir!' he gasped.

'Eh! What of it, then? Has it returned to life, and flapped off through the kitchen window?' Holmes twisted himself round upon the sofa to get a fairer view of the man's excited face.

'See here, sir! See what my wife found in its crop!' He held out his hand, and displayed upon the centre of the palm a brilliantly scintillating blue stone, rather smaller than a bean in size, but of such purity and radiance that it twinkled like an electric point in the dark hollow of his hand.

Sherlock Holmes sat up with a whistle. 'By Jove, Peterson,' said he, 'this is treasure-trove indeed! I suppose you know what you have got?'

'A diamond, sir! A precious stone! It cuts into glass as though it were putty.'

'It's more than a precious stone. It's *the* precious stone.'

'Not the Countess of Morcar's blue carbuncle?' I ejaculated.

'Precisely so. I ought to know its size and shape, seeing that I have read the advertisement about it in

The Times every day lately. It is absolutely unique, and its value can only be conjectured, but the reward offered of a thousand pounds is certainly not within a twentieth part of the market price.'

'A thousand pounds! Great Lord of mercy!' The commissionaire plumped down into a chair, and stared from one to the other of us.

'That is the reward, and I have reason to know that there are sentimental considerations in the background which would induce the Countess to part with half of her fortune if she could but recover the gem.'

'It was lost, if I remember aright, at the Hotel Cosmopolitan,' I remarked.

'Precisely so, on the 22nd of December, just five days ago. John Horner, a plumber, was accused of having abstracted it from the lady's jewel-case. The evidence against him was so strong that the case has been referred to the Assizes. I have some account of the matter here, I believe.' He rummaged amid his newspapers, glancing over the dates, until at last he smoothed one out, doubled it over, and read the following paragraph:

'"Hotel Cosmopolitan Jewel Robbery. John Horner, 26, plumber, was brought up upon the charge of having upon the 22nd inst., abstracted from the jewel-case of the Countess of Morcar the valuable gem known as the blue carbuncle. James

Ryder, upper-attendant at the hotel, gave his evidence to the effect that he had shown Horner up to the dressing-room of the Countess of Morcar upon the day of the robbery, in order that he might solder the second bar of the grate, which was loose. He had remained with Horner some little time but had finally been called away. On returning, he found that Horner had disappeared, that the bureau had been forced open, and that the small morocco casket in which, as it afterwards transpired, the Countess was accustomed to keep her jewel, was lying empty upon the dressing-table. Ryder instantly gave the alarm, and Horner was arrested the same evening; but the stone could not be found either upon his person or in his rooms. Catherine Cusack, maid to the Countess, deposed to having heard Ryder's cry of dismay on discovering the robbery, and to having rushed into the room, where she found matters were as described by the last witness. Inspector Bradstreet, B Division, gave evidence as to the arrest of Horner, who struggled frantically, and protested his innocence in the strongest terms. Evidence of a previous conviction for robbery having been given against the prisoner, the magistrate refused to deal summarily with the offence, but referred it to the Assizes. Horner, who had shown signs of intense emotion during the proceedings, fainted away at the conclusion, and was carried out of court."

'Hum! So much for the police-court,' said Holmes thoughtfully, tossing aside his paper. 'The question for us now to solve is the sequence of events from a rifled jewel-case at one end to the crop of a goose in Tottenham Court Road at the other. You see, Watson, our little deductions have suddenly assumed a much more important and less innocent aspect. Here is the stone; the stone came from the goose, and the goose came from Mr. Henry Baker, the gentleman with the bad hat and all the other characteristics with which I have bored you. So now we must set ourselves very seriously to finding this gentleman, and ascertaining what part he has played in this little mystery. To do this, we must try the simplest means first, and these lie undoubtedly in an advertisement in all the evening papers. If this fail, I shall have recourse to other methods.'

'What will you say?'

'Give me a pencil, and that slip of paper. Now, then: "Found at the corner of Goodge Street, a goose and a black felt hat. Mr. Henry Baker can have the same by applying at 6.30 this evening at 221 B Baker Street." That is clear and concise.'

'Very. But will he see it?'

'Well, he is sure to keep an eye on the papers, since, to a poor man, the loss was a heavy one. He was clearly so scared by his mischance in breaking the window, and by the approach of Peterson, that he thought of nothing but flight; but since then he must have bitterly regretted the impulse which caused him to drop his bird. Then, again, the introduction of his name will cause him to see it, for every one who knows him will direct his attention to it. Here you are, Peterson, run down to the advertising agency, and have this put in the evening papers.'

'In which, sir?'

'Oh, in the *Globe, Star, Pall Mall, St James's Gazette, Evening News, Standard, Echo,* and any others that occur to you.'

'Very well, sir. And this stone?'

'Ah, yes. I shall keep the stone. Thank you. And, I say, Peterson, just buy a goose on your way back, and leave it here with me, for we must have one to give to this gentleman in place of the one which your family is now devouring.'

When the commissionaire had gone, Holmes took up the stone and held it against the light. 'It's a bonny thing,' said he. 'Just see how it glints and sparkles. Of course it is a nucleus and focus of crime. Every good stone is. They are the devil's pet baits. In the larger and older jewels every facet may stand for a bloody deed. This stone is not yet twenty years old. It was found in the banks of the Amoy River in Southern China, and is remarkable in having every characteristic of the carbuncle, save that it is blue in shade, instead of ruby red. In spite of its youth, it has already a sinister history. There have been two murders, a vitriol-throwing, a suicide, and several robberies brought about for the sake of this forty-grain weight of crystallized charcoal. Who would think that so pretty a toy would be a purveyor to the gallows and the prison? I'll lock it up in my strong-box, now, and drop a line to the Countess to say that we have it.'

'Do you think this man Horner is innocent?'

'I cannot tell.'

'Well, then, do you imagine that this other one, Henry Baker, had anything to do with the matter?'

'It is, I think, much more likely that Henry Baker is an absolutely innocent man, who had no idea that the bird which he was carrying was of considerably more value than if it were made of solid gold. That, however, I shall determine by a very simple test, if we have an answer to our advertisement.'

'And you can do nothing until then?'

'Nothing.'

'In that case I shall continue my professional round. But I shall come back in the evening at the hour you have mentioned, for I should like to see the solution of so tangled a business.'

'Very glad to see you. I dine at seven. There is a woodcock, I believe. By the way, in view of recent occurrences, perhaps I ought to ask Mrs. Hudson to examine its crop.'

I had been delayed at a case, and it was a little after half-past six when I found myself in Baker Street once more. As I approached the house I saw a tall man in a Scotch bonnet, with a coat which was but-toned up to his chin, waiting outside in the bright semicircle which was thrown from the fanlight. Just as I arrived, the door was opened, and we were shown up together to Holmes's room.

'Mr. Henry Baker, I believe,' said he, rising from his armchair, and greeting his visitor with the easy air of geniality which he could so readily assume. 'Pray take this chair by the fire, Mr. Baker. It is a cold night, and I observe that your circulation is more adapted for summer than for winter. Ah, Wat-son, you have just come at the right time. Is that your hat, Mr. Baker?'

'Yes, sir, that is undoubtedly my hat.'

He was a large man, with rounded shoulders, a massive head, and a broad, intelligent face, sloping down to a pointed beard of grizzled brown. A touch of red in nose and cheeks, with a slight tremor of his extended hand, recalled Holmes's surmise as to his habits. His rusty black frock-coat was buttoned right up in front, with the collar turned up, and his lank wrists protruded from his sleeves without a sign of cuff or shirt. He spoke in a low staccato fashion, choosing his words with care, and gave the impression generally of a man of learning and letters who had had ill-usage at the hands of fortune.

'We have retained these things for some days,' said Holmes, 'because we expected to see an advertisement from you giving your address. I am at a loss to know now why you did not advertise.'

Our visitor gave a rather shame-faced laugh. 'Shillings have not been so plentiful with me as they once were,' he remarked. 'I had no doubt that the gang of roughs who assaulted me had carried off both my hat and the bird. I did not care to spend more money in a hopeless attempt at recovering them.'

'Very naturally. By the way, about the bird—we were compelled to eat it.'

'To eat it!' Our visitor half rose from his chair in his excitement.

'Yes; it would have been no use to anyone had we not done so. But I presume that this other goose upon the sideboard, which is about the same weight and perfectly fresh, will answer your purpose equally well?'

'Oh, certainly, certainly!' answered Mr. Baker, with a sigh of relief.

'Of course, we still have the feathers, legs, crop, and so on of your own bird, if you so wish—'

The man burst into a hearty laugh. 'They might be useful to me as relics of my adventure,' said he, 'but beyond that I can hardly see what use the *disjecta membra* of my late acquaintance are going to be to me. No, sir, I think that, with your permission, I will confine my attentions to the excellent bird which I perceive upon the sideboard.'

Sherlock Holmes glanced sharply across at me with a slight shrug of his shoulders.

'There is your hat, then, and there your bird,' said he. 'By the way, would it bore you to tell me where you got the other one from? I am somewhat of a fowl fancier, and I have seldom seen a better-grown goose.'

'Certainly, sir,' said Baker, who had risen and tucked his newly-gained property under his arm. 'There are a few of us who frequent the "Alpha" Inn near the Museum—we are to be found in the Museum itself during the day, you understand. This year our good host, Windigate by name, instituted a goose-club, by which, on consideration of some few pence every week, we were each to receive a bird at Christmas. My pence were duly paid, and the rest is familiar to you. I am much indebted to you, sir, for a Scotch bonnet is fitted neither to my years nor my gravity.' With a comical pomposity of manner he bowed solemnly to both of us, and strode off upon his way.

'So much for Mr. Henry Baker,' said Holmes, when he had closed the door behind him. 'It is quite certain that he knows nothing whatever about the matter. Are you hungry, Watson?'

'Not particularly.'

'Then I suggest that we turn our dinner into a supper, and follow up this clue while it is still hot.'

'By all means.'

It was a bitter night, so we drew on our ulsters and wrapped cravats about our throats. Outside, the stars were shining coldly in a cloudless sky, and the breath of the passers-by blew out into smoke like so many pistol shots. Our footfalls rang out crisply and loudly as we swung through the doctors' quarter, Wimpole Street, Harley Street, and so through Wigmore Street into Oxford Street. In a quarter of an hour we were in Bloomsbury at the "Alpha" Inn, which is a small public-house at the corner of one of the streets which run down into Holborn. Holmes pushed open the door of the private bar, and ordered two glasses of beer from the ruddy-faced, white-aproned landlord.

'Your beer should be excellent if it is as good as your geese,' he said.

'My geese!' The man seemed surprised.

'Yes. I was speaking only half an hour ago to Mr.

Henry Baker, who was a member of your goose-club.'

'Ah! yes, I see. But you see, sir, them's not *our* geese.'

'Indeed! Whose, then?'

'Well, I got the two dozen from a salesman in Covent Garden.'

'Indeed! I know some of them. Which was it?'

'Breckinridge is his name.'

'Ah! I don't know him. Well, here's your good health, landlord, and prosperity to your house. Good-night!

'Now for Mr. Breckinridge,' he continued, buttoning up his coat, as we came out into the frosty air. 'Remember, Watson, that though we have so homely a thing as a goose at one end of this chain, we have at the other a man who will certainly get seven years' penal servitude, unless we can establish his innocence. It is possible that our inquiry may but confirm his guilt; but, in any case, we have a line of investigation which has been missed by the police, and which a singular chance has placed in our hands. Let us follow it out to the bitter end. Faces to the south, then, and quick march!'

We passed across Holborn, down Endell Street, and so through a zigzag of slums of Covent Garden Market. One of the largest stalls bore the name of Breckinridge upon it, and the proprietor, a horsey-looking man with a sharp face and trim side-whiskers, was helping a boy to put up the shutters.

'Good evening, it's a cold night,' said Holmes.

The salesman nodded, and shot a questioning glance at my companion.

'Sold out of geese, I see,' continued Holmes, pointing at the bare slabs of marble.

'Let you have five hundred to-morrow morning.'

'That's no good.'

'Well, there are some on the stall with the gas flare.'

'Oh, but I was recommended to you.'

'Who by?'

'The landlord of the "Alpha".'

'Ah, yes; I sent him a couple of dozen.'

'Fine birds they were, too. Now where did you get them from?'

To my surprise the question provoked a burst of anger from the salesman.

'Now then, mister,' said he, with his head cocked and his arms akimbo, 'what are you driving at? Let's have it straight, now.'

'It is straight enough. I should like to know who sold you the geese which you supplied to the "Alpha".'

'Well, then, I shan't tell you. So now!'

'Oh, it is a matter of no importance; but I don't know why you should be so warm over such a trifle.'

'Warm! You'd be as warm, maybe, if you were pestered as I am. When I pay good money for a good article there should be an end of the business; but it's "Where are the geese?" and "Who did you sell the geese to?" and "What will you take for the geese?" One would think they were the only geese in the world, to hear the fuss that is made over them.'

'Well, I have no connection with any other people who have been making inquiries,' said Holmes carelessly. 'If you won't tell us the bet is off, that is all. But I'm always ready to back my opinion on a matter of fowls, and I have a fiver on it that the bird I ate is country bred.'

'Well, then, you've lost your fiver, for it's town bred,' snapped the salesman.

'It's nothing of the kind.'

'I say it is.'

'I don't believe you.'

'D'you think you know more about fowls than I, who have handled them ever since I was a nipper? I tell you, all those birds that went to the "Alpha" were town bred.'

'You'll never persuade me to believe that.'

'Will you bet, then?'

'It's merely taking your money, for I know that I

am right. But I'll have a sovereign on with you, just to teach you not to be obstinate.'

The salesman chuckled grimly. 'Bring me the books, Bill,' said he.

The small boy brought round a small thin volume and a great greasy-backed one, laying them out together beneath the hanging lamp.

'Now then, Mr. Cocksure,' said the salesman, 'I thought that I was out of geese, but before I finish you'll find that there is still one left in my shop. You see this little book?'

'Well?'

'That's the list of the folk from whom I buy. D'you see? Well, then, here on this page are the country folk, and the numbers after their names are where their accounts are in the big ledger. Now, then! You see this other page in red ink? Well, that is a list of my town suppliers. Now, look at that third name. Just read it out to me.'

'Mrs. Oakshott, 117, Brixton Road—249,' read Holmes.

'Quite so. Now turn that up in the ledger.'

Holmes turned to the page indicated. 'Here you are, "Mrs. Oakshott, 117, Brixton Road, egg and poultry supplier."'

'Now, then, what's the last entry?'

'"December 22. Twenty-four geese at 7s 6d."'

'Quite so. There you are. And underneath?'

' "Sold to Mr. Windigate of the 'Alpha' at 12*s*." '

'What have you say now?'

Sherlock Holmes looked deeply chagrined. He drew a sovereign from his pocket and threw it down upon the slab, turning away with the air of a man whose disgust is too deep for words. A few yards off he stopped under a lamp-post, and laughed in the hearty, noiseless fashion which was peculiar to him.

'When you see a man with whiskers of that cut and the "*Pink 'Un*" protruding out of his pocket, you can always draw him by a bet,' said he. 'I dare say that if I had put a hundred pounds down in front of him that man would not have given me such complete information as was drawn from him by the idea that he was doing me on a wager. Well, Watson, we are, I fancy, nearing the end of our quest, and the only point which remains to be determined is whether we should go on to this Mrs. Oakshott tonight, or whether we should reserve it for to-morrow. It is clear from what that surly fellow said that there are others besides ourselves who are anxious about the matter, and I should—'

His remarks were suddenly cut short by a loud hubbub which broke out from the stall which we had just left. Turning round we saw a little rat-faced fellow, standing in the centre of the circle of yellow light which was thrown by the swinging lamp, while Breckinridge the salesman, framed in the door of his stall, was shaking his fists fiercely at the cringing figure.

'I've had enough of you and your geese,' he shouted. 'I wish you were all at the devil together. If you come pestering me any more with your silly talk I'll set the dog at you. You bring Mrs. Oakshott here and I'll answer her, but what have you to do with it? Did I buy the geese off you?'

'No: but one of them was mine all the same,' whined the little man.

'Well, then, ask Mrs. Oakshott for it.'

'She told me to ask you.'

'Well, you can ask the King of Proosia, for all I care. I've had enough of it. Get out of this!' He rushed fiercely forward, and the inquirer flitted away into the darkness.

'Ha, this may save us a visit to Brixton Road,' whispered Holmes. 'Come with me, and we will see what is to be made of this fellow.' Striding through the scattered knots of people who lounged round the flaring stalls, my companion speedily overtook the little man and touched him upon the shoulder. He sprang round, and I could see in the gaslight that every vestige of colour had been driven from his face.

'Who are you, then? What do you want?' he asked in a quavering voice.

'You will excuse me,' said Holmes, blandly, 'but I could not help overhearing the questions which you put to the salesman just now. I think that I could be of assistance to you.'

'You? Who are you? How could you know anything of the matter?'

'My name is Sherlock Holmes. It is my business to know what other people don't know.'

'But you can know nothing of this?'

'Excuse me, I know everything of it. You are endeavouring to trace some geese which were sold by Mrs. Oakshott, of Brixton Road, to a salesman named Breckinridge, by him in turn to Mr. Windigate, of the "Alpha", and by him to his club, of which Mr. Henry Baker is a member.'

'Oh, sir, you are the very man whom I have longed to meet,' cried the little fellow, with outstreched hands and quivering fingers. 'I can hardly explain to you how interested I am in this matter.'

Sherlock Holmes hailed a four-wheeler which was passing. 'In that case we had better discuss it in a cosy room rather than in this windswept marketplace,' said he. 'But pray tell me, before we go further, who it is that I have the pleasure of assisting.'

The man hesitated for an instant. 'My name is

John Robinson,' he answered, with a sidelong glance.

'No, no; the real name,' said Holmes sweetly. 'It is always awkward doing business with an *alias*.'

A flush sprang to the white cheeks of the stranger. 'Well, then,' said he, 'my real name is James Ryder.'

'Precisely so. Head attendant at the Hotel Cosmopolitan. Pray step into the cab, and I shall soon be able to tell you everything which you would wish to know.'

The little man stood glancing from one to the other of us with half-frightened, half-hopeful eyes, as one who is not sure whether he is on the verge of a windfall or of a catastrophe. Then he stepped into the cab, and in half an hour we were back in the sitting-room at Baker Street. Nothing had been said during our drive, but the high, thin breathing of our new companion, and the claspings and unclaspings of his hands, spoke of the nervous tension within him.

'Here we are!' said Holmes cheerily, as we filed into the room. 'The fire looks very seasonable in this weather. You look cold, Mr. Ryder. Pray take the basket chair. I will just put on my slippers before we settle this little matter of yours. Now, then! You want to know what became of those geese?'

'Yes, sir.'

'Or rather, I fancy, of that goose. It was one bird, I

imagine, in which you were interested—white, with a black bar across the tail.'

Ryder quivered with emotion. 'Oh, sir,' he cried, 'can you tell me where it went to?'

'It came here.'

'Here?'

'Yes, and a most remarkable bird it proved. I don't wonder that you should take an interest in it. It laid an egg after it was dead—the bonniest, brightest little blue egg that was ever seen. I have it here in my museum.'

Our visitor staggered to his feet, and clutched the mantelpiece with his right hand. Holmes unlocked his strong-box, and held up the blue carbuncle, which shone out like a star, with a cold, brilliant, many-pointed radiance. Ryder stood glaring with a drawn face, uncertain whether to claim or to disown it.

'The game's up, Ryder,' said Holmes quietly. 'Hold up, man, or you'll be into the fire. Give him an arm back into his chair, Watson. He's not got blood enough to go in for felony with impunity. Give him a dash of brandy. So! Now he looks a little more human. What a shrimp it is, to be sure!'

For a moment he had staggered and nearly fallen, but the brandy brought a tinge of colour into his cheeks, and he sat staring with frightened eyes at his accuser.

'I have almost every link in my hands, and all the proofs which I could possibly need, so there is little which you need tell me. Still, that little may as well be cleared up to make the case complete. You had heard, Ryder, of this blue stone of the Countess of Morcar's?'

'It was Catherine Cusack who told me of it,' said he, in a crackling voice.

'I see. Her ladyship's waiting-maid. Well the temptation of sudden wealth so easily acquired was too much for you, as it has been for better men before you; but you were not very scrupulous in the means you used. It seems to me, Ryder, that there is the making of a very pretty villain in you. You knew that this man Horner, the plumber, had been concerned in some such matter before, and that suspicion would rest the more readily upon him. What did you do, then? You made some small job in my lady's room—you and your confederate Cusack—and you managed that he should be the man sent for. Then, when he had left, you rifled the jewel-case, raised the alarm, and had this unfortunate man arrested. You then—'

Ryder threw himself down suddenly upon the rug, and clutched at my companion's knees. 'For God's sake, have mercy!' he shrieked. 'Think of my father! Of my mother! It would break their hearts. I never went wrong before! I never will again. I swear it. I'll swear it on a Bible. Oh, don't bring it into court! For Christ's sake, don't!'

'Get back into your chair! said Holmes sternly. 'It is very well to cringe and crawl now, but you thought little enough of this poor Horner in the dock for a crime of which he knew nothing.'

'I will fly, Mr. Holmes. I will leave the country, sir. Then the charge against him will break down.'

'Hum! We will talk about that. And now let us hear a true account of the next act. How came the stone into the goose, and how came the goose into the open market? Tell us the truth, for there lies your only hope of safety.'

Ryder passed his tongue over his parched lips. 'I will tell you it just as it happened, sir,' said he. 'When Horner had been arrested, it seemed to me that it would be best for me to get away with the stone at once, for I did not know at what moment the police might not take it into their heads to search me and my room. There was no place about the hotel where it would be safe. I went out, as if on some commission, and I made for my sister's house. She had married a man named Oakshott, and lived in Brixton Road, where she fattened fowls for the market. All the way there every man I met seemed to me to be a policeman or a detective, and for all that it was a cold night, the sweat was pouring down my face before I came to the Brixton Road. My sister asked me what was the matter, and why I was so pale; but I told her that I had been upset by the jewel robbery at the hotel. Then I went into the backyard, and smoked a pipe, and wondered what it would be best to do.

'I had a friend once called Maudsley, who went to the bad, and has just been serving his time in Pentonville. One day he had met me, and fell into talk about the ways of thieves and how they could get rid of what they stole. I knew that he would be true to me, for I knew one or two things about him, so I made up my mind to go right on to Kilburn, where he lived and take him into my confidence. He would show me how to turn the stone into money. But how to get to him in safety? I thought of the agonies I had gone through in coming from the hotel. I might at any moment be seized and searched, and there would be the stone in my waistcoat pocket. I was leaning against the wall at the time, and looking at the geese which were waddling about round my feet, and suddenly an idea came into my head which showed me how I could beat the best detective that ever lived.

'My sister had told me some weeks before that I might have the pick of her geese for a Christmas present, and I knew that she was always as good as her word. I would take my goose now, and in it I would carry my stone to Kilburn. There was a little shed in the yard, and behind this I drove one of the birds, a fine big one, white, with a barred tail. I caught it, and, prising its bill open, I thrust the stone down its throat as far as my finger could reach. The bird gave a gulp, and I felt the stone pass along its gullet and down into its crop. But the creature flapped and struggled, and out came my sister to know what was the matter. As I turned to speak to her the brute broke loose, and fluttered off among the others.

' "Whatever were you doing with that bird, Jem?" says she.

' "Well," said I, "you said you'd give me one for Christmas, and I was feeling which was the fattest."

' "Oh," says she, "we've set yours aside for you. Jem's bird, we call it. It's the big, white one over yonder. There's twenty-six of them, which makes one for you, and one for us, and two dozen for the market."

' "Thank you, Maggie," says I; "but if it is all the same to you I'd rather have that one I was handling just now."

' "The other is a good three pound heavier," she said, "and we fattened it expressly for you."

' "Never mind. I'll have the other, and I'll take it now," said I.

' "Oh, just as you like," said she, a little huffed. "Which is it you want, then?"

' "That white one, with the barred tail, right in the middle of the flock."

' "Oh, very well. Kill it and take it with you."

'Well, I did what she said, Mr. Holmes, and I carried the bird all the way to Kilburn. I told my pal what I had done, for he was a man that it was easy to tell a thing like that to. He laughed until he choked, and we got a knife and opened the goose. My heart turned to water, for there was no sign of the stone, and I knew that some terrible mistake had occurred. I left the bird, rushed back to my sister's, and hurried into the back yard. There was not a bird to be seen there.

' "Where are they all, Maggie?" I cried.

' "Gone to the dealer's."

' "Which dealer's?"

' "Breckinridge, of Covent Garden."

' "But was there another with a barred tail?" I asked, "the same as the one I chose?"

' "Yes, Jem, there were two barred-tailed ones, and I could never tell them apart.'

'Well, then, of course, I saw it all, and I ran off as hard as my feet would carry me to this man Breckinridge; but he had sold the lot at once, and not one word would he tell me as to where they had gone.

You heard him yourselves tonight. Well, he has always answered me like that. My sister thinks that I am going mad. Sometimes I think that I am myself. And now—now I am myself a branded thief, without ever having touched the wealth for which I sold my character. God help me! God help me!' He burst into convulsive sobbing, with his face buried in his hands.

There was a long silence, broken only by his heavy breathing, and by the measured tapping of Sherlock Holmes's finger-tips upon the edge of the table. Then my friend rose, and threw open the door.

'Get out!' said he.

'What, sir! Oh, heaven bless you!'

'No more words. Get out!'

And no more words were needed. There was a rush, a clatter upon the stairs, the bang of a door, and the crisp rattle of running footfalls from the street.

'After all, Watson,' said Holmes, reaching up his hand for his clay pipe, 'I am not retained by the police to supply their deficiencies. If Horner were in danger it would be another thing, but this fellow will not appear against him, and the case must collapse. I suppose that I am commuting a felony, but it is just possible that I am saving a soul. This fellow will not go wrong again. He is too terribly frightened. Send him to gaol now, and you make him a gaol-bird for life. Besides, it is the season of forgiveness. Chance has put in our way a most singular and whimsical problem, and its solution is its own reward. If you will have the goodness to touch the bell, Doctor, we will begin another investigation, in which also a bird will be the chief feature.'

The Bachelor's Christmas

ROBERT GRANT

Thomas Wiggin, or Tom Wiggin, as everyone called him, sat alone in his bachelor quarters on Christmas-eve waiting for a carriage. The carriage was not late, but Tom, who was a methodical man in everything he did, had finished his preparations a little sooner than need be. His fur coat and hat and gloves lay on a chair beside him, ready to put on the moment Bridget, the maid, should knock at the door and tell him that Perkins, the cabby at the corner, was blocking the way. Tom had already taken out of his pocket two ten-dollar gold pieces and laid them on the centre-table beside an array of packages done up with marvellous care in the whitest of paper and the reddest of ribbon. One of the gold pieces was for Bridget and the other for Perkins. Twice the sum would not have replaced the crockery and objects of virtu which the Hibernian handmaiden, who brought up his breakfast and was supposed to keep his room tidy, had smashed since he had tipped her last; and Tom had, only two months before, undergone the melancholy experience of falling through the bottom of Perkins's coupé, because of the pertinacity with which that common carrier of passengers clung to the delusion that no repairs to a vehicle were necessary until it dropped to pieces. But as Tom would have said if interrogated on the subject by a subtler mind, Christmas comes but once a year, and though Bridget's best was her worst, she had tried to do it, and Perkins, shiftless as he was, had driven his poor old nag one day into a pink lather in endeavoring to catch a train for him, which he had just missed after all.

Besides, Tom had had a remarkably good business year, so that a ten-dollar gold piece did not seem to him the dazzlingly large sum he had regarded it ten years earlier. He had lived in these same bachelor lodgings for ten years and during that time had built up a very neat business by his own unaided effort, as his contemporaries (and contemporaries are apt to be stern critics) were ready to admit. He had worked hard and steadily, taking only enough vacation to enable him to keep well, and shunting everything to the background which threatened to interfere with the object he had in view—that is, everything but one thing. And this one thing he had made up his mind five years ago was out of the question. Consequently he had shunted it to the background with everything else, and devoted himself more unreservedly than ever to the real estate business.

Ten years is quite a piece out of any man's life, and though Tom Wiggin was the picture of health, he was, as we say colloquially, no longer a chicken. He was stouter than he had been and had lost some of his hair, which gave him rather a middle-aged appearance, or at least suggested that he never would see thirty-five again. When he had taken his present room he had been a slim and almost delicate-looking stripling without a copper whom any girl might be likely to fancy. To-day, in his own estimation and in that of his friends and acquaintances, he was a well-seasoned old bachelor who was not likely to ask any one feminine to share his comfortable competency.

Christmas comes but once a year, and Tom had for several years past been in the habit of recognizing the fact in his special way. He was extensively an uncle. That is to say, he had two married sisters, one with five and the other with three children of tender age, and each of his two married brothers had presented him with a nephew and niece of the name of Wiggin. Categorically speaking, he had seven nephews and five nieces to provide with Christmas gifts, not to mention his two sisters and his two sisters-in-law, all of whom had grown accustomed to expect a package in white paper tied with pink ribbon and marked "with love and a merry Christmas from Tom." Here were sixteen presents to begin with, and there were apt to be almost as many more. On this particular Christmas evening there were thirty-five parcels in all, each done up with immaculate care, for Tom, like most old bachelors, prided himself on doing everything in a thorough, deliberate fashion. He had made his last purchase a fortnight ago, and had spent two entire evenings in putting the array of toys and fancy goods in presentable order. They were of all sorts and sizes, for Tom had paled neither before bulk nor price. There was a safety bicycle for a nephew who had set his heart on one, and the tiniest of gold watches for his eldest niece. There was a warm fur-lined cloak for his dead mother's oldest friend, a spinster lady who had small means wherewith to keep herself comfortable in a cold world, and a case of marvellous port for his old chum, Belden, who would see that it was not wasted on unappreciative palates. Everything was ready for the summons from Perkins, the cabby, and Tom, bald-headed bachelor that he was, was fuming a little in spite of the fact that it still lacked three minutes of the hour appointed for departure.

The clock in the neighboring church tower, whose tones were plainly audible in the sky parlors which he called his home, had only just struck five when the tramp of feet followed by a knock announced the joint arrival of Bridget and Perkins, to whom he had intrusted the duty of helping him to carry his precious parcels down three flights of stairs to the attendant cab. This was the sixth consecutive year which Bridget and Perkins had done the same thing, and they thought they knew what to expect. But they had counted without their host. A year ago they had chuckled for forty-eight hours over a five-dollar bill apiece. Now, when they opened the door and presented their grinning countenances, their benefactor, after shouting at them a merry Christmas, proceeded to daze their intellects, of every particle of which they stood in sore need for the purpose of a safe descent, by tossing to each of them a gold coin of twice the denomination. For some moments they stood in bewildered, sheepish silence examining their treasure, as though to make certain it was genuine; then Bridget, taxing her intelligence for a suitable expression for the wealth of feeling at her heart, exclaimed:

"And sure, Mr. Wiggin, it's Bridget Lanagan that's hoping that before the good Lord brings anither Christmas-day the proudest lady in the land will be yer wife. It's me and Perkins would be the first to say God bless her, though we lost a good job by it." At this prodigal outburst of expectation Tom Wiggin's countenance grew rosy-red, notwithstanding the incredulous laugh with which he received the blessing of his warm-hearted handmaiden and the nods of the less nimble-witted cab-man. Then a shadow crossed it as though of unhappy recollection, and there was a tinge of real hopelessness in his half-jocular protestation.

"Many thanks, Bridget, for your good wishes, but there's no such luck in store for me. I shall live and die an old bachelor such as you see me now, and you and Perkins will be able to count on a ten-dollar gold piece on Christmas-eve for the rest of your lives. That is," Tom added by way of timely warning, "provided you don't smash any of these things of mine in carrying them downstairs. You remember that the pair of you last year between you broke a teacup worth its weight in gold, and the year before that large vase broke itself. If everything were to go down safely I should almost begin to believe that what Bridget hopes might come true. Careful now, and be sure not to lay that bicycle right on top of the gilt-edged dinner-plates for my sister Mary."

Whether it was that Tom's strictures in regard to the clumsiness of his assistants were exaggerated, or they were bent upon causing him to repose trust in Bridget's prophecy, the thirty-five packages reached the cab and were stowed within and without, under

their owner's supervising eye, without a single casu-
alty.

"Faith, Mr. Wiggin, they'll be taking yer this time
for Santa Claus, sure," said Perkins when the last precious parcel had been deposited. "Yer'll have to ride
outside, sir, as yer did last year."

Evidently the gaping file of small boys which had
formed itself on each side of the doorway was of the
opinion that, if the gentleman in the fur coat was
not Santa Claus, he was one of his blood-relations,
for, as Tom climbed carefully to his post beside
Perkins so as not to hazard the safety of the bicycle
and the box of port, for which there was no room
inside, they broke out into a shrill hurrah. Perhaps
they too, or at least some of them, knew what they
had to expect, for before Santa Claus seated himself
on the box he plunged his hands into the side pockets of his fur overcoat, and then reproducing them,
seemed to toss them high to the winds, as he cried,
with gay good-will:

"Scramble now, you little devils, scramble, and
wish you merry Christmas!"

What Tom flung to the winds was neither his fingers nor his thumbs, but a plethora of bright nickels
which he had drawn from the bank for the express
purpose. As the glittering shower of brand-new five-
cent pieces fell to the icy sidewalk, the band of

urchins threw themselves upon it with a shout of transport which drew tears from the eyes of the tender-hearted Bridget, who had remained to witness this established ceremony, and ought to have warmed the cockles of the donor's heart, if indeed they needed warming. Twice again he replunged his hands into his pockets and twice again the yell was repeated. Then seating himself beside Perkins, Tom gave the signal for departure, and as the cab rounded the corner a score of little lungs gave him back his merry Christmas with all their might.

It was a genuine Christmas-eve. The ground was covered with snow and the sleigh-bells were jangling merrily. The lamps were already lighted and many a parlor window gave out the reflection of wreaths of holly, and now and again sparkled with little rows of candles in token of the precious Christmas anniversary. Perkins's coupé was on wheels, and his equine paradox was imperfectly caulked into the bargain, so that the world seemed to be rushing by them as they jogged along. Tom had a list which he from time to time consulted by the allied light of the moon and the street-lamps, in order to see that his itinerary was accurately followed and no one forgotten. At every house he dismounted in person and handed in his present. When he reached the residence of his sister, Mary Ferris, who was the mother of the five children, he had to make four trips up and down the door-steps. His sister, who was listening, recognized his voice and came into the vestibule to meet him, and her children, bounding in her wake like an elated pack of wolves, shouted with one tongue,

"Hurrah! it's Uncle Tom."

Mrs. Ferris sent them scampering upstairs in double-quick time on pain of dire penalties if they peeped or listened, and fondly drew her brother into the small sitting-room which opened out of the hall.

"I can't stop, Mary," he said, "I'm on my annual circuit. Now let's see if I've got everything. Here's the bicycle for Roger, junior. They call it 'a safety,' and I trust it may prove so. And the Noah's ark, the largest one made, for Harry; and a musical box, which plays eight tunes, for Dorothy; and a doll which sings 'Ta-ra-boom-de-ay' for little Mary; and a woolly lamb for baby Ned. And here's a trifle in the crockery line for you, my dear. If you don't like the pattern you can change them. Now I must be off. How's Roger, senior? Give him my love and a merry Christmas."

"He'll be at home very soon, Tom, and dreadfully sorry to have missed you. The children are just crazy about their stockings, and little Roger had given up all hope of a bicycle. You are too generous to them and to all of us. And, oh, Tom," she added, laying her hand upon his arm, "I feel dreadfully that we shan't have you with us at dinner to-morrow, but old Mr.

Ferris depends on Roger and me for Christmas. He says it may be the last time, and that Christmas is the Ferris day. Thanksgiving is the Wiggin day, you know, and we did have a jolly time then; yet I just hate to think of your not dining with one of us on Christmas. How can it be helped, though, if all the things-in-law have family parties?"

"Why, that's all right, Mary. As you say, Thanksgiving is the Wiggin day, and things-in-law have rights, as well as those they marry. Merry Christmas, dearest, and let me go, or I shall never get through my list."

"Ah, but, Tom love, I do wish you were married," she cried, putting her arms around his neck to detain him. She was his favorite sister, and free to introduce dangerous topics with due discretion. "You would be so much happier."

"Do I seem so miserable?" he inquired, as he looked down at her and stroked her hair. "That's an old story, Mary. I've heard you express the same wish every six months for the last ten years. Every family should have one old bachelor, at least, and I shall be ours."

She was silent for an instant. "Do you ever see Isabelle Hardy, nowadays?" she asked, with brave insistence. "I have sometimes thought"—she stopped, deterred from completing her sentence by the shadow which had come over Tom's face.

He gently, but firmly, removed his sister's arms from his neck, and answered gravely, almost stiffly, "Very rarely indeed." Then, with a fresh access of gayety, as though he were resolved that nothing foreign to the occasion should mar its spirit, he cried lustily, "A merry Christmas to you, Mary!" and departed.

Continuing steadily on his round, Tom delivered safely the case of port, and the fur-lined cloak, and brought up in the next street, in front of his brother Joe's house. Here he was to leave the gold watch for his eldest niece, a generous box of bonbons for his sister-in-law, a tool-chest for young Joe, and a first edition of "Vanity Fair" for Joe himself, who, though not particularly well off, was a rabid book collector. Tom had dogged an auctioneer for two days to make sure of obtaining the volume in question, which, so far as he could see, was like as two peas to the subsequent issues of the same book to be bought anywhere for a song. He was convinced of his mistake when he saw his brother's face light up at sight of the treasure-trove and heard his delighted inquiry, "Where on earth did you pick this up, Tom? You couldn't have given me anything I'd rather have."

"Glad you like it, Joe. If it isn't the real thing, I'll have the hide of that fellow, Nevins, who sold it to me."

"The real thing? It's a genuine first edition and a splendid specimen. It's adorable. I say, old fellow, it's an outrage that we're to dine with Julia's father to-morrow and leave you out in the cold. Another year I mean to strike and have a Wiggin Christmas dinner, Thanksgiving or no Thanksgiving. Mary and I were comparing notes yesterday and vowing it was an infernal shame."

"Now, it's all right as it is, Joe. I've just left Mary, and I understand perfectly. You've got enough to do to digest your father-in-law's mince pie and Madeira without having me on your stomach."

"A regular old-fashioned ten-course feed, where you sit down at seven and get up at half-past ten feeling like lead. Ugh! Where are you going to dine, Tom?"

"No matter. That's my secret. I shall have a good dinner, never you fear. I must be off now and deliver the rest of my goods."

"It's an outrage—an infernal outrage," growled Joe. "Before you go, old man," he said, hooking his arm into his brother's, and dragging him in the direction of the dining-room, "we'll have a drink. I put a pint of fizz on the ice this morning for your special benefit. It won't take two minutes to mix the cock-tail." Thereupon Joe gave the bell-handle a wrench, and directed that the bottle in the ice-chest should be brought up together with the cracked ice which he had ordered to be in readiness, and in a very short space of time the white-capped maid reappeared with a waiter laden with all the necessary ingredients for the delectable beverage in question. Joe carefully measured out some bitters, pop went the cork of the Perrier Jouet, and presently the brothers were looking at each other over two brimming glasses.

"Wish you merry Christmas, Joe."

"Wish you merry Christmas, Tom. And here's to *her*." Joe paused an instant before he drank to add, "It's a big mistake you're not married, Tom. All I can say is some girl is losing a first-class husband. I say here's to *her*."

Tom, who had waited at the words, raised his glass solemnly. "There is no her and there never will be," he said, with quiet decision. "Still, since you give the toast, Joe, I'll drink it. It's not poisonous," he added, with a wry smile—"so here's to *her*." He drained his glass and set it down on the waiter, then for an instant stood ruminantly with his back to the open fire. "The drink was better than the toast in my case, Joe. My her must have died in infancy."

"Honest Injun, Tom?" asked Joe, as he gripped his brother's hand held out for a parting shake and looked into his face.

Tom's eyes quailed before the honest gaze. His lip quivered. "I'm an infernal liar, Joe, and you know it.

But what's the use? She wouldn't have me, man—and there's no one else whom I want to have. So, merry Christmas, Joe, and God bless you and yours."

As he went out into the frosty night the clock in the hall struck half-past six. There were only five parcels left and the coupé was nearly empty. Tom opened the door and stepping inside, lay back wearily. Presently he picked up one of the parcels—it was a book apparently, from its shape—and laid it at his side. When Perkins drew up the next time, Tom gathered the remaining four and ran up the steps with them. They were for his sister Kitty and her little company, and he spent a few moments indoors to explain matters. When he reappeared he said to his conductor, "114 Farragut Place, and then to the Club."

Tom sat inside with the remaining package resting on his lap, nervously watching for the cab to stop. They halted presently before a spacious house, the old-fashioned aspect of which was heightened by the curved iron railing which ran along the flight of steps leading up to it. Just before the cab stopped, Tom had taken a note from his breast pocket, and after looking round him stealthily in the darkness, had kissed the envelope. Now he tucked it under the red ribbon of the remaining package and walking gravely up the steps, rang the bell. There was nothing in the envelope but his visiting card, on which he had written, "with best wishes for a merry Christmas." When the servant came to the door Tom said, "Will you please give this to Miss Isabelle Hardy." Then the door closed in his face and he went solemnly down the steps again. On reaching the now empty cab he glanced over his shoulder as though in hope of catching a face at the window, but every shade was down, and the wreaths of holly were the nearest semblance to faces, and they seemed almost to grin at him. And well they might. It was the fifth year in succession that he had gone through exactly this same pantomime. Tom heaved one deep sigh; then he straightened his shoulders and passed his hand across his eyes as though he were sweeping away an unprofitable vision.

"To the club," he repeated sturdily to Perkins. "And now," he said to himself, as he shrouded himself in his fur coat and put up his feet on the opposite cushion, "the question is how to make the best of a devilish poor outlook. I mean to have a merry Christmas somehow."

II.

Though it was dinner time, there were few men in the club when Tom entered it. Still there was a half-dozen familiar spirits lounging in the sitting-room, most melancholy among whom was Frazer Bell, a bachelor far gone in the forties, an epicure, but poor as a church mouse.

"Just the man," said Tom to himself, and he drew him aside.

"Will you dine with me to-night, Frazer?"

"Er—I have just ordered dinner, but—"

"Then I'll countermand it," interposed Tom blithely, by way of relieving his would-be guest from the quandary of accepting the invitation without loss of self-respect. "It's Christmas-eve and this is my outfit; I'm going in for as good a dinner as they can give us in honor of the occasion. I say, old man, will you do me the favor to order it? You know fifty times better than I what we ought to have to get the best."

Frazer Bell grinned melodiously. One could almost see his mouth water.

"I'll do it if you like," he said.

"I wish you would. And be sure to put down the finest there is, and to pick out something gilt-edged in the way of wine; something cobwebby and precious."

"I'll try," said Frazer, with another grin, and he ambled off in the direction of the office.

Tom went into the reading-room and picked up a magazine. Presently he passed his hands across his eyes again, for the wreaths in the windows of the house in Farragut Place were grinning at him still.

He said to himself that he guessed he needed another drink, and pressed the electric button at his side.

"Ask Mr. Frazer Bell what he'll have and bring me a Martigny cocktail," he said to the servant. Then he shut his eyes and the grinning wreaths changed into a girl's face, a face which had haunted him day in and day out for seven years. He knew that he ought to brush that away also, but he could not bring himself to do it on Christmas-eve. He would give himself that little luxury at least, before he tried to obliterate it by talking gastronomy with Frazer Bell. Nearly seven years, verily, since he had seen her first! She was then a girl of nineteen, and he at the bottom of the real estate ladder without a dollar to his name, as it were. He had been crazy to marry her, and for two years he had followed her from ball-room to ball-room with a feverish assiduity which threatened to revolutionize his business habits and make light of his business principles. He was not the only one in love with her; there were half a dozen; but the one whose devotion he dreaded most was Charles Leverett Saunders, a handsome dashing beau, a scion of a rich and conspicuous house. He had watched her behavior toward his rival with the eye of a lynx, and as he compared the notes of one evening with the notes of the next he had felt that she was more gracious to Saunders than to him. And yet sometimes she was so sweet and kind to him. But then, again she would be cold and distant, almost icy, in short; on which occasions he had felt as though he would like to cut his throat. A half-dozen times he had made up his mind to offer himself to her and know his fate, but somehow his determination, which was so prodigious in other affairs, had failed him. So matters had gone for a year and a half, and he had seemed no nearer and no less near to the goal than ever. He had said to himself severely that this thing must not go on.

On December 31st, just five years ago, there was to be a famous ball, the crack party of the season. He had resolved that before the old year was out he would know his fate once and for all. Ten-dollar gold pieces did not grow for him then on every bush, but he ordered from the florist the handsomest bouquet of roses and violets which native horticultural talent could devise, and sent it to Miss Isabelle Hardy on the eve of the ball. She had promised to dance the German with him, and when he entered the ballroom his eyes saw no one until they rested on her. A frown had creased his brow, for she was on the arm of Charles Leverett Saunders, and was looking up into his face with a smile of happy excitement which had suggested to Tom that he was as far from her thoughts as the Emperor of Japan. What was more and worse, she carried three gorgeous bouquets, but his was not among them. Where was it?

Had it not been sent? If so, he would ruin that florist's trade for ever and ever. Or had she left it at home on purpose?

He fought shy of her until the German and there was no longer an excuse for him to keep away. Almost at once she thanked him for his lovely flowers.

"But you have not brought them."

"No," she said, sweetly. "I was unable to—I," and she had paused in her embarrassment.

"There were so many, of course."

"No, it was not that, Mr. Wiggin, I assure you." But she had looked a little hurt at his gruff words. "I had a very good reason for not bringing them."

There had been a piteous look in the girl's eyes as she spoke, which he had often recalled since; but then he had thought of nothing but his anger and the slight which had been put upon him. He felt like asking why she had not left Charles Leverett Saunders's flowers at home instead of his. It was clear that she did not care for him, and it became clearer and clearer in the course of the evening; for after a while they had sat almost tongue-tied beside each other. He had tried his best not to be disagreeable, but in spite of himself cynical sentences had slipped from between his teeth in close succession. He had seen that she was hurt and he had rather gloried in it, and presently an embarrassed silence had followed, broken by the arrival of his rival with a magnificent favor which he proffered beamingly to the girl of Tom's heart. She had sailed away, and looking back over her shoulder, given Tom one glance—one of those icy glances which made him yearn to cut his throat. That was bad enough, but to crown all, when her turn came to bestow a boutonnière she made Tom carry her straight up to Leverett Saunders, in the buttonhole of whose coat she proceeded to fasten the rosebud for which Tom would have given twelve months of his life.

Five years ago on the first of January! He had gone home that night certain that Isabelle Hardy did not love him, and resolved that she should play fast and loose with him no longer. In the first hours of the new year he vowed that he would forget her, and devote himself to his business heart and soul. Henceforth he would close eye and brain to all distractions. He would cease forever to be a plaything for a woman's caprice.

He had kept his word. That is to say, his attentions had ended from that hour. The festivities which had known him knew him no more. He went nowhere, and the reason whispered under the rose was that Isabelle Hardy had given him the mitten. The whispers reached him, but little he cared that rumor was not strictly accurate. Was it not practically so? She had to all intents and purposes thrown him over, and he had stamped her image from his heart and gone on with his business, looking neither to the right nor to the left. Occasionally he passed her in the street, and on every Christmas-eve since the night of his resolution, he had left a trifling remembrance at the house in Farragut Place, just, as it were, to show that there was no ill feeling. Otherwise they never met, and here he was to-day, an old bachelor close on the confines of forty, getting bald and set in his ways, with a splendid business and a secret ache at his heart. And she? Tom had never known why she had not married Charles Leverett Saunders, as everybody expected and said she was going to do. Yet suddenly, without warning, that dashing gallant had gone abroad and had remained there ever since, doing the Nile, and Norway, and hunting tigers in the jungles of India, according as the humor seized him. And she? She was beginning to show just a little the traces of time, to suggest what she would look like if she never married and remained after all an old maid. He had been struck by it the last time he had passed her in the street. An old maid! Isabelle Hardy an old maid! There was bitter humor in it for Tom, and he laughed aloud in the reading-room, then, starting at his own performance, looked around him confusedly. He was alone, and his untasted drink stood at his elbow. No one had heard his harsh, strange outburst. He tossed off the cocktail and sank back in his easy chair to confront the vision. An old maid. And he was an old bachelor. And it was Christmas-eve. And what a gloomy, diabolical anniversary it was for old maids and old bachelors. They had no things-in-law to invite them to dinner. They were out in the cold and their room was better than their company. Jokes? Jollities? They were all matrimonial and centered about baby's teeth or Noah's arks. The only thing for an old bachelor or old maid to do was to ransack toy shops and then stand aside. Merry Christmas? How in the name of Santa Claus was an old bachelor or an old maid to have a merry Christmas? And why in time shouldn't they be merry if they could?

Five minutes later, the servant had to announce twice that dinner was served before Tom turned his head, which caused that functionary to reflect that Mr. Wiggin was getting a little deaf. He was looking straight before him into the fire, as though he were interested in the processes of combustion or the price of coal. He turned at the second summons with a start.

"What's that, Simon? Mr. Bell waiting for me? Oh, of course; dinner is ready. Tell him—tell him," he added with a feverish, excited manner as he sprang to his feet, "that I'll be with him in a moment. I must use the telephone first. I'll put it through," he added to himself as he dashed from the room, "if it takes a leg."

Whatever Tom was bent on almost cost him a bone of some sort at the start, for just beyond the door of the reading-room he bumped full into George Hapgood, a stout, dignified-looking man of about fifty. When Tom realized who it was his eyes gleamed joyously, and in lieu of an apology he blurted out:

"You're just the man I'm looking for, Hapgood. Will you do me the favor to dine with me to-morrow? Now don't say you can't for you must."

"To-morrow? To-morrow's Christmas, isn't it?" was the inquiry, with just a shade of melancholy in the tone.

"Yes. And we're out of it—two old bachelors like you and me. I'm going to bring a few choice spirits together to prove that the things-in-law can't have all the fun. Say you'll come. Here, at seven."

"I—I was going to dine with my brother, but I got a telegram from him this afternoon saying that the children had broken out with scarlet fever and—"

"I understand, old man. So did mine. I mean—we're all in the same boat. Then I shall count on you at seven."

"Thank you kindly, Wiggin. I'll be glad to come," answered Hapgood, with a grave, courteous bow. Tom remembered having heard it said that Hapgood had never really smiled since his lady-love, Marian Blake, married Willis Bolles twenty-five years before. He was a brilliant lawyer and an influential man, but he had never been known to smile, and he habitually fought shy of all entertainments where the other sex was to be encountered, as though he feared contagion.

"I thought I wouldn't tell him that there might be women. It'll do him good to meet a few," chuckled Tom, as he pursued his way to the telephone box.

"Is that Albion Hall?"

"Yes, seh."

"Is Mr. Maxwell there?"

"No, seh, Mr. Maxwell is gone home."

"Who are you?"

"The janitor, seh."

"Is the hall engaged for to-morrow night?"

"Can't say, seh. Haven't any orders. You mean Christmas night, seh?"

"Yes, to-morrow, Christmas."

"Likely not, seh."

"Where does Mr. Maxwell live?"

"Plainville, seh."

"Humph! Do you wish to make a ten-dollar bill, janitor? Very well. Take a carriage and drive out to Plainville as tight as you can fetch it, and find out if Mr. Thomas Wiggin—he knows me—can have the hall to-morrow night. Tell Mr. Maxwell that if he'll meet me at my rooms at eight o'clock to-morrow, Christmas morning, I'll add twenty-five per cent to the price. Do you understand? Now repeat what I've said to you. That's right. Go along now and report to me at the Blackstone Club as soon as you get back, and for every five minutes which you take from an hour and a half I'll add an extra dollar to the ten."

Tom looked at his watch reflectively. It was a quarter past seven. He must dine first, if only not to break faith with Frazer Bell, whom he had kept waiting abominably long already. He stopped an instant, however, at the office on his way to join Frazer, so as to make sure that he could have the large green dining-room for the following evening.

"To-morrow's Christmas, you know, Mr. Wiggin?" suggested the steward, respectfully.

"I know it, Dunklee. Is there any reason why I shouldn't give a dinner party on Christmas day?"

"No, sir, of course not. I merely thought that perhaps you were going to dine elsewhere and had forgotten it was Christmas day."

"I dine here, and—I wish a dinner for, say sixteen—I can't tell the precise number yet—a ladies' dinner. And I wish it to be as handsome as possible. You mustn't fail me," he added, noticing that the steward looked rather dismayed. "Start your messengers at once and spare no expense, if you have to drag the butchers from their beds to get what you need. I'll see to the flowers myself; I have a greenhouse in my mind's eye which I intend to buy solidly for the occasion."

"Very well, Mr. Wiggin, I'll do my best, though it's late to begin, sir."

Frazer Bell was sitting before his raw oysters the picture of polite despair, seeing in his mind's eye the delicate dinner which he had ordered being done to death and getting lukewarm.

"My dear fellow, I owe you a thousand pardons, but I had to telephone. If our dinner is spoiled, or whether it is or not, I want you to promise to dine with me to-morrow night. I have evolved a scheme while we were waiting, which I will unfold to you presently. Go on with your oysters. I hope you will forgive me."

"To-morrow, Christmas?"

"Yes. I propose to give an entertainment to all the old bachelors and maiden ladies of my acquaintance, if they'll come. A dinner here followed by a dance at Albion Hall, and Dunklee is arranging for the dinner. I'm going to invite all the old timers, and I need your advice as to the list. For a starter I'll put down the three Bellknap girls."

Tom whipped out his pencil and proceeded to utilize the back of the bill of fare which Frazer had had drawn up to gloat over.

"See first what you're going to eat, old man."

"It's sure to be admirable if you ordered it. It has

always been a matter of wonder to me that neither of those Bellknap girls have married. Then there's Georgiana Dixon, in the same block. Glad I remembered her. Charming girl too. She ought to have been married years ago. Come to think of it, you used to be a friend of hers, Frazer."

"Yes, I did. What on earth are you up to, Tom? Are you in earnest?"

"Never more so in my life. I tell you there's a tacit conspiracy in this town—I dare say it's all over the planet—against us poor wretches who are old enough to be married and haven't, and they—the married ones I mean—like to keep us out in the cold, as a sort of punishment, may be, because we've chosen to remain single. I'm sick of it for one, and I'm going to organize a revolution. I'm going to have a grand family meeting of all the poor lonely spirits like you and me and the Bellknap girls and Georgiana Dixon and George Hapgood, and—and the things-in-law may go to the devil. Now put your wits on this thing, Frazer, while you disintegrate your terrapin. Come, girls first."

"Do you suppose they'll ever come?" asked Frazer, with an amazed grin. He was essentially a conventional man without a spark of imagination, and he could scarcely believe that Tom was really in earnest.

"They've got to come. Why shouldn't they come?"

"They'll think it queer."

"It isn't queer. It's righteous."

"All right. Put down Miss Mamie Scott. She will never see thirty again."

"Capital. Poor soul! A girl to make any man happy."

"There's Susan Davis."

"To be sure. She isn't pretty, but she's good. Joe Elliott used to be partial to her before he ran a rig with that smug-faced doll who jilted him. What a fool he was! We'll ask him too."

To tell the truth, even the gastronomic Frazer Bell, in spite of the fact that the dinner was very far from spoiled, presently forgot what he was eating and drinking in the absorbing process of selection. By the time the cheese and a rare glass of Burgundy arrived the list was finished, and Tom was eager to escape to the reading-room to prepare the notes of invitation, which must be sent at once. There were forty-six in all to be invited, out of which he hoped to secure enough for a full-fledged dinner-party. Those who could not come to dinner were to be urged to join them at Albion Hall later.

The matter of wording the invitation was a serious one, and Tom sat feeling of the bald spot on his crown for several minutes. At last, with a desperate air he plunged his pen into the inkstand and wrote as follows to Miss Madeline Bellknap:

"My dear Miss Bellknap: I beg as a favor that you and both your sisters will honor me with your company at dinner to-morrow, December 25th, at the Blackstone Club, at seven o'clock. I am bringing together, in celebration of a bachelor's Christmas, a number of kindred spirits who have no things-in-law to cater to their sympathetic needs, and yet who have a no less equal right to a merry Christmas. After dinner we shall adjourn to Albion Hall to dance, to which I trust that you or some of you, if unable to dine with me, will come at ten o'clock. With the compliments of the season and the sincere hope that you will oblige me, I am,

"Very sincerely yours,

"Thomas Wiggin."

"How is that, Frazer?"

"I guess it's all right," said Frazer, in a tone which suggested that he was far from sure whether it was not all wrong.

"Perfectly respectful and to the point, isn't it?"

"Yes. Hold on, Tom. How about a chaperon? They won't come without a chaperon."

Tom bit his lip. "I won't have a chaperon. I'll be—if I will have a chaperon." He puckered his brow gloomily; then, with a sudden wave of his hand, he cried,

"I have it."

Thereupon he dashed off this postscript:

"P.S. We are all old enough to take care of ourselves."

For the next two hours Tom and Frazer devoted themselves with feverish industry to the task of writing the two-score invitations. In such an emergency forgery seemed allowable, and, without attempting to imitate the Wiggin chirography, Frazer boldly signed the name of Thomas. As soon as every half-dozen notes were finished they were hurried to their destination by special messengers. The clock struck half-past ten when the last was done. Tom handed over to the boy in attendance the final batch, all save a single one. While he was writing this he could have written half a dozen of the others, and now that it was written and addressed he drew it from the envelope to read once more the words which he had penned so carefully. Their tenor was essentially the same, but he had stricken out a phrase or two here, and added a phrase or two there, to make sure that she would understand the nature of the invitation. Then he arose with it in his hand and said, "Good-night, Frazer. A thousand thanks. I'll leave this one myself. Wish you merry Christmas."

III.

At half past six on the evening of Christmas day Tom Wiggin stood in the large green dining-room of the Blackstone Club, surveying a magnificently appointed table. Roses, pansies, and violets from the green-house which he had bought out at ten o'clock that morning, lay tastefully banked and scattered upon the cloth, intertwined with masses of ever-green and holly gay with berries. Christmas wreaths and festoons were lavishly arranged around the walls. Dunklee had assured him that there should be no dearth of palatable viands, and, most important fact of all, there had been twenty acceptances for dinner, happily just ten men and ten women, and nearly a dozen more acceptances for the dance. He had been in a mad whirl since daybreak, but he believed now that he had accomplished everything except to arrange the seats at table, which needed a little quiet reflection.

The answers had begun to arrive shortly after breakfast. The first had been a refusal, a little curt and stiff in tone, as though the lady in question, notwithstanding the fact that she had promised to dine with one of her family, wished to give him to understand that she took herself too seriously to accept such an invitation under any circumstances. Tom's heart sank within him, and he said to himself that he had made a mess of it. Five minutes later his features were as complacent as those of a Cheshire cat. The Misses Bellknap were coming, all three of them. They had ordered dinner at home, but were coming notwithstanding, to help Mr. Wiggin pass a merry Christmas and confound the things-in-law.

"They are three noble sports," Tom had said to himself, as he danced around his apartment waving the mildly-scented note.

Other answers came thick and fast. Of course many had engagements, but most of these expressed deep regret at their inability to attend, and several who could not come to dinner promised to put in an appearance at the dance. There were a few other chilling refusals. Miss Susan Davis, whom Tom had characterized as not pretty but good, let him perceive very plainly that she considered the invitation indelicate. On the other hand, Miss Mamie Scott, who would never see thirty again, had written him spiritedly that it was a comfort to know that she was old enough to take care of herself, and that she was coming without her mother for the first time in her life.

And she? Tom had not heard until nearly noon,

and he had realized, as he held the little neatly-sealed note in his hand, that if she was going to fail him his pleasure in the whole business would be utterly gone. His wrist shook as though he had the palsy, and he hated to look. She was coming; yes, she was coming. Her father and mother were going to dine with her brother-in-law, and though she had promised to do the same she thought she would enjoy better the very original dinner to which he had invited her. "And, as you say," she wrote in conclusion, "we are certainly old enough to take care of ourselves." She was coming; yes, she was coming, and whatever happened now, he was going to have a merry Christmas.

And how was he to seat them? It was rather a nice problem. To begin with, Tom sandwiched in George Hapgood between the eldest Miss Bellknap and Miss Mamie Scott, which was as delightful a situation as any man could wish to have. Frazer Bell must go beside Georgiana Dixon, and Harry Abercombie, who had been dangling for years in the train of Angelina Phillips until everybody was tired, should take her in and have the second Miss Bellknap on his other side. Tom was making pretty good progress, but what really troubled him was whether it would do for him to place Isabelle Hardy next to himself. Would not such a proceeding be quite inconsistent with the vow which he had been living up to for the past five years? What sense would there be in putting himself in the way of temptation, when he knew perfectly well that she did not care a button for him? What use, indeed? And yet, as he said to himself, Christmas comes but once a year, and this was his party, and—and had not she herself stated that they certainly were old enough now to take care of themselves? Why shouldn't he sit next to her? He was no longer the sentimental, hot-headed boy of five years ago. They would enjoy themselves like any other sober bachelor and old maid. It would only be for one evening, and beginning with to-morrow he would stick to his vow as sturdily as ever. Yes, he would take in the eldest Miss Bellknap, who would be the oldest woman present, and he would put Isabelle Hardy on his left.

When he had made this important decision Tom found the arrangement of his other guests a simple matter, and after one final scrutinizing, but tolerably contented, glance around the table, he walked into the ladies' drawing-room to await the arrival of his company.

Punctually on the stroke of seven, the three Misses Bellknap swept into the room in a merry flutter. They were tall bean-poles of girls, who had naturally a prancing style, and they were in their very best bib and tucker, which included great puffed sleeves and nodding plumes in their hair. In one breath they told

Tom that they considered it a grand idea, that they had been practically nowhere for years, and that it was a real pleasure to be thought of and taken down from the shelf, if only for a single evening. It was evident that they had come determined to have at least a good time, if not a riot, for when their eyes rested on George Hapgood standing in the door-way the picture of blank amazement, all three giggled convulsively as though they were eighteen.

"Come in, George, don't be afraid," said Tom. "They won't bite."

"We really won't hurt you, Mr. Hapgood," said Miss Madeline, the eldest; "do come in."

It was too late for the woman-hater to draw back now, so, like the man he was, he braced his muscles and faced the music. He bowed with grave courtesy to the youngest Miss Bellknap; he bowed with a faint smile—just a ghostly glimmer, but, nevertheless, a smile—to Miss Arabella, the second Miss Bellknap; and when he faced the eldest Miss Bellknap, who happening to be the furthest away from him was the last to be reached, his features broke down completely, and he positively laughed—laughed for the first time in twenty years.

"Do shake hands, Mr. Hapgood," said Miss Madeline, "this is like old times."

And now everybody began to arrive in a bunch in the midst of a general handshaking and chorus of merriment. The arrival of each old stager, masculine or feminine, was greeted with fresh exclamations of delight, and a spirit of contagious frivolity was rampant from the very start.

Tom was already bubbling over with enjoyment, but his eyes were glued on the doorway. There she was at last, looking—yes, looking younger and prettier than he had ever seen her in his life, and dressed bewitchingly. An old maid! It was impossible. It was monstrous.

"It was very good of you to come, Miss Hardy."

"I am very much pleased to be here, Mr. Wiggin."

Most conventional phraseology, and there was really no reason why Tom should keep repeating the words over to himself in a dazed sort of fashion until he was called to account by the opening of the doors.

"Dinner is served, sir."

Then readjusting his faculties, Tom gave his arm to Miss Madeline Bellknap, every Jack did the same to his appointed Jill, and the company filed gayly into the dining-room.

Beginning with the oysters, there was almost a pandemonium of conversation, and tongues wagged fast and eagerly. There were to be no speeches— Tom had determined on that—or rather only a single one, and this was an after-thought. When the champagne was passed, and all the glasses were filled, Tom rose in his seat. Everyone stopped talking, and there was an expectant hush.

"I wish to offer a toast," he said, "a toast for the old bachelors to drink. Wish you merry Christmas and—and here's to *her*!"

There was a brief pause, and then George Hapgood, and in his wake the whole table, rose like one man and emptied their brimming glasses.

"Here's to *her*!"

Tom did not look to right nor to left, not even out of the corner of his eye, as he drained to the last drop the sparkling wine. He would keep to his vow and drink to her in secret. Some of the ladies giggled slightly, and all looked at their plates. It was just a little awkward, even for the most unattached, until Miss Madeline Bellknap rose, glass in hand, and said valiantly, with a wave of her napkin:

"My dears, I give you a toast for you to drink. Wish you merry Christmas. We are old enough to take care of ourselves; and—and here's to *him*!"

Then there was babel. The women stood up to a woman, and the toast was consummated.

Miss Hardy laughed gayly with the rest. Presently she turned to Tom and said, as if it had suddenly occurred to her, though they had been sitting side by side talking commonplaces ever since dinner began:

"I have not really seen you for years, Mr. Wiggin."

"I have been busy—very busy," said Tom, in a tone which, though he did not intend it to be so, was almost brusque.

"So I have heard. I understand you have been very successful in your business."

"I have stuck to it, that's all."

"I really don't think we have met so as to talk together since Mrs. Carter's ball, and that was—let me see—five years ago this coming New Year's eve. I remember we danced the German together, and—you sent me some flowers which I didn't carry. Perhaps you have forgotten all about it, for five years is a long time and you have been so busy; but I should like to explain to you about those flowers—why I didn't carry them. We are both old enough now to take care of ourselves, so there can't be any objection to my telling you, and—and you won't be offended at this late day, I'm sure. I had several bouquets that night, and Fannie Perkins, who was staying with me, had none. Fannie was shy and sensitive, and it occurred to me to offer one of mine to her. She wouldn't think of it at first, but mother urged her so strongly that she gave in at last. 'Which shall I take, Isabelle?' she asked. I thought a moment and then said, 'Take your pick, Fannie.' And she chose yours. And that is why I didn't carry it to the party. But I think you have forgotten all about it, Mr. Wiggin."

Tom looked as though he had. His chin rested on his collar, and he seemed to be staring at the table-cloth.

"I remember it as if it were yesterday," he said, sadly. "I was a fool."

Miss Hardy colored. "We were both young," she answered, "but now that we are older and wiser, I don't mind admitting on my side that it was stupid of me, to begin with, to give one of my bouquets to anybody, and stupid when I saw that you were put out not to tell you the truth. But wisdom is the reward of years, isn't it?" She talked easily, almost gayly. Tom suddenly realized that he had made a piece of bread which he had been clutching into a sodden ball.

"I'd like to ask you a single question." He was trying to talk easily too. "Why did you let Miss Perkins have her pick? Did you value them all equally?"

"It was because I did not value them all equally that I told her to choose. I did not wish her to think that I cared for one more than the others."

"And whose was that?"

"Five years is a long time, Mr. Wiggin. You said a single question, and this is two. Alas! It is the only point in the story which I have quite forgotten."

"Then why did you tell me?"

"Because I hoped that we might be friends again. When people get to be as old as you and I we value our old friends. There are none exactly like them."

"And that is all?"

"What more is there, Mr. Wiggin? Except to thank you for your lovely book, and to wish you a merry Christmas."

"The carriages are waiting," said a servant in Tom's ear.

The dinner was over and it was time to set out for Albion Hall. The ladies filed into the drawing-room in order, as Miss Madeline phrased it, to give the old bachelors a chance for a short cigar. When that was over Tom bundled his company into carriages, and away they all went in the gayest of spirits.

Whatever belonging to the greenhouse had not been spread over the dinner-table adorned the walls of the dancing-room, and presently as joyous and hilarious a company as anyone would wish to see was tripping to the rhythm of the waltz over a perfect floor. There was just the right number for delightful dancing, no young inexperienced couples to bump into everybody, no things-in-law to stand in the way and look stupid; no one but genuine old stagers taken down from the shelf for one last glorious frolic. You should have seen George Hapgood spinning round with Miss Madeline! How Frazer Bell grinned as he whirled Miss Mamie Scott from one corner of the hall to the other! And Tom? Where was Tom?

As some of you who have danced at Albion Hall

may remember, there is a very small bower-like ante-room, or off-shoot, or whatever you choose to call it, a sort of adjunct to the supper-room, fit for just one couple to withdraw to. On this Christmas evening it was a veritable hiding-place, for the entrance to it was screened by two noble evergreens which stood as sentinels to demand a pass-word. If the gay company suspected that Tom Wiggin was there, no one was rash enough to peep within and ascertain. Tom Wiggin *was* there, and quite contrary to the spirit of the occasion, he was down on his knees unbosoming the love which he had been smothering for five years to the girl of his heart. Only think of it! And he, a bald-headed old bachelor, and she an old maid old enough to take care of herself. There she sat with her hands before her and a smile on her face, letting him go on. And then, strangest part of all, when he had finished and told how miserable he had been while he was so very busy and absorbed in his business, she suddenly remembered whose bouquet it was she had valued most five years before, although she had declared an hour earlier that she had totally forgotten. And then—but the rest is a secret, known only to the sentinel evergreens and themselves. That is, the rest save one thing. It was after they had agreed to live as bachelor and maid no longer, and Tom was sitting looking at Isabelle as if he had had no dinner, he remarked, with a sudden outburst, as though he was angry with destiny and a much outraged being:

"Why on earth did I not find out five years ago that you loved me?"

"Because," said the pretty spinster in question, "you never asked me, Tom, dear."

Tom Wiggin looked a trifle sheepish in spite of his joy. "I never thought of that," he said. "I'm afraid I never did."

How Santa Claus Came to Simpson's Bar

BRET HARTE

It had been raining in the valley of the Sacramento. The North Fork had overflowed its banks and Rattlesnake Creek was impassable. The few boulders that had marked the summer ford at Simpson's Crossing were obliterated by a vast sheet of water stretching to the foothills. The up stage was stopped at Grangers; the last mail had been abandoned in the *tules*, the rider swimming for his life. "An area," remarked the *Sierra Avalanche*, with pensive local pride, "as large as the State of Massachusetts is now under water."

Nor was the weather any better in the foothills. The mud lay deep on the mountain road; wagons that neither physical force nor moral objurgation could move from the evil ways into which they had fallen encumbered the track, and the way to Simpson's Bar was indicated by broken-down teams and hard swearing. And farther on, cut off and inaccessible, rained upon and bedraggled, smitten by high winds and threatened by high water, Simpson's Bar on the eve of Christmas day, 1862, clung like a swallow's nest to the rocky entablature and splintered capitals of Table Mountain, and shook in the blast.

As night shut down on the settlement, a few lights gleamed through the mist from the windows of cabins on either side of the highway now crossed and gullied by lawless streams and swept by marauding winds. Happily most of the population were gathered at Thompson's store, clustered around a red-hot stove, at which they silently spat in some accepted sense of social communion that perhaps rendered conversation unnecessary. Indeed, most methods of diversion had long since been exhausted on Simpson's Bar; high water had suspended the regular occupations on gulch and on river, and a consequent lack of money and whiskey had taken the zest from most illegitimate recreation. Even Mr. Hamlin was fain to leave the Bar with fifty dollars in his pocket—the only amount actually realized of the large sums won by him in the successful exercise of his arduous profession. "Ef I was asked," he remarked somewhat later, "ef I was asked to pint out a party little village where a retired sport as didn't care for money could exercise hisself, frequent and lively, I'd say Simpson's Bar; but for a young man with a large family depending on his exertions, it don't pay." As Mr. Hamlin's family consisted mainly of female adults, this remark is quoted rather to show the breadth of his humor than the exact extent of his responsibilities.

Howbeit, the unconscious objects of this satire sat that evening in the listless apathy begotten of idleness and lack of excitement. Even the sudden splashing of hoofs before the door did not arouse them. Dick Bullen alone paused in the act of scraping out his pipe, and lifted his head, but no other one of the group indicated any interest in, or recognition of, the man who entered.

It was a figure familiar enough to the company, and known in Simpson's Bar as the "Old Man." A man of perhaps fifty years; grizzled and scant of hair, but still fresh and youthful of complexion. A face full of ready, but not very powerful, sympathy, with a chameleon-like aptitude for taking on the shade and color of contiguous moods and feelings. He had evidently just left some hilarious companions and did not at first notice the gravity of the group, but clapped the shoulder of the nearest man jocularly and threw himself into a vacant chair.

"Jest heard the best thing out, boys! Ye know Smiley, over yar—Jim Smiley—funniest man in the Bar? Well, Jim was jest telling the richest yarn about—"

"Smiley's a—fool," interrupted a gloomy voice.

"A particular—skunk," added another in sepulchral accents.

A silence followed these positive statements. The Old Man glanced quickly around the group. Then his face slowly changed. "That's so," he said reflectively, after a pause, "certingly a sort of a skunk and suthin' of a fool. In course." He was silent for a moment as in painful contemplation of the unsavoriness and folly of the unpopular Smiley. "Dismal weather, ain't it?" he added, now fully embarked on the current of prevailing sentiment. "Mighty rough papers on the boys, and no show for money this season. And tomorrow's Christmas."

There was a movement among the men at this announcement, but whether of satisfaction or disgust was not plain. "Yes," continued the Old Man in the lugubrious tone he had, within the last few moments, unconsciously adopted, "yes, Christmas, and tonight's Christmas eve. Ye see, boys, I kinder thought—that is, I sorter had an idee, jest passin' like, you know—that maybe ye'd all like to come over to my house tonight and have a sort of tear round. But I suppose, now, you wouldn't? Don't feel like it, maybe?" he added with anxious sympathy, peering into the faces of his companions.

"Well, I don't know," responded Tom Flynn with

some cheerfulness. "P'r'aps we may. But how about your wife, Old Man? What does *she* say to it?"

The Old Man hesitated. His conjugal experience had not been a happy one, and the fact was known to Simpson's Bar. His first wife, a delicate, pretty little woman, had suffered keenly and secretly from the jealous suspicions of her husband, until one day he invited the whole Bar to his house to expose her infidelity. On arriving, the party found the shy, petite creature quietly engaged in her household duties and retired abashed and discomfited. But the sensitive woman did not easily recover from the shock of this extraordinary outrage. It was with difficulty she regained her equanimity sufficiently to release her lover from the closet in which he was concealed and escape with him. She left a boy of three years to comfort her bereaved husband. The Old Man's present wife had been his cook. She was large, loyal, and aggressive.

Before he could reply, Joe Dimmick suggested with great directness that it was the "Old Man's house" and that, invoking the Divine Power, if the case were his own, he would invite whom he pleased, even if in so doing he imperiled his salvation. The Powers of Evil, he further remarked, should contend against him vainly. All this delivered with a terseness and vigor lost in this necessary translation.

"In course. Certainly. Thet's it," said the Old Man with a sympathetic frown. "Thar's no trouble about *thet*. It's my own house, built every stick on it myself. Don't you be afeard o' her, boys. She *may* cut up a trifle rough, ez wimmin do, but she'll come round." Secretly the Old Man trusted to the exaltation of liquor and the power of courageous example to sustain him in such an emergency.

As yet, Dick Bullen, the oracle and leader of Simpson's Bar, had not spoken. He now took his pipe from his lips. "Old Man, how's that yer Johnny gettin' on? Seems to me he didn't look so peart last time I seed him on the bluff heavin' rocks at Chinamen. Didn't seem to take much interest in it. Thar was a gang of 'em by yar yesterday—drownded out up the river—and I kinder thought o' Johnny, and how he'd miss em! May be now, we'd be in the way ef he wus sick?"

The father, evidently touched not only by this pathetic picture of Johnny's deprivation, but by the considerate delicacy of the speaker, hastened to assure him that Johnny was better and that a "little fun might liven him up." Whereupon Dick arose, shook himself, and saying, "I'm ready. Lead the way, Old Man: here goes," himself led the way with a leap, a characteristic howl, and darted out into the night. As he passed through the outer room he caught up a blazing brand from the hearth. The action was repeated by the rest of the party, closely following and elbowing each other, and before the astonished proprietor of Thompson's grocery was aware of the intention of his guests, the room was deserted.

The night was pitchy dark. In the first gust of wind their temporary torches were extinguished, and only the red brands dancing and flitting in the gloom like drunken will-o'-the-wisps indicated their whereabouts. Their way led up Pine-Tree Cañon, at the head of which a broad, low, bark-thatched cabin burrowed in the mountainside. It was the home of the Old Man, and the entrance to the tunnel in which he worked when he worked at all. Here the crowd paused for a moment, out of delicate deference to their host, who came up panting in the rear.

"P'r'aps ye'd better hold on a second out yer, whilst I go in and see thet things is all right," said the Old Man, with an indifference he was far from feeling. The suggestion was graciously accepted, the door opened and closed on the host, and the crowd, leaning their backs against the wall and cowering under the eaves, waited and listened.

For a few moments there was no sound but the

dripping of water from the eaves, and the stir and rustle of wrestling boughs above them. Then the men became uneasy, and whispered suggestion and suspicion passed from the one to the other. "Reckon she's caved in his head the first lick!" "Decoyed him inter the tunnel and barred him up, likely." "Got him down and sittin' on him." "Prob'ly bilin' suthin' to heave on us: stand clear the door, boys!" For just then the latch clicked, the door slowly opened, and a voice said, "Come in out o' the wet."

The voice was neither that of the Old Man nor of his wife. It was the voice of a small boy, its weak treble broken by that preternatural hoarseness which only vagabondage and the habit of premature self-assertion can give. It was the face of a small boy that looked up at theirs—a face that might have been pretty and even refined but that it was darkened by evil knowledge from within, and dirt and hard experience from without. He had a blanket around his shoulders and had evidently just risen from his bed. "Come in," he repeated, "and don't make no noise. The Old Man's in there talking to mar," he continued, pointing to an adjacent room which seemed to be a kitchen, from which the Old Man's voice came in deprecating accents. "Let me be," he added querulously to Dick Bullen, who had caught him up, blanket and all, and was affecting to toss him into the fire. "Let go o' me, you damned old fool, d'ye hear?"

Thus adjured, Dick Bullen lowered Johnny to the ground with a smothered laugh, while the men, entering quietly, ranged themselves around a long table of rough boards which occupied the center of the room. Johnny then gravely proceeded to a cupboard and brought out several articles which he deposited on the table. "Thar's whiskey. And crackers. And red herons. And cheese." He took a bite of the latter on his way to the table. "And sugar." He scooped up a mouthful en route with a small and very dirty hand. "And terbacker. Thar's dried appils too on the shelf, but I don't admire 'em. Appils is swellin'. Thar," he concluded, "now wade in, and don't be afeard. I don't mind the old woman. She don't b'long to *me*. S'long."

He had stepped to the threshold of a small room, scarcely larger than a closet, partitioned off from the main apartment and holding in its dim recess a small bed. He stood there a moment looking at the company, his bare feet peeping from the blanket, and nodded.

"Hello, Johnny! You ain't goin' to turn in agin, are ye?" said Dick.

"Yes, I are," responded Johnny, decidedly.

"Why, wot's up, old fellow?"

"I'm sick."

"How sick?"

"I've got a fevier. And childblains. And roomatiz," returned Johnny, and vanished within. After a moment's pause, he added in the dark, apparently from under the bedclothes, "and biles!"

There was an embarrassing silence. The men looked at each other, and at the fire. Even with the appetizing banquet before them, it seemed as if they might again fall into the despondency of Thompson's grocery, when the voice of the Old Man, incautiously lifted, came deprecatingly from the kitchen.

"Certainly! Thet's so. In course they is. A gang o' lazy drunken loafers, and that ar Dick Bullen's the ornariest of all. Didn't hev no more *sabe* than to come round yar with sickness in the house and no provision. Thet's what I said: 'Bullen,' sez I, 'it's crazy drunk you are, or a fool,' sez I, 'to think o' such a thing.' 'Staples,' I sez, 'be you a man, Staples, and 'spect to raise hell under my roof and invalids lyin' round?' But they would come—they would. Thet's wot you must 'spect o' such trash as lays round the Bar."

A burst of laughter from the men followed this unfortunate exposure. Whether it was overheard in the kitchen, or whether the Old Man's irate companion had just then exhausted all other modes of expressing her contemptuous indignation, I cannot say, but a back door was suddenly slammed with great violence. A moment later and the Old Man reappeared, haply unconscious of the cause of the late hilarious outburst, and smiled blandly. "The old woman thought she'd jest run over to Mrs. McFadden's for a sociable call," he explained, with jaunty indifference, as he took a seat at the board.

Oddly enough it needed this untoward incident to relieve the embarrassment that was beginning to be felt by the party, and their natural audacity returned with their host. I do not propose to record the convivialities of that evening. The inquisitive reader will accept the statement that the conversation was characterized by the same intellectual exaltation, the same cautious reverence, the same fastidious delicacy, the same rhetorical precision, and the same logical and coherent discourse somewhat later in the evening, which distinguish similar gatherings of the masculine sex in more civilized localities and under more favorable auspices. No glasses were broken in the absence of any; no liquor was spilt on floor or table in the scarcity of that article.

It was nearly midnight when the festivities were interrupted. "Hush," said Dick Bullen, holding up his hand. It was the querulous voice of Johnny from his adjacent closet: "Oh, Dad!"

The Old Man arose hurriedly and disappeared in

the closet. Presently he reappeared. "His rheumatiz is coming on agin bad," he explained, "and he wants rubbin'." He lifted the demijohn of whiskey from the table and shook it. It was empty. Dick Bullen put down his tin cup with an embarrassed laugh. So did the others. The Old Man examined their contents and said hopefully, "I reckon that's enough; he don't need much. You hold on all o' you for a spell, and I'll be back." He vanished in the closet with an old flannel shirt and the whiskey. The door closed but imperfectly, and the following dialogue was distinctly audible:

"Now, sonny, whar does she ache worst?"

"Sometimes over yar and sometimes under yer; but it's most powerful from yer to yer. Rub yer, Dad."

A silence seemed to indicate a brisk rubbing. Then Johnny:

"Hevin' a good time out yer, Dad?"

"Yes, sonny."

"Tomorrer's Chrismiss—ain't it?"

"Yes, sonny. How does she feel now?"

"Better. Rub a little furder down. Wot's Chrismiss, anyway? Wot's it all about?"

"Oh, it's a day."

This exhaustive definition was apparently satisfactory, for there was a silent interval of rubbing. Presently Johnny again:

"Mar sez that everywhere else but yer everybody

gives things to everybody Chrismiss, and then she jist waded inter you. She sez thar's a man they call Sandy Claus, not a white man, you know, but a kind o' Chinemin, comes down the chimbley night afore Chrismiss and gives things to chillern—boys like me. Put's 'em in their butes! Thet's what she tried to play upon me. Easy now, Pop, whar are you rubbin' to—thet's a mile from the place. She jest made that up, didn't she, jest to aggrewate me and you? Don't rub thar. . . . Why, Dad?"

In the great quiet that seemed to have fallen upon the house the sigh of the near pines and the drip of leaves without was very distinct. Johnny's voice, too, was lowered as he went on, "Don't you take on now, fur I'm gettin' all right fast. Wot's the boys doin' out thar?"

The Old Man partly opened the door and peered through. His guests were sitting there sociably enough, and there were a few silver coins and a lean buckskin purse on the table. "Bettin' on suthin'— some little game or 'nother. They're all right," he replied to Johnny and recommenced his rubbing.

"I'd like to take a hand and win some money," said Johnny, reflectively, after a pause.

The Old Man glibly repeated what was evidently a familiar formula, that if Johnny would wait until he struck it rich in the tunnel he'd have lots of money, and so forth.

"Yes," said Johnny, "but you don't. And whether you strike it or I win it, it's about the same. It's all luck. But it's mighty cur'o's about Chrismiss—ain't it? Why do they call it Chrismiss?"

Perhaps from some instinctive deference to the overhearing of his guests, or from some vague sense of incongruity, the Old Man's reply was so low as to be inaudible beyond the room.

"Yes," said Johnny, with some slight abatement of interest, "I've heerd o' *him* before. Thar, that'll do, Dad. I don't ache near so bad as I did. Now wrap me tight in this yer blanket. So. Now," he added in a muffled whisper, "sit down yer by me till I go asleep." To assure himself of obedience, he disengaged one hand from the blanket and, grasping his father's sleeve, again composed himself to rest.

For some moments the Old Man waited patiently. Then the unwonted stillness of the house excited his curiosity, and without moving from the bed he cautiously opened the door with his disengaged hand and looked into the main room. To his infinite surprise it was dark and deserted. But even then a smoldering log on the hearth broke, and by the upspringing blaze he saw the figure of Dick Bullen sitting by the dying embers.

"Hello!"

Dick started, rose, and came somewhat unsteadily toward him.

"Whar's the boys?" said the Old Man.

"Gone up the cañon on a little *pasear*. They're coming back for me in a minit. I'm waitin' round for 'em. What are you starin' at, Old Man?" he added with a forced laugh. "Do you think I'm drunk?"

The Old Man might have been pardoned the supposition, for Dick's eyes were humid and his face flushed. He loitered and lounged back to the chimney, yawned, shook himself, buttoned up his coat, and laughed. "Liquor ain't so plenty as that, Old Man. Now don't you git up," he continued as the Old Man made a movement to release his sleeve from Johnny's hand. "Don't you mind manners. Sit jest whar you be; I'm goin' in a jiffy. Thar, that's them now."

There was a low tap at the door. Dick Bullen opened it quickly, nodded good night to his host, and disappeared. The Old Man would have followed him but for the hand that still unconsciously grasped his sleeve. He could have easily disengaged it; it was small, weak, and emaciated. But perhaps because it *was* small, weak, and emaciated he changed his mind and, drawing his chair closer to the bed, rested his head upon it. In this defenseless attitude the potency of his earlier potations surprised him. The room flickered and faded before his eyes, reappeared, faded again, went out, and left him—asleep.

Meantime Dick Bullen, closing the door, confronted his companions. "Are you ready?" said Staples. "Ready," said Dick. "What's the time?" "Past twelve," was the reply. "Can you make it? It's nigh on fifty miles, the round trip hither and yon." "I reckon," returned Dick, shortly. "Whar's the mare?" "Bill and Jack's holdin' her at the crossin'." "Let 'em hold on a minit longer," said Dick.

He turned and re-entered the house softly. By the light of the guttering candle and dying fire he saw that the door of the little room was open. He stepped toward it on tiptoe and looked in. The Old Man had fallen back in his chair, snoring, his helpless feet thrust out in a line with his collapsed shoulders and his hat pulled over his eyes. Beside him, on a narrow wooden bedstead, lay Johnny, muffled tightly in a blanket that hid all save a strip of forehead and a few curls damp with perspiration. Dick Bullen made a step forward, hesitated, and glanced over his shoulder into the deserted room. Everything was quiet. With a sudden resolution he parted his huge mustaches with both hands and stooped over the sleeping boy. But even as he did so a mischievous blast swooped down the chimney, rekindled the hearth, and lit up the room with a shameless glow from which Dick fled in bashful terror.

His companions were already waiting for him at the crossing. Two of them were struggling in the darkness with some strange misshapen bulk, which as Dick came nearer took the semblance of a great yellow horse. It was the mare. She was not a pretty picture. From her Roman nose to her rising haunches, from her arched spine hidden by the stiff *machillas* of a Mexican saddle to her thick, straight, bony legs, there was not a line of equine grace. In her half-blind but wholly vicious white eyes, in her protruding underlip, in her monstrous color, there was nothing but ugliness and vice.

"Now then," said Staples, "stand cl'ar of her heels, boys, and up with you. Don't miss your first holt of her mane, and mind ye get your off stirrup *quick*. Ready!"

There was a leap, a scrambling struggle, a bound, a wild retreat of the crowd, a circle of flying hoofs, two springless leaps that jarred the earth, a rapid play and jingle of spurs, a plunge, and then the voice of Dick somewhere in the darkness, "All right!"

"Don't take the lower road back onless you're hard pushed for time! Don't hold her in downhill! We'll be at the ford at five. G'lang! Hoopa! Mula! GO!"

A splash, a spark struck from the ledge in the road, a clatter in the rocky cut beyond, and Dick was gone.

It was one o'clock, and yet he had only gained Rattlesnake Hill. For in that time Jovita had rehearsed to him all her imperfections and practiced all her vices. Thrice had she stumbled. Twice had she thrown up her Roman nose in a straight line with the reins and, resisting bit and spur, struck out madly across country. Twice had she reared and, rearing, fallen backward; and twice had the agile Dick, unharmed, regained his seat before she found her vicious legs again. And a mile beyond them, at the foot of a long hill, was Rattlesnake Creek. Dick knew that here was the crucial test of his ability to perform his enterprise, set his teeth grimly, put his knees well into her flanks, and changed his defensive tactics to brisk aggression. Bullied and maddened, Jovita began the descent of the hill. Here the artful Richard pretended to hold her in with ostentatious objurgation and well-feigned cries of alarm. It is unnecessary to add that Jovita instantly ran away. Nor need I state the time made in the descent; it is written in the chronicles of Simpson's Bar. Enough that in another moment, as it seemed to Dick, she was splashing on the overflowed banks of Rattlesnake Creek. As Dick expected, the momentum she had acquired carried her beyond the point of balking, and holding her well together for a mighty leap, they dashed into the middle of the swiftly flowing current. A few moments of kicking, wading, and swimming, and Dick drew a long breath on the opposite bank.

The road from Rattlesnake Creek to Red Mountain was tolerably level. Either the plunge in Rattlesnake Creek had dampened her baleful fire, or the art which led to it had shown her the superior wickedness of her rider, for Jovita no longer wasted her surplus energy in wanton conceits. Once she bucked, but it was from force of habit; once she shied, but it was from a new freshly painted meetinghouse at the crossing of the county road. Hollows, ditches, gravelly deposits, patches of freshly springing grasses flew from beneath her rattling hoofs. She began to smell unpleasantly, once or twice she coughed slightly, but there was no abatement of her strength or speed. By two o'clock he had passed Red Mountain and begun the descent to the plain. Ten minutes later the driver of the fast Pioneer coach was overtaken and passed by a "man on a Pinto hoss"—an event sufficiently notable for remark. At half past two Dick rose in his stirrups with a great shout. Stars were glittering through the rifted clouds, and beyond him, out of the plain, rose two spires, a flagstaff and a straggling line of black objects. Dick jingled his spurs and swung his *riata*, Jovita bounded forward, and in another moment they swept into Tuttleville and drew up before the wooden piazza of "The Hotel of All Nations."

What transpired that night at Tuttleville is not strictly a part of this record. Briefly I may state, however, that after Jovita had been handed over to a sleepy ostler, whom she at once kicked into unpleasant consciousness, Dick sallied out with the barkeeper for a tour of the sleeping town. Lights still gleamed from the few saloons and gambling houses; but, avoiding these, they stopped before several closed shops, and by persistent tapping and judicious outcry roused the proprietors from their beds and made them unbar the doors of their magazines and expose their wares. Sometimes they were met by curses, but oftener by interest and some concern in their needs, and the interview was invariably concluded by a drink. It was three o'clock before this pleasantry was given over, and with a small waterproof bag of India rubber strapped on his shoulders Dick returned to the hotel. But here he was waylaid by Beauty—Beauty opulent in charms, affluent in dress, persuasive in speech, and Spanish in accent! In vain she repeated the invitation in "Excelsior," happily scorned by all Alpine-climbing youth and rejected by this child of the Sierras—a rejection softened in this instance by a laugh and his last gold coin. And then he sprang to the saddle and dashed down the lonely street and out into the lonelier plain, where presently the lights, the black line of houses, the spires, and the flagstaff sank into the earth behind him again and were lost in the distance.

The storm had cleared away, the air was brisk and cold, the outlines of adjacent landmarks were distinct, but it was half past four before Dick reached the meetinghouse and the crossing of the county road. To avoid the rising grade he had taken a longer and more circuitous road, in whose viscid mud Jovita sank fetlock deep at every bound. It was a poor preparation for a steady ascent of five miles more; but Jovita, gathering her legs under her, took it with her usual blind, unreasoning fury, and a half hour later reached the long level that led to Rattlesnake Creek. Another half hour would bring him to the creek. He threw the reins lightly upon the neck of the mare, chirruped to her, and began to sing.

Suddenly Jovita shied with a bound that would have unseated a less practiced rider. Hanging to her rein was a figure that had leaped from the bank, and at the same time from the road before her arose a shadowy horse and rider. "Throw up your hands," commanded this second apparition, with an oath.

Dick felt the mare tremble, quiver, and apparently sink under him. He knew what it meant and was prepared.

"Stand aside, Jack Simpson, I know you, you damned thief. Let me pass or—"

He did not finish the sentence. Jovita rose straight

in the air with a terrific bound, throwing the figure from her bit with a single shake of her vicious head, and charged with deadly malevolence down on the impediment before her. An oath, a pistol shot, horse and highwayman rolled over in the road, and the next moment Jovita was a hundred yards away. But the good right arm of her rider, shattered by a bullet, dropped helplessly at his side.

Without slackening his speed he shifted the reins to his left hand. But a few moments later he was obliged to halt and tighten the saddle girths that had slipped in the onset. This in his crippled condition took some time. He had no fear of pursuit, but looking up he saw that the eastern stars were already paling and that the distant peaks had lost their ghostly whiteness and now stood out blackly against a lighter sky. Day was upon him. Then, completely absorbed in a single idea, he forgot the pain of his wound and mounting again dashed on toward Rattlesnake Creek. But now Jovita's breath came broken by gasps, Dick reeled in his saddle, and brighter and brighter grew the sky.

Ride, Richard; run, Jovita; linger, O day!

For the last few rods there was a roaring in his ears. Was it exhaustion from loss of blood, or what? He was dazed and giddy as he swept down the hill, and did not recognize his surroundings. Had he taken the wrong road, or was this Rattlesnake Creek?

It was. But the bawling creek he had swum a few hours before had risen, more than doubled its volume, and now rolled a swift and resistless river between him and Rattlesnake Hill. For the first time that night Richard's heart sank within him. The river, the mountain, the quickening east swam before his eyes. He shut them to recover his self-control. In that brief interval, by some fantastic mental process, the little room at Simpson's Bar and the figures of the sleeping father and son rose upon him. He opened his eyes wildly, cast off his coat, pistol, boots, and saddle, bound his precious pack tightly to his shoulders, grasped the bare flanks of Jovita with his bared knees, and with a shout dashed into the yellow water. A cry rose from the opposite bank as the heads of a man and a horse struggled for a few moments against the battling current, and then were swept away amidst uprooted trees and whirling driftwood.

The Old Man started and woke. The fire on the hearth was dead, the candle in the outer room flickering in its socket, and somebody was rapping at the door. He opened it, but fell back with a cry before the dripping, half-naked figure that reeled against the doorpost.

"Dick?"

"Hush! Is he awake yet?"

"No—but Dick—"

"Dry up, you old fool! Get me some whiskey *quick*!" The Old Man flew and returned with an empty bottle. Dick would have sworn, but his strength was not equal to the occasion. He staggered, caught at the handle of the door, and motioned to the Old Man.

"Thar's suthin' in my pack yer for Johnny. Take it off. I can't."

The Old Man unstrapped the pack and laid it before the exhausted man.

"Open it, quick!"

He did so with trembling fingers. It contained only a few poor toys—cheap and barbaric enough, goodness knows, but bright with paint and tinsel. One of them was broken; another, I fear, was irretrievably ruined by water; and on the third—ah me! there was a cruel spot.

"It don't look like much, that's a fact," said Dick, ruefully, "but it's the best we could do. Take 'em, Old Man, and put 'em in his stocking, and tell him—tell him, you know—hold me, Old Man—" The Old Man caught at his sinking figure. "Tell him," said Dick, with a weak little laugh, "tell him Sandy Claus has come."

And even so, bedraggled, ragged, unshaven, and

unshorn, with one arm hanging helplessly at his side, Santa Claus came to Simpson's Bar and fell fainting on the first threshold. The Christmas dawn came slowly after, touching the remoter peaks with the rosy warmth of ineffable love. And it looked so tenderly on Simpson's Bar that the whole mountain, as if caught in a generous action, blushed to the skies.

The Man Who Was Like Shakspeare

WILLIAM BLACK

THE DOCTOR DREAMS

O n the 24th of December last year Dr.
Maurice Daniel left his home in Brompton, London, for his accustomed after-
breakfast stroll. First of all he walked down to
Chelsea Bridge, and had a look at the gray river, the
gray skies, and the gray shadows of London in the
distance. Then he wandered on until he found himself at Victoria Station. Apparently having no business to do there—or any where else, for the matter
of that—he turned, and proceeded to make the best
of his way back to his own house.

Now it happened that he strayed into a somewhat
narrow and dingy street, the narrowness and dingi-
ness of which he did not perceive, for his mind was

occupied with his familiar hobby, which was phrenology. This hale old gentleman of sixty-five had himself some notion of completing the labors of Gall and Spurzheim, and had already collected some variety of materials in his odd little hermitage at Brompton. He was thinking of all these things in a somewhat absent way, when his attention was suddenly drawn to a small shop in this gloomy thoroughfare through which he was passing. It was a tailor's shop. There were no signs of a large trade in the place; in fact, one could only tell that it was a tailor's shop because the tailor himself was visible through the dirty window; seated on a board, and industriously plying needle and thread. It was the appearance of this man that had startled Dr. Daniel out of his reverie. The tailor bore an extraordinary resemblance to the Droeshout portrait of Shakspeare, insomuch that the old gentleman outside could only stand and stare at him. There were points of difference, of course. The head was narrower than Shakespeare's, but the forehead was quite as lofty. The hair was red. What the tailor's eyes were he could not see, for they were fixed on his work; but they were probably light blue.

"Comparison and causality enormous," the old Doctor said to himself. "Hope and wonder also large. Number and time deficient. Language, I fear, not much to speak of. But what a head—what a brain! Fifty-five ounces, I will take my oath—six ounces over the average of the European male. Why, Lord Campbell had only fifty-three; and then the splendid possibilities that lie in the difference! What is Bain's phrase? that 'while the size of brain increases in arithmetical proportion, intellectual range increases in geometrical proportion.' Here is a man with brain-power sufficient to alter the history of a nation."

The old Doctor walked on, dreaming harder than ever. And now there arose in his mind a project, of which the origin was twofold. The night before he had been reading in his bachelor study a heap of Christmas literature that had been sent him by his sister, an old maiden lady, who lived mostly at Bath, and who took this means of marking her friendly sentiments toward her brother. She was not a sentimental old lady, but she was correct and methodical in her ways, and believing that Christmas literature was proper at Christmas, she had dispatched to her brother a fairly large quantity of it. Having received the gift, he was bound to make use of it; so he sat down after dinner by his study fire, and pored over the stories, old and new, that she had sent. He began to feel that he ought to do something for Christmas. He did not wish to be classed among those persons who, in the stories, were described as sordid, mean, black-hearted, and generally villainous because they were indifferent about Christmas, or unable to weep over it. Moreover, Dr. Daniel was really an amiable old gentleman, and some of the stories of charity touched him. He was determined that nobody should say he was a Mr. Scrooge, if only he had an opportunity of doing any body a good turn.

Now, as he walked home to Brompton this forenoon, that vague desire of doing some benevolent deed co-operated with his deep-lying interest in phrenology to lead him to a daring resolve. Although not a very wealthy man, he was pretty well off, and always had sufficient funds in hand for an exceptional call. He would now, he said, try what could be done with this poor tailor. He would give to that splendid brain its opportunity. Who could tell how many village Hampdens and mute inglorious Miltons had not been lost to this country simply because we had no sufficient system of national education, by which the chance of declaring himself was elsewhere given to any capable youth? There could be little doubt but that the tailor was a victim to this lack of early instruction. In making his acquaintance, in becoming his patron, in placing before him opportunities of acquiring the power of expression, a good deed would be done to the poor man in any case, while there was also the beautiful and captivating hope that in course of time a great genius would reveal himself to his country, all through the kindly ministrations of a philosopher who should be nameless.

Inspired by this hope to overcome his natural shyness and timidity, Dr. Daniel came out again in the afternoon, and made his way down to the tailor's shop. The man still sat there—more ignoble drudgery could not be imagined. The Doctor entered.

"I did not observe your name over the door?" said he, hesitatingly, to the tailor, who had turned quickly round, and was staring at him with a pair of small, piercing, light blue eyes.

"'Tis Gearge O'Leary, Sor," said the tailor, looking rather afraid.

The Doctor's hopes were slightly dashed: the man was an Irishman. But then, he instantly reflected, Ireland had not yet produced her Shakspeare; perhaps this was he.

"An Irishman, I presume?"

"Yis, Sor," said the tailor, somewhat recovering from his astonishment, and proceeding to get down from the board. "Is there anny thing, now, that—"

"Oh yes," cried the old Doctor, immensely relieved to find a subterfuge suggested to him. "I wanted to see if you would repair some things for me. Dear, dear me, and so you are an Irishman! I am sure I don't know what I wish done to them. Could you call this evening on me, about half past eight? Oh, I don't wish you to work tomorrow—far from it; but I should like to have the things taken away. Could you oblige me, Mr. O'Leary, by calling yourself?"

That evening Mr. O'Leary, wearing an elegant black frock-coat and a beautiful bright green necktie, was shown into the Doctor's study, where the old gentleman was seated by the fire, with a decanter of port and a couple of wine-glasses on the table.

"Now, Mr. O'Leary," said this cunning old gentleman, with a fine affectation of manner, "I have my ways, you know, and I never do business with any man without having a glass of wine over it. Sit down and help yourself. 'Twas my grandfather left me that; you needn't be afraid of it. And how long have you been a tailor, Mr. O'Leary?"

"Is it how long I have been a tailor, Sor?" said Mr. O'Leary, helping himself to the port, and taking care to have the glass pretty well filled; "why, Sor, since ever I could spake, barrin' the five years I was in the army, until me father bought me out."

"You have been in the army too? Don't be afraid to try another glass of that port, Mr. O'Leary."

"Well, sure enough, 'tis Christmas-toime, Sor," said Mr. O'Leary, turning to the table right willingly.

Matters having been thus satisfactorily settled, the

wily Doctor gradually began to get out of O'Leary all the facts concerning his history which he chose to tell. The Doctor's housekeeper had certainly brought in a number of old and shabby garments, which were flung on a sofa hard by; but the Doctor made no reference to them, while his guest seemed sufficiently pleased to sit in a comfortable arm-chair, with a decanter of port-wine at his elbow. Perhaps it was the wine that had made him a trifle garrulous; but at all events he talked about himself and his various experiences of life with a charming frankness. Here was a man, the Doctor said to himself, of infinite observation. Cuvier, with his sixty-four ounces of brain, could only stow away facts about birds, beasts, and fishes; here was a man, with probably nine ounces less, who had stored up invaluable experiences of mankind, their habits, customs, and humorous ways. O'Leary was as much at home among the fishermen of his native village as among the democratic tailors of London. At one time he was describing his life in the army, at another telling how he had served as a gamekeeper when trade was bad. The more loosely his tongue wagged, the more daring became his epithets; but the Doctor was aware that Shakespeare himself had not always been cautious in his language. But when O'Leary came to describe his present circumstances, he grew less buoyant. Affairs were not going well with him. He could barely screw the rent of that humble shop out of his earnings. And then, with some shyness, he admitted the existence of a young woman who had a great interest in his welfare, and he said he thought they would never be able to get married if his small business did not improve.

"Ah, you have a sweetheart," said Dr. Daniel, slyly. "I dare say, now, Mr. O'Leary, you have written some bits of poetry about her, haven't you?"

"Is it poethry?" said O'Leary, with a loud laugh; "'tis a mighty quars sort o' poethry, Sor, an' no mistake; but, oh yes, Sor, I've sent her many's the bit o' poethry, and 'tis very fond of it she is, Sor."

The old Doctor's face gleamed with delight; step by step the whole affair was marching on well. His fairest hopes were being realized.

"I have a great interest in literary matters, Mr. O'Leary, and I should like to see some of your poetry, but I fear I could not ask you to show me any of the verses you have sent to your sweetheart. Is there no other subject, now, that you have thought of trying? A man of your quick observation ought to aim at something better than sewing clothes. Do I speak too plainly?"

"Divil a bit," said Mr. O'Leary, frankly.

"And, to tell you the truth, I should be glad to do any thing in the way of helping you that I could. I don't say give up your trade at once; that is a dangerous step. To attain eminence in literature you require long and careful preparation—a wide experience that is only to be gained by diligent study of men in all walks of life—a freedom of expression only to be acquired by practice. And these things, Mr. O'Leary, are only the railway lines. The brain is the engine. You have got a good head."

"There's manny a stick has been broken by coming against it, Sor," said O'Leary, modestly.

"I do not wish to raise false hopes," continued the Doctor, feeling it his duty to express a doubt which he did not himself entertain for a moment; "but this I may say, that I am interested in you, and am willing to help you if I can. You may take these clothes, Mr. O'Leary, and look over them at your convenience. I am in no hurry for them. But if within the next few days you care to write a few verses, just to give one a notion of the bent of your mind and of your faculty of expression, I should be glad to see them."

"About what, Sor?"

"Any thing, any thing," said the Doctor. "Obey the free impulse of your own imagination. By the time you see me again I shall be able to tell you more definitely what I propose to do for you; but in the mean time I think you ought to keep the matter to yourself. Do you understand me?"

"Indeed I do, Sor," said Mr. O'Leary, getting up, and discovering that either the port-wine or the

Doctor's plan had rather confused his head. However, he got the clothes together, thanked the Doctor most profusely, and left.

That night Dr. Daniel went to bed as happy as a man could be, and all night long he dreamed of brilliant receptions of public meetings, of Queen's drawing rooms, and more than all of his own great pride and glory in introducing to the world a new Shakspeare.

THE FIRST TRIAL

Three days thereafter the Doctor received a letter, and as he opened it an inclosure dropped out. It contained Mr. O'Leary's first experiments in professional verse writing. The Doctor seized it with avidity, and would have read it forthwith, but, being a methodical man, he placed it on the table, and read the letter first.

Mr. O'Leary was a bad penman; it was with much difficulty that the old gentleman could make out the sense of the rambling lines. But when he did so, he was pleased. O'Leary confessed that he had not the impudence to bring his verses personally to the Doctor. He knew they were worthless. He was ashamed of them; he even fancied he could do better. And then he added something about the condition of the Doctor's coats and trousers.

Here is the first composition, which the Doctor now proceeded to read, with some necessary alterations in Mr. O'Leary's spelling:

> *"The moon was clear, the stars were white,*
> *The wind blew o'er the sea,*
> *When Mary left her cottage home*
> *To go on board with me.*
> *"Alas! the ship was going fast,*
> *The storm did rage and roar,*
> *And Mary stood upon the deck*
> *And looked back to the shore.*
> *"The moon was covered with the dark,*
> *The wind did blow aloud;*
> *She struck a rock and straight went o'er,*
> *And all on board were drowned."*

"The poetry of the simple and uncultured mind," said the Doctor to himself, "naturally takes the lyrical form. Nations begin with *Chevy Chase* and end with *Hamlet*. In this artless composition the chief feature is its simplicity and directness of phrase. The stars are white; the ship goes fast; the girl, the central figure, stands upon the deck and looks back to the shore. It appears to me that there is genuine poetic sentiment in this very reticence of phrase, and in the stern sincerity and conciseness of the narrative. The professional critic, some disappointed poetaster, would remark, of course, that '*drowned*' does not rhyme with '*aloud*,' he would also make merry, doubtless, over the fact that if all on board were drowned, the narrator, being himself on board, would not have lived to tell the tale. But such is the criticism that stifles genius in its cradle. We can not expect to have our young poets express themselves according to their inspiration, if we proceed to treat them with a godless banter. What I perceive in this composition of Mr. O'Leary's is a most promising naturalness and simplicity, coupled with a good deal of melody, especially in the first verse. Let us see what he has done with his remaining effort."

Mr. O'Leary's second composition had evidently been written in compliance with a suggestion of the Doctor that a true poet should deal with the actual life around him—that he should tell us what he sees, and put into powerful verse the experiences, fears, and hopes of his fellows. Here it is:

"'*Tis the gray of the evening in Vauxhall Road.*
Alas! what sounds do I hear?
A crowd is around the public-house door;
It is a quarrel, I fear.
He is drunk; he doth lift up his hand!
In vain the policeman doth run!
Before he arrives the woman is struck down,
And all the mischief is done!"

The Doctor was not so sure about these lines. They contained, he reasoned with himself, a perfect picture of the scene which the poet had attempted to describe. But there was a want of form, of method, of melody, apparent in the lines. They wanted the sweet idyllic charm of the verses describing Mary as she stood on the deck of the ship. But was he not himself responsible for this composition's failure? He had thoughtlessly discoursed to O'Leary about the virtues of realism. He had endeavored to guide and direct the poetic instinct instead of leaving it free choice. Now the bent of O'Leary's mind was clearly synthetic and romantic; he would not follow in the wake of Crabbe and Wordsworth. Doctor Daniel would omit further consideration of the lines about the Vauxhall Road. He would pin his faith to the charming ballad about Mary.

He sent a message to O'Leary that he wished to see him that evening. When O'Leary entered the study he was inclined to be at once bashful and nervous; but his patron speedily re-assured him.

"You know," said he, with a smile—"you know, Mr. O'Leary, I did not expect you to be able to write poetry all at once, I merely wished to see if you had any leaning that way; and I must honestly say that there is a good deal of promise about the little ballad you sent me. Whether you may develop any very special gift remains to be seen; but if you care to make the experiment, I shall be willing, as I told you, to help you as much as I can. You must read and study the great fountain-heads of poetry; you must have leisure to go about and observe all varieties of men and things; you must have your mind relieved from anxiety in order to receive without dictation the materials for contemplation. I suppose you have few books. Have you read Shakspeare?"

"Is it Shakspeare?" said O'Leary, doubtfully. "Well, Sor, 'tis little I know av him in print, but sure I've seen him in the theatre. There's *Macbeth*, now, and the foightin' wi' swords; and as for the *Colleen Bawn*, 'tis a mighty foine piece entirely. Shakspeare, Sor! 'tis little av him I've seen mesilf; but he was a great man annyhow."

"I see I must present you with a copy of his works, Mr. O'Leary. I may say, however, that Shakspeare did not write the *Colleen Bawn*, which is a modern piece, I believe. But first of all I think you ought to begin and study the ballad literature of our country; then you might proceed to Coleridge and Byron, and finally devote yourself to Shakspeare. You should also cultivate a habit of observation during your leisure rambles, not confining yourself to things which interest merely yourself. When you come to read Shakspeare, you will find how strangely he would enter into the opinions, senti-ments, and aspirations of an ambitious monarch, and next minute how he could show himself familiar with the speech and thought of some common-minded peasant or justice of the peace. You must widen your atmosphere. You must forget Pimlico and Vauxhall Bridge Road occasionally. Now if you had next Saturday free, I would myself go with you to Kew Gardens and Richmond; there you would see beautiful garden scenes and the quiet beauties of the river; while at Richmond you would see some of the grand houses of rich people, and observe some-thing of their ways of living."

"Faix, it's mesilf would be deloighted to go wid ye," said O'Leary, with a rueful expression of face, "for 'tis little I'm doin' now with the shop; but little as it is, Sor—"

"Don't let that stand in your way," the old Doctor said, generously. "I'm an old man, and have few claims on me in the way of friendship or benevo-lence. I told you I would give you an opportunity of rising to something beyond the sewing of clothes, useful and necessary as that occupation is. Now to put your mind at rest for at least this week, Mr. O'Leary, suppose I ask you to accept this little sum. Why, I hope you don't misunderstand me? I believed you rather wished to enter into this project."

O'Leary was neither angry nor indignant; he was

simply bewildered. He had received into the palm of his hand five golden sovereigns, and he could only stare at these in mute astonishment.

"Do ye mane it, Sor?" said he, fearing to put them in his pocket.

"Dear, dear me; it is no such great matter!" Dr. Daniel said, smiling at his companion's perplexity. "Put the money in your pocket, Mr. O'Leary. It is Christmas-time, you know, when the giving of little presents is permissible."

"Am I to write anny more poethry, Sor?" said O'Leary, putting the sovereigns in his pocket.

"If you have any impulse that way, I should be glad if you would trust to it. But in any case you will call on me at ten next Saturday morning?"

"That I will, Sor!" said O'Leary, not quite sure but that this was all a dream.

When he got outside, he went to a lamp, and took out the sovereigns. Sovereigns they certainly were; and yet he was puzzled. He went into a public-house and had a glass of ale, in order to have one of the golden coins changed; the man gave him a heap of silver in return. He came out again with a lighter heart.

"Bedad," said he to himself, "and 'tis a poet I am. Me mother knew nothin' about it; me father, rest his sowl, was accustomed to bate me if ivver I'd a pen in me hand. But what would they say to thim blissed five gowld pieces, and all for a dirthy scrap o' writin'? Oh, 'tis a moighty foine thing to be a poet, an' no mistake. And now 'tis to Biddy I'm goin'; and will she belave it?"

A CONSPIRATOR

Now there was not any where in London a more amiable, simple-minded, and pious young woman than Biddy Flanagan, who was the poet's sweetheart. She was a domestic servant, rather good-looking with a fair, freckled face, hair nearly as red as her lover's, and a brogue much less pronounced than his. But when O'Leary told this poor girl all the story of his adventure with Dr. Daniel, her quick invention and pathetic hope rather got the better of her conscience. She did not tell her sweetheart that she considered Dr. Daniel a good-natured old maniac, but she acted on that assumption. By this time, be it observed, O'Leary had begun to share in the Doctor's illusions or aspirations. He showed Biddy copies of the verses he had written, for which she professed a great admiration, though she could not read them very accurately. But after O'Leary had described the Doctor's project, and shown her the four gold sovereigns and the silver, and talked about the holiday at Kew, and so forth, then she gave him, with an artful ingenuousness, her advice.

It was this. Her sweetheart, she faintly hinted, might in time turn out to be a great man, and that would be a fine thing for him at least. As for her, she could not expect him to go out walking with her after he had been to grand houses. On this, of course, O'Leary protested that whatever rank and wealth might fall to his lot, he would never desert the girl who had remained true to him so long and waited so patiently for that better fortune which seemed now to be approaching. Biddy, continuing, gently reminded him that rich people might be fickle in their patronage, and might not care to wait for years to see the end of their projects. O'Leary had written two poems; the result was £5. Would it not be better to continue writing these as rapidly as possible, so that as much ready money as Dr. Daniel might be willing to give could be secured at once? And then, if her sweetheart did care about getting married—

The suggestion was not lost on O'Leary. After all, he reflected, however great were the possibilities of the future, a little money just now and a marriage with his faithful Biddy were far more attractive.

"But divil the bit can I think of anny thing more to write," said her sweetheart. " 'Tis a moighty hard thing, the writing of poethry; and that's the truth, Biddy darling."

"Arrah, now," said Biddy, impatiently, "what harm would there be in taking a bit here or there, just to keep up the gintleman's spirits, and by-and-by 'tis many a fine bit of poethry you'll give him into the bargain, when it comes aisier to ye."

"There's something in that, Biddy," said O'Leary, not only listening to the tempter, but anxious to find reasons for agreeing with her. "'Tis mesilf that knows that ye can't make a pair of throwsers till ye've learned to thread the needle, and sorra a bit do I know of the making of poethry. But, Biddy, d'ye see, if he was to come on the poethry—"

"What!" cried Biddy, "an ould gintleman like that! 'Tis not a loine of our good ould Irish songs will he know; and 'tis no chating of him, Gearge dear, for you'll make it up to him whin the writing of your own poethry comes in toime. Now there's the *Cruiskeen Lawn*—"

"Get along wid ye, Biddy!" said O'Leary, rather angrily; "and is it a fool you'd make av me? Why, the old gentleman has been to all the plays and the theatres, and isn't it out av the ould songs like that that they make the plays? Sure and it's the police-office I'd foind mesilf in, and not in Kew Gardens at all, at all."

"There's manny more," said Biddy, shrewdly, not pressing the point.

O'Leary pondered over this suggestion for a day or two. He did not think he would be really imposing on the old gentleman by occasionally quoting a verse from some one else as his own. It was merely borrowing to be repaid back with interest. At some future time, when the writing of poetry had become easier to him, he would confess the true authorship of these verses, get them back, and offer in their stead large and completed poems.

He dressed himself very smartly to call on Dr. Daniel on that Saturday morning. He had even gone the length of getting a tall hat—an ornament which he seldom wore, because the peculiar shape of his head made it almost impossible for him to wear such a hat with safety, especially if the day were windy. The Doctor was glad to see him; the morning was a pleasant one; they both set out in an amiable frame of mind.

In the railway carriage O'Leary took a piece of paper from his pocket. His guilty conscience revealed itself in his forehead—that lofty forehead that had caused the old Doctor to dream dreams. The color that appeared in his face Dr. Daniel took to be an evidence of modesty; and is not all true genius modest?

"So you have been busy again," said his Mentor,

with a pleased smile. "You must not write as if you wished to gratify me. It is your own future of which I am thinking."

He read the lines, which were these:

> *"As charming as Flora*
> *Is beauteous young Norah,*
> *The joy of my heart*
> *   And the pride of Kildare!*
> *I ne'er would deceive her,*
> *For sad it would grieve her*
> *To know that I sighed*
> *   For another less fair."*

"Very pretty—very pretty indeed," the Doctor said, approvingly, and O'Leary breathed again. "There is much simple melody in the verse; and the ending of it, taking it for granted that any other must be less fair than she, is quaint and effective. Did you say your sweetheart's name was Norah, Mr. O'Leary?"

"Biddy, Sor," said his companion.

"That is not quite so poetical," said the Doctor; and then he continued the reading:

> *"Where'er I may be, love,*
> *I'll ne'er forget thee, love,*
> *Though beauties may smile*

> *And try to insnare;*
> *But ne'er will I ever*
> *My heart from thine sever,*
> *Dear Norah, sweet Norah,*
> *The pride of Kildare!"*

"Very good—very good also," said the Doctor; "although there is just a touch of self-conscious vanity—you will excuse me, Mr. O'Leary—in the notion that beauties would endeavor to insnare the hero of the lines. But perhaps I am wrong. You do not write these lines as the utterance of yourself. The poem, so far as it goes, is dramatic—an impersonation. Now the majority of men, when they are young, are vain enough to believe that beauties do try to insnare them: hence the sentiment expressed by this person is, I believe, true; and I beg your pardon."

At this point, it must be admitted, O'Leary's conscience was touched. He felt that it was a shame to impose on this good-natured and generous old gentleman. He could almost have thrown himself on his knees on the floor of the carriage, and confessed that he was a scoundrel and a knave.

Some recollection of Biddy, and her pretty, honest, anxious face prevented him. The poor girl had waited patiently for that better luck which never came. The milk-man had offered to walk out with her, the postman had offered to marry her this very Christmas, but she had remained true to this hapless tailor, on whom Fortune seemed resolved to send not the briefest ray of her favor. And now when he saw within his reach a means of bettering himself somewhat, and of releasing her from the bondage of that overcrowded house in Lambeth to give her a couple of rooms—small, indeed, but her own—he tried to stifle that feeble protest of his conscience. He saw Dr. Daniel fold up the paper and put it in his pocket-book; and he knew that the die was at length cast.

All that day the friendly Doctor took his pupil about, showing him how differently different people lived, pointing out the beauties of the gray and wintry landscape, and talking to O'Leary of how he should set about his self-education. In the evening the poet dined with the Doctor, much to the amazement of the old housekeeper, who was indignant, but silent. At night he went away with a whole armful of books.

Next evening he saw Biddy, and he was in a downcast mood.

"Biddy," said he, " 'tis moighty afeard I am we are thieving from the good ould gintleman. There is another five pounds to come to me next week; and, bedad, the mate that I'll buy with it'll go near to choking me, it will."

Biddy was for a moment a little frightened; but presently she said:

"And is it you, Gearge O'Leary, that would be setting yourself up as a better judge of poethry than the ould gintleman, and him a Doctor too? And if it is the poethry he wants, can't ye give him enough of it in times to come, and a good pennyworth over, so there'll be no repentin' of the bargain betune ye? And, indeed, it is not another year, Gearge dear, that I could stop in that house. What with the noine children, and the washin' all day, and the settin' up for the master till three in the mornin', 'tis me coffin, next you'll be for buying, Gearge dear, and not anny wedding-ring."

O'Leary's doubts were banished for the moment, but not destroyed.

FOREBODINGS

It must be said for O'Leary that he honestly did his best to requite the Doctor's care. He devoted every minute of his leisure time to that self-education which had been recommended to him; he industriously labored at the books which had been given him. Somehow or other, however, the big brain behind that splendid forehead would not work. When he tried to understand certain things the Doctor told him in explanation, a sort of fog appeared to float before his eyes. When he tried to write verses of his own composition, blankness surrounded him. He would sit helplessly by his table for hours, no suggestion of any subject occurring to him. He grew irritable and impatient. The Doctor noticed that his pupil, when they walked out together, had lost much of his old gayety of spirits. He began to wonder whether tailoring and study combined were not proving too much for O'Leary's health.

Otherwise all seemed to go well with him. The old Doctor was as much in love with his project as ever, and had grown to take a very keen and personal interest in the affairs of this poor man. Finding out that much of O'Leary's anxiety was apparently connected with the question of his marriage, he suddenly resolved upon setting his friend's mind at rest on that point by an act of exceptional generosity. He told O'Leary that he evidently wanted change of air and scene. When he got married he would have to leave his present humble lodgings. Now what did he think of living a few miles out of London—say about Hammersmith or Barnes—where the Doctor would purchase for him a small cottage, and furnish the same? The walk in of a morning would improve his health, and afford him ample time for thinking. If he would see Biddy Flanagan, and arrange about the marriage, the Doctor would proceed forthwith to seek out and purchase some small cottage.

When he told Biddy of this proposal there were tears in his eyes.

"Biddy," said he, " 'tis a jail and not a cottage that I'm fit for. Sure there's not a day I go up to the ould gintleman's house now that I'm not trimbling from me head to me foot—with shame, yes, with shame. Biddy, what o'clock is it?"

" 'Tis after ten, I belave."

"This very minnit I'll go and tell him what a rogue I've been," O'Leary said, stopping short on the pavement.

The girl looked at him, frightened and silent; but her hand was on his arm, and he did not move. Then she spoke to him. She did not attempt to justify what had been done; she only pleaded that, now it was done, he should wait and accept this cottage—as a loan, not a gift. They would be most economical. She knew how to tend a small kitchen-garden. She would take in washing. O'Leary would save up what he could in the shop, and then by-and-by he could go to Dr. Daniel, confess his forgeries, and pay the first installment of the money which he had to refund. Dr. Daniel had already given him £20 in money, besides an immense number of books; they would accept this climax of his generosity, and being installed in the cottage, would work faithfully to pay back the whole.

O'Leary consented, with evil forebodings in his mind, and resumed his imposture. He had almost began to despair of ever being able to do any thing himself; he did not even try now; he merely copied a verse or two of one of Moore's songs, and took that to the Doctor to encourage the old gentleman's hopes. Fortunately Dr. Daniel showed none of these contributions to his friends. They had got vaguely to know that he had recently picked up some odd protégé; but the Doctor was not communicative on the point, wishing to have some finished work of O'Leary's before introducing him to the world.

But each time that the tailor copied out some verses and carried his stolen wares to the house in Brompton, he grew more and more agitated. A feeling of sickness came over him as he rang the bell; when he came away, he felt inclined to walk down to Chelsea Bridge and end his anxieties in the river. The remorse that he felt seemed to be increased by each fresh proof of the old Doctor's generosity, while the fear of detection became almost unbearable. He grew haggard in face. He was peevish and irritable, so that Biddy was almost afraid to speak to him when they went out walking together. At last, one night, he turned and declared to her fiercely that it was all her fault, and that she had made a thief of him.

The girl burst out crying, and spoke in a wild way of drowning herself. She quitted him abruptly, and walked off in the direction of the bridge.

For some time he gloomily regarded her, uncertain what he should do; then he ran after her and stopped her. He would do what she wanted. He would say nothing more about the whole affair till they had the cottage. So he gradually pacified her; but from that moment each felt that the mutual confidence which had existed between them had suffered a serious shock, and that at any moment something might occur to sunder it altogether.

So the days and weeks went by. The small cottage was at last got hold of; and so great was the interest of the Doctor in this project that he sent for his sister to come up from Bath to help him in selecting some pieces of furniture and the necessary saucepans and dishes. Should O'Leary turn out to have the poetical power which the shape of his head promised, might not this little cottage come to be in future times regarded with interest by travelers from all parts of the world?

But the near approach of this marriage, and the prospect of possessing this tiny residence, did not seem greatly to raise the spirits of O'Leary and his betrothed. Biddy now began to look anxious too—anxious and apprehensive, as if she lived in constant dread of something happening. She made fewer appointments with O'Leary; sometimes they walked for an evening together with scarcely a word passing between them. The old delight of these meetings had passed away.

One night he was to have met her, but he did not come—a most unusual circumstance in his case, for he was a dutiful lover. More strangely still, no word of explanation came next morning. All the next day she waited and worried, harassed by a hundred fears; and at last, in the evening, she went to her mistress and begged to be set at liberty for a couple of hours. The request was sulkily granted.

Rapidly, indeed, did she run across the bridge and up through the gaunt and silent streets of Pimlico. With a beating heart she knocked at the door of O'Leary's lodgings; the landlady, who knew her, came. She had scarcely breath left to ask if Mr. O'Leary was at home. The landlady, a fat, good-natured, shabbily dressed woman, drew her inside, and motioned her to keep quiet.

"He was took werry ill yesterday, the poor young man, in a fever like, and to-day he has been wandering. There's something on his mind, miss, that is troubling the poor young man—about them books he has, and some money; and law! the way he has been goin' on about you! But I knew as you was sure to come over this hevenin'—and will you go up stairs?"

Biddy followed the landlady up stairs as if she was in a dream. In a bewildered sort of way she saw the door opened before her, and found herself being taken noiselessly into the small room, which was dimly lit with a solitary candle. In the bed in the corner O'Leary lay, apparently asleep, with a bright flush in his face. He turned round uneasily; he stared at her, but did not recognize her; then he turned away again, muttering something about Dr. Daniel and Chelsea Bridge.

Biddy seemed to recover herself. She went deliberately over to the bed, her face pale and determined, and said,

"George, me darlin', don't ye know 'tis me? Where's the money? Give me the money; and 'tis every farden av it and every blessed wan o' the books that I'll take back to the Doctor this very minnit. Don't ye hear me, Gearge dear?"

The sick man groped underneath his pillow, and feebly brought out a leather purse. He gave it her, without looking at her, and said.

"Take it all back, Biddy."

The landlady could not understand the fierce look of determination on the girl's face. Biddy put the purse in her pocket. She gathered up the books from the corner of the room, piled them on the table, and then whipped the table-cover round them, and tied up the ends. With this heavy load on her back she staggered down stairs, and along the narrow passage.

" 'Tis the books and the money have brought the fever on him," she was muttering to herself; "wirra, wirra, but 'twas a bad day that he met that ould gintleman, wid his books and his money. And, sure, whin I give him them back, 'tis to Father Maloney I'm goin,' to tell him that Gearge O'Leary is down wid the fever."

THE DOCTOR'S SISTER

The Doctor's sister came up from Bath—a thin, precise little woman, with silver-gray curls and shrewd gray eyes. She wanted to know more about this protégé of her brother's, of whom she had vaguely heard. Thereupon the Doctor, forgetting his shyness, grew quite garrulous about his project, described O'Leary's magnificent forehead, told her all that he hoped from it, and said that already he had received ample proofs of the man's poetical leanings. To all this Miss Daniel listened attentively, but silently. When he had finished, she asked him if she might look at some of Mr. O'Leary's pieces.

The Doctor was at first inclined to refuse. It would be unfair to take these compositions as evidence of what O'Leary might hereafter do. But Miss Daniel was so firm in demanding to see some actual work of the new poet's that her brother at last consented to go and fetch some of it.

She had scarcely begun to read the first of the pieces when he observed an extraordinary expression come into her face. She stared at the paper; then a flush of anger appeared on her forehead; finally she looked at himself with something more near to contempt than pity.

"How can you, Maurice," she said to the frightened Doctor—"how can you let people make a fool of you so? Year after year it is always the same—some new craze, and some new impostor taking advantage of you. Last year it was those relics of Sedan: they were no more relics of Sedan than I am. Why, don't you know that this man has been palming off on you verses of Moore's songs—songs that every schoolgirl knows? Oh yes, your Mr. O'Leary is not a fool; his big forehead can do something for him."

The Doctor would not believe it. He was inclined to be violently angry. Then his sister walked out of the room.

In a few minutes she returned. She had managed to unearth an old copy of *Moore's Irish Melodies*, which she had left in the house in days gone by. Without a word, she opened the page, put her finger at a certain passage, and placed it before her brother. Doubt was no longer possible. Here was O'Leary's

"Oh, believe me, if all those endearing young charms;" there was Moore's version of the same. Miss Daniel rapidly run over O'Leary's manuscripts. She could identify nearly all the pieces, though some of them were disguised. The very first of them—that which described Mary standing on the deck of the doomed ship—she declared was stolen from a Scotch song.

It was really some time before the full sense of O'Leary's perfidy was impressed on the good old Doctor. He showed no signs of anger; but he was deeply pained and humiliated. It was not so much that his own pet scheme had fallen through, but that one whom he had tried to benefit should have betrayed him so grossly.

Miss Daniel was of another mind. She demanded to have the man punished. She insisted on the Doctor, although it was nearly ten o'clock, taking her to see this traitorous tailor, so that he might be confronted and his ingratitude and meanness pointed out to him. She talked of a policeman, and the crime of obtaining money on false pretenses, her brother all the while listening in a confused and absent way, as if he did not even yet understand it all.

At this moment Dr. Daniel's housekeeper tapped at the door, opened it, and announced that a young woman called Flanagan wished to see the Doctor, having a message from Mr. O'Leary.

A gleam of virtuous indignation leaped into Miss Daniel's eyes; she bade the housekeeper show her in at once.

The next moment Biddy Flanagan, still with something of a wild look in her face, entered the room. She did not see that there was any stranger present. She hastily undid the table-cover, placed the heap of books on the table, and counted out beside them eighteen sovereigns; and then she turned to the Doctor.

"Thim's the books, Sor," she said, in an excited way, "and there's the money—all but two of the gould pieces annyhow, and to-morrow you'll have thim too—and sure 'tis the light heart I have in putting thim there. And the cottage, Sor—plaze your honor, we'll have nawthin' to do wid the cottage—"

"My good girl, what is all this about? What do you mean?" the Doctor said.

"What do I mane?" Biddy cried, with her lips getting tremulous and her eyes filling with tears, "why, 'tis Gearge O'Leary, Sor; he's down wid the fever; and what has brought the fever on him but the books, and the money, and all the chatin'. And 'twas me that did it, Sor; indeed, it was mesilf, and not him at all; and the poethry, Sor, he brought you, sure 'twas all stolen; and I made him do it, for 'twas the weddin' I was thinkin' of—"

Here Biddy burst out crying; but she quickly recovered herself, and made some wild effort to express her contrition. She had no time to lose. She was going off for Father Maloney. It was the ceaseless anxiety, she explained, about the imposture that had worried her lover into a fever; now she had brought them back, and confessed her fault, she was going to fetch the doctor and the priest.

When she had left, Miss Daniel said to her brother.

"Will you go and see this poor man?"

"To upbraid him when he is down with a fever?" said the Doctor, indignantly.

"No; to relieve his mind by telling him you forgive him. And you have not a great deal to forgive, Maurice. You must have driven the man into deceiving you. Suppose you were to tell him now— or as soon as he can understand you—that you don't wish him to earn that cottage by writing poetry, but that you will give it him as soon as he is well enough to get back to his tailoring; don't you think that would help to get him better?"

It did; and George and Biddy are at this moment installed in the cottage, the latter quite contented that her lover should not have turned out a great poet, and he glad to be relieved from a task which was too much for his brain. As for the old Doctor, he has not given up his faith in phrenology, of course, merely because it apparently failed in one instance. He has still a lingering suspicion that O'Leary has thrown his opportunity away. However, if the world has lost, O'Leary has gained: there is not a happier tailor any where.

Sources

"The Gift of the Magi," by O. Henry. From *The New York World*, 1905.

"Christmas Jenny," by Mary Wilkins Freeman. From *A New England Nun and Other Stories* (Harper & Brothers, 1891).

"Christmas Every Day," by William Dean Howells. From *Christmas Every Day and Other Stories Told to Children* (Harper & Brothers, 1893).

"From the Garden of a Friend," by Mary Agnes Tincker. From *The Atlantic Monthly*, October 1886.

"The Christmas Club," by Edward Eggleston. From *Scribner's Monthly*, January 1873.

"Vanka," by Anton Chekhov. From *The Cook's Wedding and Other Stories*, trans. Constance Garnett (Chatto & Windus, 1922).

"Reginald's Christmas Revel," by Saki. From *Reginald* (Methuen, 1904).

"Mrs. Podgers' Teapot," by Louisa May Alcott. From *Saturday Evening Gazette*, December 24, 1864.

"The Story of the Goblins Who Stole a Sexton," by Charles Dickens. From *The Pickwick Papers* (Chapman and Hall, 1837)

SOURCES

"The Christmas Shadrach," by Frank R. Stockton. From
The Century, December 1891.

"Dancing Dan's Christmas," by Damon Runyon. From
Collier's, 1932.

"Christmas Storms and Sunshine," by Elizabeth Gaskell.
From *Howitt's Journal*, 1848.

"The Blue Carbuncle," by Arthur Conan Doyle. From
Strand Magazine, January 1892.

"The Bachelor's Christmas," by Robert Grant. From
Scribner's Magazine, December 1893.

"How Santa Claus Came to Simpson's Bar," by Bret Harte.
From *The Atlantic Monthly*, March 1872.

"The Man Who Was Like Shakspeare," by William Black.
From *Harper's New Monthly Magazine*, January 1875.